# EVERYTHING THERE IS

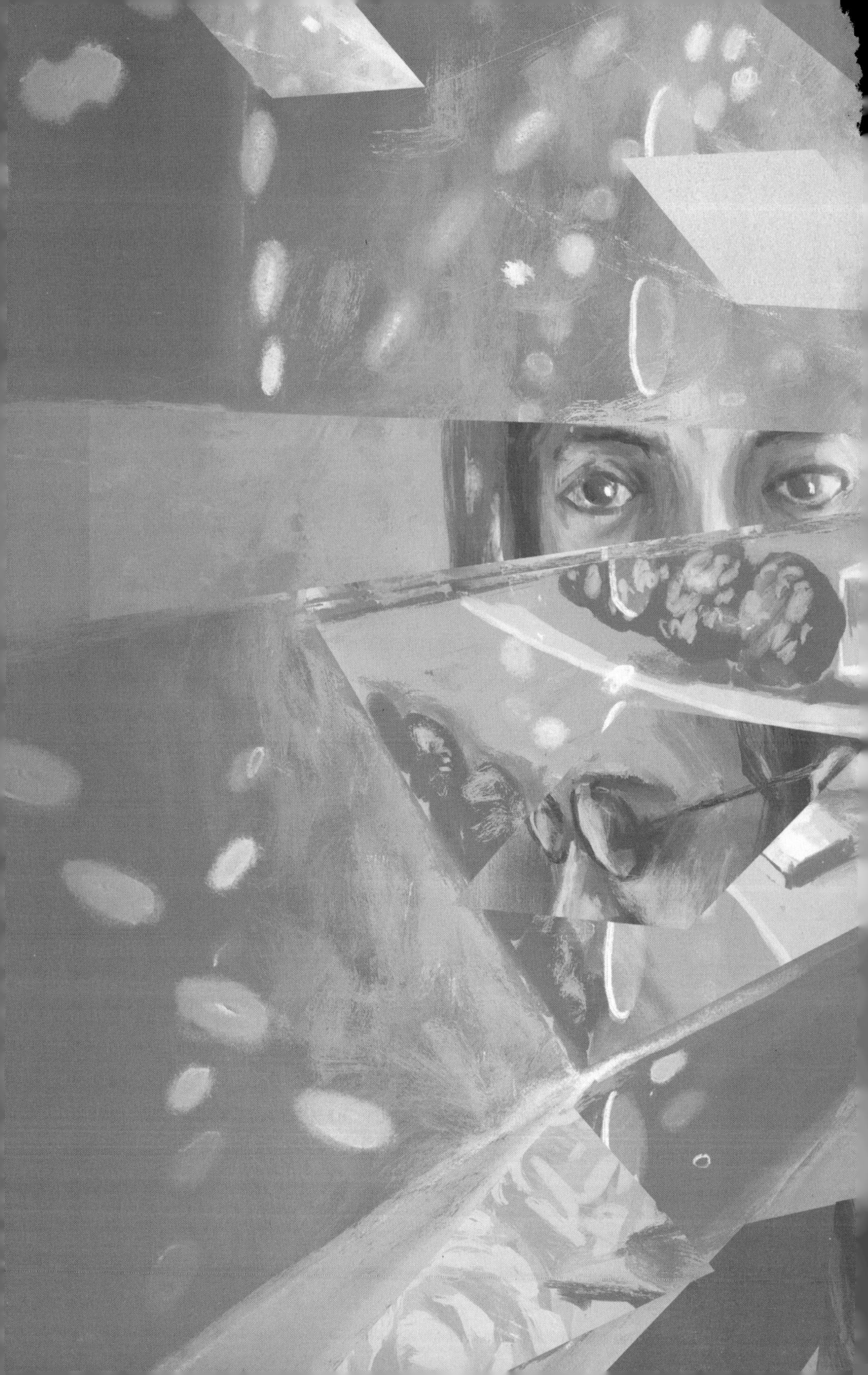

cntxt
EVERYTHING
THERE IS
A Novel
M.G. VASSANJI

cntxt

First published in hardback by Doubleday Canada in 2023

First published in paperback by Anchor Canada in 2024

Published by Context, an imprint of Westland Books, a division of Nasadiya Technologies Private Limited, in 2024

No. 269/2B, First Floor, 'Irai Arul', Vimalraj Street, Nethaji Nagar, Alapakkam Main Road, Maduravoyal, Chennai 600095



ISBN: 9789360451745

10 9 8 7 6 5 4 3 2 1

This is a work of fiction. Names, characters, organisations, places, events and incidents are either products of the author's imagination or used fictitiously.



Typeset by Jojy Philip

Printed at Manipal Technologies Limited, Manipal

for Adil,
with fond memories

The duty of the man who investigates the writings of scientists, if learning the truth is his goal, is to make himself an enemy of all that he reads, and … attack it from every side. He should also suspect himself as he performs his critical examination of it, so that he may avoid falling into either prejudice or leniency.

Ibn Al-Haytham [Alhazen] B. 965 CE

I feel also not able to imagine some will or goal outside the human sphere. My views are near to those of Spinoza: admiration for the beauty of and belief in the logical simplicity of the order and harmony which we can grasp humbly and only imperfectly.

Albert Einstein

The aim of physics, or at least one branch of physics, is after all to find the principles … that explain everything we see in nature, to find the ultimate rational basis of the universe. And that gets fairly close in some respects to what people have associated with the word 'God.'

Steven Weinberg

*'Nurul Islam, come and drink your milk and then be off to sleep!'*

*The boy, stretched out on the floor with his writing slate close to a paraffin lamp, didn't pay heed. His mother, Halima Begum, went muttering away, at which Hamid, the older brother, came by and snatched away the slate from under Nurul's pen. Seeing the figures written or drawn upon it, Hamid broke out into a cackle of teenage laughter.*

*'You ass, what nonsense have you written! Copied algebra from my book and not understanding a thing!'*

*Tears rolled down the younger brother's cheeks. He stood up, paused a moment, and without touching his milk hurried away to the inner room and stretched out on his sleeping mat.*

*'You should not be so cruel,' Halima Begum chided her older son.*

*In the dark, in the inner room, Nurul, grieving on his mat, resolved to learn those mysteriously dancing symbols of algebra which so intrigued him, and to be able to juggle and play with them better than anybody else. He swore to himself, as only a boy of six can swear, that he would be the champion algebraist of Punjab. No, of India. Of the entire world. Of all the seven worlds.*

*And for a time, he became one.*

'I told them that you were perhaps one of the world's greatest physicists,' Abe Rosenfeld said very casually to Nurul Islam, when they were settled in the car heading out from Boston's airport.

Nurul Islam raised an eyebrow at him.

'I had to tell them something,' Abe explained apologetically, to Nurul's broad amusement. Abe Rosenfeld was not one for superlatives or even the mildest flattery. Not even for Einstein, going by a famous instance at Princeton, and who was Nurul Islam of Pakistan in comparison to *him*?

'Well, thank you, even if you didn't mean it,' Nurul replied. 'But why would immigration detain me? Do I look like a radical to you? Don't I look respectable, a middle-aged professor in my tweed jacket and tie, my fresh haircut and half of an English accent?'

Not quite accurate, of course. His passport and his features often provoked England's gatekeepers at London Heathrow to detain him a mite longer than normal, and a lot longer when a fresh batch of immigrants arrived from the former colonies. He'd never had a problem entering the United States before.

It took a moment before Abe said with a wry smile, 'Could be that wild mustachio of yours.' Then he added, 'Or it could be the 'Islam' in your name. You know, the Nation of Islam and so on. Malcolm X. It's nothing, I wouldn't worry.'

Nurul brushed his famous moustache, which had the look of two black jets shooting off in opposite directions from his face and matched his thick crop of curly hair. He was somewhat stout in body and wore on this November day a wool overcoat and red paisley scarf.

It was fall 1971.

'*You* wouldn't worry,' he retorted to the other's nonchalance. 'But evidently I have to … I thought that was all over, the student riots, the race riots …?'

'Not quite over. We still get an occasional flare-up on the Square.'

Nurul watched Abe: the crumpled baby face, the red hair greying. The well-worn brown jacket. The posture already bending. And barely forty. They had their differences due to their temperaments—Abe had been called a logician, Nurul a magician—and there was their unstated rivalry, but they shared mutual respect, and surely some affection? Nurul sometimes wondered what Abe's private thoughts were, outside of physics. Abe was not political, which was admirable—give him a paper and something to write, and like a child doodling with a crayon he would be lost to the world, contented—and often come up with something truly startling. Recently though he had allowed himself some public opinions. So, for that matter, had Nurul. As we age and lose our mental agility we pick up our causes.

Outside, it was dark and wet, the highway mesmerizing, a brilliant train of moving lights, like a beam of elementary particles made visible, each vehicle a bundle of energy. A quantum. At each exit, some of this vehicular beam separated off, deflected by a suburban force. He knew this route well, he thought he knew Boston, at least Cambridge, reasonably well, which was why the detention at immigration had been an annoyance. The Prudential Building glittered familiarly in the distance, its radio mast winking intermittently on top; the MIT dome glowed dimly the other side of the Charles, and Nurul thought of the people he knew at the institute. They'd offered him a position once during a previous visit. Come, they said, and Rosenfeld will be just down the river at that Ivy place, and the two of you together can produce the miracle, unify the four forces in the universe. That was old Viki Weisskopf's offer; a paternal figure, the great Wolfgang Pauli's student, still aching for his Nobel. And if Abe entices me to join him there, down the river? Nurul had teased. All right, better stay in London then.

'You don't mind the Holiday Inn?' Abe asked. 'It's close enough for you to walk to the department, if you want to. Or be near all the action on the Square. You're always welcome to stay at our home, there's plenty of room, but I assume you'll need your privacy.'

He looked pointedly at Nurul.

'Yes, thank you, the Holiday Inn is fine. And I'll have dinner in my room tonight, don't worry about me, old chap.'

To spar tomorrow they had to approach each other afresh from a distance, their equations their feints. Nurul's thrust and jab to Abe's enticing, calculating chain … was that quite accurate?

There were messages awaiting him at the hotel. Academic acquaintances with invitations to speak, random students desperate to meet, a proposal for a radio interview. Invitation from the Quincy mosque. His room door having closed behind the tipped bellboy, he stared regretfully at his bulging briefcase leaning against the centre table—it would not be possible to catch up on anything tonight. His work was his hashish, he often said. Even if it was merely to glance at the contents page of a student thesis, or a learned paper he had been asked to referee for a journal. Keep him away from work and he started having a reaction, that depressed feeling in the pit of his stomach. Time was fleeting. Is forty too late?

He washed and came out in his long shirt, he took out his small prayer mat from his bag, gently unfolded it and laid it on the floor; then with his ancient skullcap—which he also unfolded—on his head he carefully, almost joyfully, fell down on his knees to pray. Y'Allah, forgive me for having missed the last one, but you know that I didn't forget you. You don't expect me to go down on my knees in the aisle of the plane, do you. I know you don't. After his prayer he ordered his supper—how can you not have hamburgers in America? With root beer and shoestring fries. Finally he sat back on the armchair and phoned Sakina Begum. Here was a different sort of parrying.

'You forget me as soon as you're away.' Affectionate. Chiding. Possessive.

'My dear, I thought you'd enjoy your independence.'

'Don't be so clever. You know I can only enjoy my independence with you here. And your two sons and daughter need you. Muni misses you.'

That hooked him.

'And how is my darling little Muni?' His voice changed. 'Is she there?'

'Yes, she's here. Speak with her.'

And he spoke tenderly with his daughter, five years old, and momentarily was a child himself, then again an adult, and made the requisite promises to bring presents and play badminton with her as soon as he returned. He should make time, the thought came. He didn't move so well these days, didn't take care of himself, one hazard of his itinerant life of the mind.

Sakina came back.

'Don't forget Salima's wedding next month. Don't go planning a trip.'

'I don't plan trips, my dear. I plan meetings. Who is Salima?'

'You don't remember Maher's daughter? My cousin Maher.'

'Yes, yes. I haven't seen her in ages.'

'I said you would give a speech at the reception. That will be nice.'

'I will not make a speech at the reception. I hardly know the girl. Who is the groom?'

'Some English boy. But he will convert and become a good Muslim, don't worry. He is a barrister. At least, can you bring a present for the wedding?'

'I am on work, my dear ... not on holiday ... and since when do I buy presents for weddings?'

'I only asked.'

'OK. Khuda hafiz, my dear. Look after yourself.'

'Allah hafiz.' And God bless you too.

And the Prophet said: *Among the Muslims the most perfect, as regards his faith, is the one whose character is excellent, and the best among you are those who treat their wives well.*

He also said: *The best of you is he who is best to his family, and I am the best among you to my family.*

As he sat back on the settee, watching the white ceiling, he felt quietly shattered, overcome by a pang of guilt. The pull of duty. All by himself in the night's solitude, engaged with equations—that was his natural state, where he was at home. She could not know it—not the way he knew it. Hers was what cosmologists might call a parallel universe—it was one where different laws prevailed, involving family rituals and relationships, all bound by emotions and duty, all alien to his nature, yet paradoxically endearing and necessary. What exercised her mind was whom to invite to dinner, what to wear on Friday, if the toothpaste or the ice cream were genuinely halal. That was her world, a world in which he too had grown up. But like a stray neutron from an atomic nucleus he had tunnelled out into his other life, his own private world of physics and mathematics, from which he returned only when reminded and beckoned. When he felt its inexorable pull.

Even his metaphors came from the world of physics and field theory, he mused. There was a time, when he was in college in Lahore, when he wrote the occasional poem, or a short story. He had edited the college magazine, *Lotus*. That was long ago, when the metaphors were different. They had to do with romantic love.

He read a few verses from the Quran and in them he heard God's voice speaking to him. He heard it in a gruff but affectionate Arabic and yet understood it in his native Urdu, speaking intimately, directly, and he felt all his agitations subside; he was in a cool embrace, and a calmness covered his heart.

He had been asked once how he reconciled the two, the Quran and fundamental physics, one an adherence to a single immutable text, the other a belief in the mutability of ideas, the deposing of texts. Aristotle's physics had been superseded, so had Newton's laws. Euclid and Archimedes had been extended. Einstein was often tested. But the Quran remained the same. Nurul had answered the obvious, the two needed no reconciliation, they were separate. One a matter of faith and conviction; the other that of observation and reason. And somehow the equations and laws of physics reflected through that sublime mirror—the human mind—the workings of God's Creation, its wonders. When you appreciated that beauty, when you saw how the fundamental particles of nature fitted into a geometric pattern, such as an octagon, when you discovered a hidden algebra of symbols to describe a phenomenon of nature such as the shape and colour of a crystal, you could not but see His hand in it and love Him. See Him laughing, feel His hand on your back. Shabash, child. Well done, now try solving the next riddle.

What do you pray to, Dr Islam? Do you believe in miracles? Do you believe the world was created in six days, Professor? I don't know, he had answered once, I wasn't there. But I believe in the laws of physics, their unity. And I know the unity of God. It is everywhere around us. Is your God the God of Einstein and Spinoza? Perhaps—did Einstein's God speak to him?

As was his habit, he woke up at four and had a light snack of crackers with coffee left over from the evening. Then in his notebook he began to develop an idea, a flash of insight he'd jotted down on the plane, on a Pan American Airways napkin, which he had later carefully stowed away. Having gone some way further with the notion, satisfied, he decided he would give the problem to a student to develop when he got back to London. Eventually in one's career one had more ideas than time to look at them; than what the aging brain could handle; but you could still use them to train younger minds …

The thought occurred, why had Abe invited him to Harvard? It was rather sudden—there was nothing much left in their theory that they could not discuss over the phone and by correspondence. Abe said as much, but he had extra funds and why not? Why not indeed, Nurul replied, I'd love to come. He was impulsive. But travel gave him time to think, explore his mind; and crossing the pond one always came away with fresh ideas, new challenges. More happened here, and faster.

He took a shower, dressed, said his prayer and went down, pleased with himself.

As he sat having his breakfast of toast, one boiled egg, and coffee—American tea was a travesty—while perusing the Boston paper before him on the table, a young woman came inside, looked around and walked towards him. He looked up. A cheering sight, he thought.

'Professor Islam?'

'Yes. You must be my designated escort.'

'I'm to walk you to Professor Rosenfeld's office. But there's no hurry, I'll wait outside while you finish your breakfast.'

'I've finished, let's go.' He got up, picked up his briefcase.

'By the way, I'm Hilary Chase … Abe's student.'

'Ah—' They walked out into a chilly fall day, overcast and windy.

'And what do you do?' Nurul asked the young woman.

She was a pretty girl in a plain, healthy sort of way, he observed, with a long pale face, her brown hair done up casually behind her with a clip. Light of step, like a dancer, but a serious kind of girl, very polite. In her mid-twenties, he guessed. In answer to his question she told him that she was working on the chemical origin of life, using a conjecture of Nomura's.

'Ah—good. You should tell me more about it sometime.'

He wasn't sincere, of course, and she knew it. She laughed uncertainly, blushing, and they walked on in silence for a while, before she asked, 'Did you have a good flight, professor?'

'Yes, I did, thank you.'

'You came directly from London?'

'Straight from London, yes.'

They crossed Mass Ave, past the newspaper vendor where he spied the *Times* of London, then walked over to the physics department.

They sat in Abe Rosenfeld's office over coffee—Abe casually sitting back behind his desk, Nurul in the vinyl-upholstered armchair across—as other members of the physics department came by to greet the famous and exotic Nurul Islam; some mathematicians, who did not feel tainted by association with physics, turned up too. They lingered and joked, exchanged brief anecdotes, before being pulled away to their duties. It was always the same wherever Nurul went, this brief eruption of fraternity among the theoretical physicists, a letting go, before each of them burrowed back to their office to work on their chosen problem, their contribution to 'the answer,' to how the universe was put together. Finally the room was quiet and only Abe's graduate students remained; there were four of them, including Hilary Chase, who had escorted Nurul earlier. The board was covered with formulae written over other formulae over a film of chalk. Abe gave permission for the board to be erased, and it was done, wiped with a wet cloth so that no sign remained of previous work. Dust motes filled the air and they all held their breaths, it seemed, waiting for it to clear. Physicists all, they probably briefly entertained the same thought: how to describe mathematically the motion of the randomly floating particles. Nervously, one by one the graduate students went to the board to explain to Nurul what they were up to. An attempt to rid the Islam-Rosenfeld theory of infinite values in some of its predictions; a calculation of the masses of the three meson particles; an attempt to calculate the mass of the electron, which no current theory could accomplish. And this from Hilary Chase, the emergence of life as the breaking of a universal symmetry of nature. Despite the brilliance and potential of these four young people, jobs were scarce in these times, and they were understandably nervous and awkward. One of them might well come to do a fellowship with him in London; and one of his own pupils could end up here, with Abe. Theirs was a small world; but it was influential. Abe advised the US president on scientific matters, and Nurul, the Pakistani government on atomic energy. Their pedigree as physical scientists went through Einstein all the way back to Newton, Galileo, and further to the Greeks. There were a lot of Arabs and Asians in between, while Europe lay in the dark ages. That was a point Nurul always liked to stress, that the understanding of our universe and the life it contained was a common need in the human race, and the excitement of discovery should be shared by all peoples. It had become more and more of a cause as he grew older.

He had lunch with the head of the department and a number of the faculty, a somewhat raucous affair, with news tidbits and gossip. Did you know Dirac spoke at Berkeley, he's into the origins of conscious life these days, such are the ways of spent genius. Isn't Wigner dotty too? And Beringer and his student at MIT, while the wife was away teaching in Pittsburgh … better not say any more about it. After lunch he went for a long stroll around the campus, ending up at a place called the Pewter Pot, where he sat down to gather his thoughts for his lecture and risked a cup of tea, which he had with half an American-size steaming fresh muffin.

The hall was overflowing, with students and faculty from apparently all the physics departments of the Boston area, as Abe escorted Nurul in. Surely I'm not *that* famous, he murmured to Abe, who said, Just wait for the surprise. And then, as Nurul Islam stood at the podium and looked out, having just been lengthily introduced, Abe paused to acknowledge two other visitors who were present that afternoon, both passing through Cambridge and having stayed on to listen to the speaker. From the far end of the first row, a rumpled-looking Richard Feynman raised a weak hand to thunderous applause. Well well well, said Nurul to himself. That's whom they've come to see. And right in front of him, in a jacket, red vest, and blue bowtie, was a beaming Murray Gell-Mann. Well well well again. But he felt a twinge; why this attention? Why a row of eminent men in the front row sitting like a jury? Merely an accident. And where's Schwinger, the grandfather of them? They say he's in Europe.

Keeping his diverse audience in mind, Nurul first gave a brief history of the weak interaction, also known as beta-decay, a phenomenon in which atomic nuclei were observed to emit electrons. He began with Henri Becquerel, the Frenchman who, sometime in the 1890s, unexpectedly observed the phenomenon as blobs on covered photographic plates upon which he had casually placed a few uranium salts; he then moved on to Wolfgang Pauli, the Austrian who conjectured on the basis of energy measurements that another particle must be emitted alongside the electron, called the neutrino, which was subsequently discovered; and the vital theoretical description of the phenomenon by the Italian Enrico Fermi; and finally its extension by these two American eminences currently present in front of him, Feynman and Gell-Mann. This then was the weak interaction, the weak force.

At the same time great strides had been made to develop a complete theory of the electromagnetic interaction, with which we are all familiar. Electric lights and so on. (He looked towards the ceiling.) Now an itch among scientists and philosophers over the millennia had been to unify different phenomena in nature—to describe them as different manifestations of one and the same thing. Electricity and magnetism had already been unified in the nineteenth century, both described by the single set of Maxwell's equations. What remained for now was to unify the four known fundamental forces, of which electromagnetism and beta decay were two. Over the past decade many physicists had worked on unifying the latter two, to see them—in a manner of speaking—as two sides of the same coin. He gave half a dozen or so more names. We don't work alone; and, to paraphrase Isaac Newton, we stand on the shoulders of giants to see what we can see. He went on to talk about his own work in London using two simple mathematical symmetries to describe the two forces with a single equation. Abe Rosenfeld, here in Cambridge, Massachusetts, had arrived at this result by a different route. A new very massive, mysterious particle called the Higgs boson was predicted by this theory—some people were already calling it the God Particle for the miracle it had accomplished. Its actual discovery would be the ultimate test. Now the problem remained to expand this theory, which he and Rosenfeld had dubbed the Lesser Unification Theory, or LUT, to embrace the two other fundamental forces of nature: the strong force, by which the protons and neutrons were bound together in an atomic nucleus—a force whose energy was responsible for the nuclear bomb;

and the gravitational force, by which we can walk on the ground without stepping off into the air. All these four forces that we experience in our lives today, we physicists believe to be manifestations of a single unified force. It would explain how our universe, how everything around us, is put together. How do we, using pen and paper, write down this unified force and what will it predict? That is what he and many others were currently working on.

At the end of the lecture, after the customary applause, during question time—the naive and gratuitous inquiries from students and the sharper ones from the senior scientists—a hand shot up from the back of the hall.

'Professor Islam—concerning this 'Lesser Unification,' as you call it—didn't Abe Rosenfeld actually beat you to it? I mean, didn't he do it before you? You revealed your work after having seen his preprint, I believe.'

A Midland English accent. A frontal attack and irrelevant to the topic. A little flustered by what was a blatant accusation of plagiarism, Nurul answered, 'My colleague David Mason and I—and a lot of other people—have been working on these ideas for the last seven years or so. The Lesser Unification Theory existed in my lecture notes and was the subject of my talk at the Oslo Symposium early last year.'

'You should publish those notes, Nur.' Richard Feynman spoke lazily from the end of the front row, slouching even further in his seat, obviously a victim of jet lag.

*Is this why he took this layover, instead of heading straight back to Pasadena? To see and judge? And the bow-tied Gell-Mann? He was in Oslo too, it was he who summed up the Symposium, why is he silent?*

'Dick, they are in the Proceedings of that Symposium!' Nurul replied to Feynman's input.

Feynman raised both hands in a *mea culpa*.

'But the dates, Professor Islam—surely the Oslo Symposium was some weeks later?' the Englishman persisted, encouraged by the attention his question had garnered.

He met the man's eye. *I know you! You were a student of mine, weren't you. For some course or other. And didn't you take a recommendation from me to go to … Amsterdam? Yes.*

'I think the matter can be discussed in a private conversation—or taken up elsewhere,' Abe Rosenfeld interrupted with an apologetic smile, drawing the session to a close.

Following his talk and the small chit-chat during the tea that followed, both Feynman and Gell-Mann having disappeared after coming to shake his hand, an exhausted Nurul Islam walked back to his hotel. He had declined Hilary Chase's offer to escort him back. Abe, telling him to take a rest after the long day, they had a session together tomorrow, had set off in the opposite direction towards his home; he had already invited Nurul for dinner later during his stay.

As Nurul walked towards the lights of Harvard Square ahead, the statue of the university's Puritan founder a shadow to his left, he was still bothered by the aspersion that had been cast upon him. You do not do that to a senior scientist. He had been deliberately attacked. There had been a buzz in the audience. A short one but noticeable. The young man must have some backing or he would not have been so bold. No one had shut him up, there were no cries of outrage at the sacrilege. Nurul had been aware of whispers behind his back, but had dismissed them as the spite of jealous hacks who had nothing to show for themselves. Pure physics may be a noble quest, but is not free of its crass elements ... there are always the jealous and the backbiters ... Or was he overreacting? Perhaps Feynman had really taken a layover during a long journey, and Gell-Mann had really come to see a student.

No matter. There was work to be done. What had begun to nag him was the thought that it was only at that moment, when fielding that absurd projectile, that he had acknowledged the contribution of his friend David Mason in public. David, who had suddenly departed for the States six years earlier, had ended up in the obscurity of a teaching position in Nairobi. Nurul always felt that the sudden departure had been a betrayal of their friendship, a betrayal of trust. Still, he should have begun his lecture with his collaboration with David, which had laid the foundation upon which Nurul Islam had built his final derivation of LUT. He had gotten carried away by all that attention. The sin of pride. Hubris. *Ghuroor*, in Urdu. He should remember for next time.

And send an apology to David, beg him to return to London. We miss you, David, we were like family.

Harvard Square was fairly quiet as Nurul crossed it, the bookstore on Mass Ave brightly lit and busy, the coffee shop next door on dimmers but quite full. To his left, the avenue faded into dark space, beyond which lurked MIT by the river; what were those guys there up to? He stopped at the news vendor at the wide mouth of the subway entrance to buy the day's copies of the *Guardian* and the *Times* and returned to his hotel.

'Professor Islam,' said the desk clerk, 'there's a message for you.'

'Ah … thank you.' Nurul picked up the slip and glanced at it.

He just missed the elevator and decided to do his heart a favour and take the stairs. He wondered what had prompted his ancestor, whichever one he was, to adopt the surname Islam in a society where everyone was presumed to be Muslim. He had an inkling that that was precisely the point: belonging to an offbeat Muslim sect, often regarded as heretical, the family had to broadcast its Islamic credentials. He had considered using some less obvious name, perhaps his father's. But at some point a name becomes you. What particle physicist worth his salt hadn't heard of Nurul Islam, formerly of Cambridge, now at Imperial? And now the name was emblazoned on the Islam-Rosenfeld Model—LUT.

And David?

He reached his room, washed, and briefly said his prayer. Perhaps too briefly. Allah Karim, look away. He ordered a light dinner. And then on a whim he put on a cassette of Urdu poetry. Few of his professional colleagues knew of his interest in romantic poetry; it had been a required subject in school, in both English and Urdu. He had mastered it better than most.

The poet Faiz, in the beautiful voice of the singer Noorjehan, sang, *Don't ask to be my first love, my darling / there are other heartaches in life than love …*

What other heartaches?

Nurul Islam ignored, as he often did, a fleeting image from his crushing youthful infatuation and reflected on his love of mathematical physics, which had taken him across the seas to England, and to many other places since, turning him into a wanderer and searcher. Indian philosophy had a concept called *maya*, the illusive nature of the world. Had he fallen victim to this goddess in his obsession with understanding nature's fundamental forces and components? Or was it merely his hunger for fame and more fame that drove him? Should he even be thinking of Indian philosophy rather than Islamic? He represented Pakistan and was proud of it. And yet before the Partition, wasn't it all one country? When he left for England, India was on the brink. Then it broke, with what cries of agony. But the world of physics had no national boundaries. It was one single nation, speaking the same language of observation and reason. But not without its malignancies, nothing was perfect.

*Verily in the creation of the heavens and of the earth, and in the alternation of the night and of the day, are there signs for men of understanding ...*

God Himself enjoined upon humankind to seek out the mysteries of the universe. This, Nurul Islam had set out to do in his life.

That aspersion at his lecture ... at the very peak of his career ... he should dismiss it. But he felt wary.

*As a student of mathematics at Government College in Lahore, his favourite equation, like a lover's face that hovers constantly on the mind, teasing, pleasing, was this awesome inspiration of the great P. A. M. Dirac:*

$$(\rho\gamma - m)u = O$$

*He would write it on notepaper for himself and gaze passionately at it, as at a love letter, his heart racing at its unique, concise beauty, its space-time symmetry, his mind conjuring possibilities and ambition; where could this beautiful equation—so simple to look at, yet so profound—not go? Unable to resist exposing his secret lover to the world he would write it on the classroom board when no one else was around, explicating the four-dimensional gamma-matrices, and leave the formulae there to mystify his fellow students, who could only guess at the identity of the madman among them.*

*After limited Lahore and its college, Cambridge University was all he could have dreamed of, a temple of learning where you did not have to love your equations in secret; a brown youth with an incomprehensible accent in the land, in the university of the great Isaac Newton, he saw himself among young Newtons all taking themselves seriously. And when dining the first time at St. John's College he saw the tall, thin and frail man sitting at high table it was as if—could he utter this?—he had seen a manifestation of God Himself. It was Dirac. Paul Adrian Maurice Dirac. The name itself with a sacred ring to it; a Sufi incantation.*

He awoke at four with the shahada on his lips, There is no God but Him. He washed and performed his formal prayer, then sat down to work, bent over the low centre table with his soft HB pencil, eraser, sharpener, and spiral-bound notebook. He opened to the page he'd last been working on, was soon drawn into a familiar world of algebraic symbols and quantum operators, with curlicues and straight lines and dotted lines representing a plethora of particles radiating and flashing and transforming—in short, interacting with each other—according to the laws and symmetries of the fundamental forces, standing to formations that melted and reformed, the energies high, the spins and colours and flavours numerous. This was his new work, grand unification of the four forces in nature that he called supersymmetry. It would embrace LUT. For it to succeed, from the ant circuses he produced on his pages he had to draw out something simple and comprehensible, something elegant, ushered in by results you could see in a laboratory—one or more new particles and perhaps a number or two. He was far from the answer, he thought, and yet very close. It needed that tiny something, an inspirational idea, to crystallize it. This kind of challenge had always lent him a thrill and, paradoxically—when he was absorbed in a page—a sense of calm. It was his communion with Creation. The Mevlevi dervishes found spiritual communion in the intensity of their dancing. The mystically inclined members of his own sect met to do the dhikr, the chant that put them into ecstasies. This before him was his dance, with pencil and paper, his ecstasy. It needed solitude and it drew him in completely.

Inadvertently, he admitted a perturbation into his mind, an impurity; the thought that it would be nice with this new formulation to show up Clever Abe Rosenfeld.

He stopped. The absorption, the ecstasy broken by this crass, polluting thought, was followed by a tide of unwanted anxieties. What if, after all the felicitations, the Islam-Rosenfeld model—as LUT was now more and more referred to—was proved to be wrong, a new experiment announced contradicting it? The miraculous God Particle shown to be a mere fancy? What if both he and Abe had barked up the wrong tree? A chunk of productive life wasted. There wasn't much of it left. But no. You know when you've hit on that something, found a solution. The realization wears you, occupies every pore in your body. LUT was it, the beginning of the grand unification. It's how, he imagined, a musician would feel upon completion of a sonata or symphony, a poet upon writing the last line of a great poem. All the nervous excitement, the edginess ceases and there remains only the bliss of accomplishment. You only have to go about it the right way, develop it logically, make it look elegant. There's no end, however. A sonata gets finished, a symphony has a finale; but a physical theory keeps growing, improving and correcting itself, moving forward in the expectation of reaching that final goal. The finale that explained everything there is, even the mind that posited it. Did anyone really believe there would be a finale rather than a continuous series of successes, failures, and more questions?

His formulation of the theory had been present in a bunch of his lecture notes, some conversations, speculation—until he saw Abe's preprint, and wrote up his own version formally and gave his talk in Oslo. Had Abe Rosenfeld, then, actually beaten him to it? But did it make sense to think that way at all? Where do you draw the line? It was petty to hold a stopwatch to advances in science. They were not running in an Olympics. But there were those who thought that way and worked to deny many a worthy physicist their recognition. That fellow who had piped the question from the back of the audience, '*Professor Islam …*' A former graduate student in his department at Imperial. Couldn't have been that good if the professor didn't recall his name. What was he doing here? What grudge did he bear? Some barb Professor Islam had thrown at him in London, perhaps, for he was known to be impatient and—admit it—arrogant. Who was behind that fellow? That jury in the front row—Feynman, Gell-Mann, Jackiw and others—had they gathered there by coincidence or to judge for themselves how he explained his theory? But, in the end, what did it matter? He had done the work, he was well into his next challenge.

He showered and dressed, then sat down to listen to his phone messages. There were two of them, both from his wife, Sakina. He had not even heard the phone the second time. The later message was in Urdu, which signified Urgent. 'Why haven't you returned my call? It's important, what I have to tell you.' He gave her a call.

'What's urgent, dear?'

'Rahim and Mirza quarrelled last night, Muni was crying.'

'So?' He paused. 'For this you call me?'

'Don't you like me to call you?'

'Call, but this was the middle of the night here, and you said it was urgent. And boys will quarrel. And don't forget, these telephone calls are expensive. We are not wealthy … I'm not selling carpets, you know!'

'They almost fought. Well, they did briefly …'

'And did you scream at them? Pull them apart?'

'Of course I did. But they are bigger than me now.'

'Let me speak to them.'

'They are in school, don't you remember?'

The thought of his little Muni in tears tore at him.

They said goodbye.

'Don't forget the presents.'

He hung up, picked up his briefcase and went down for breakfast.

Where was I? What was I thinking? Presents. Little Muni …

The note he had picked up from the receptionist the previous evening was from someone called Dr Masoud of MIT reminding Nurul about his lecture, scheduled at that institution that afternoon at four. He had accepted the invitation several weeks before. Dr Masoud would pick him up at three at his hotel, unless Nurul had another preference. Nurul telephoned him to say not to bother, he would be at the auditorium in time—Room 10-250, wasn't it? He remembered it. And he would stay for the tea and coffee afterwards, of course, but not dinner, he would be tired. Nurul had chosen to speak from a chapter he was writing for his book on the golden age of science and philosophy in Islam spanning the period from the tenth to the fourteenth centuries. It was an age of giants, of open-ended liberal thought and discovery, and controversies—Avicenna against al-Biruni, Averroes versus Ghazali—not unlike the excitement of discovery in the last two centuries in the West. But that work on history was slow-going, real physics, his own current work, always managed to pull him away; recently, however, he had resolved to give it two hours every Sunday, and hire a student to visit the Bodleian and the British libraries in his stead. The history he would dwell upon in his lecture would be more of an exhortation: Muslims, wake up! Do great things again! The Prophet didn't come to you so you would end up pumping petrol and driving taxis.

At ten, Nurul and Abe met at the latter's office to discuss the bit that remained to be done to complete their model. It looked simple—in principle—something a student might accomplish to earn a Ph.D. But so far it had proved intractable.

They had first met about ten years ago at Imperial College in London, where Nurul was professor and Abe Rosenfeld came to spend a month. Abe was four years younger, had just been made associate professor at MIT. A modest commentary in the journal *Physics Letters* had resulted from their interaction. Following this acquaintance, they would meet occasionally at international conferences and exchange friendly words. Each had made his reputation, had his own style and achievements, and was aware of what the other fellow across the ocean was up to.

Six months after the Oslo Symposium, Abe had called him in London. By this time Abe's work on LUT had been published, and news about Nurul's presentation of his own formulation of the theory in Oslo had also spread. The result was the same, their approaches were different.

'Hi, Nurul—you don't mind me calling you Nurul, do you? This is Abe Rosenfeld.'

'Abe Who?' They both laughed.

'Some coincidence, this Lesser Unification Theory of ours. Is it a theory or a model?—I think theory. Anyway, I thought you'd moved into more ambitious territory … supersymmetry.'

'Well, you know I had been working on the Lesser—as they call it nowadays—with David Mason following Schwinger's conjecture, then we dropped it and later I returned to it … long story, but it's been there always. Now it's supersymmetry, of course.'

'We should meet … the renormalization—have you given it more thought? Perhaps two heads …'

A renormalization of any field theory was the process by which unwanted infinite-value terms could be removed from its formalism. These infinite terms had plagued particle physics for a few decades now, but they were usually removable with clever algebra.

'Agreed. You just echoed my own thoughts. I have a student working on it, no success so far.'

'Listen, I'm giving a seminar at Cambridge—I could drop over at Imperial.'

'You should, but I'm planning to be at your seminar. I'll see you there first. Not that we'll get an opportunity to talk.'

They did meet in Cambridge at dinner, with a lot of other people, and Abe said, 'Why don't you come and give us a talk at our Cambridge? Everyone would love to hear you.' And so here he was.

They became friends, when others thought they were merely competitors. Abe was an unassuming fellow who was simply very, very clever. There was an understanding between them that arose partly from their similarly modest beginnings. Abe's father had been a tailor in Baltimore; the family was from Russia, where his maternal grandfather had been a cantor. Nurul's father was a perfumer and part-time muezzin at the mosque, calling out to the faithful to pray when the regular fellow could not make it, for which he received token payment. Sometimes Nurul would sit on the ground outside the mosque steps, behind a small stool on which were displayed his father's concoctions in little bottles in various bright colours. He enjoyed shuffling the bottles around to produce different combinations of colour. Next to him sat a voluble young man selling garish paintings of holy places; and then the fruit vendor. Nurul often said that he almost became an organic chemist. But math got the better of him, it was pure; chemistry was messy, not to say flashy in more ways than one. But when a quantum number was named 'colour,' he had an anecdote for his lectures, describing his technicolour perfume stand outside the mosque of his hometown. Physics was approaching chemistry, perhaps cookery, he would add—some physicists were even speaking of quantum soups!

In Abe's office now, they discussed the renormalization problem for a while, and then somewhat hesitantly Rosenfeld paused to make a suggestion.

'It's a hairy calculation, admittedly. You know ... Alf Greiner of Amsterdam says he can do it. He was present at your lecture yesterday. I met him afterwards. He says he has written a computer program that can do complex algebra ... he can do it faster than we can.'

'I saw him sitting beside Feynman. He doesn't like me. And vice versa. We've had altercations, and I don't figure at all in his little primer on particle physics, while he has a whole page on you with a photo. Sounds petty, I know. Never mind—but does he really have a computer program that can do all that algebra?'

'He's worked on it for a couple of years, he says.'

'OK, then. We leave that problem to him. Let's see if he's right. We move on.'

'If he accomplishes it, that would be the icing on Islam-Rosenfeld. Never mind personal differences.'

'Agreed. We should meet and make up, he and I.'

'You should. We have bigger things to occupy us ... And by the way, that rude interruption at your lecture, ignore it. Such crazies are always around.'

'Always will be, I know.'

The physics part of their meeting over, they chatted for a while, exchanged news about the world of physics, and then Nurul said he wanted to do a bit of shopping, where was the best place to start? Abe suggested a couple of places downtown. 'Take one of my students with you—Hilary should be able to help you. The guys only know army-and-navy besides the Coop.'

He picked up his phone, made a call, and Hilary Chase soon appeared at the door, ready to escort the guest.

'Professor—' began Hilary as they walked through Harvard Yard, and Nurul interrupted, 'Nurul—please. Call me that—the American way, isn't it?'

She turned red. 'I'm so embarrassed, how can I—OK, Nurul … is that right?'

'Good enough. Rhymes with new-rule. You were saying?'

'Prof—Nurul, why don't we shop around the Square first. I'm sure you will find something interesting—something original, you know?—and useful. If not, we can go to Filene's or Jordan Marsh in Boston.'

They went to the little shops and stalls around the Square, inspecting possible gifts for him to take home. She was more at ease in this local element, the outbursts of chatter a sign of remaining nerves and uncertainty. She was from somewhere in Massachusetts. She hated the current president of the country and his cabal of warmongers. She had opinions about big-money physics, technology and physics, humans in space. In much of these she was echoing her mentor, Abe. He was her god.

'Mine was Dirac,' he said simply, though not without practice. The girl beside him gasped, stopped in her tracks, so he had to turn around. 'Have you met him?' she almost whispered. 'I mean, do you know him … well?' Of course he did, he had studied under the great man in Cambridge, at St. John's College, and later briefly he'd been a colleague. When he arrived there, Dirac had already made his great discovery and was legendary.

He told her an anecdote about Dirac.

'Did you hear this one—at a symposium a physicist had just given a lecture, when someone from the audience said, "John, I believe you introduced a sign error in your calculation." And Paul Dirac said quietly, "An odd number of them."'

She burst out laughing, then stopped in embarrassment.

'Is he really like that—Dirac?'

'Yes. Have you heard about the three fishermen who couldn't divide their catch because there was one fish extra?'

She laughed again. 'Yes. Abe told us that one.'

There was something charming about her, on one hand so proper and yet so spontaneous. She had been accepted to work with one of the great scientists of the time and therefore was somebody special in her own right. He stopped, turned to her, and said, 'Listen, it's all right to have gods when you are young. It's good. One day you will be a god—or goddess—to young physicists.'

Let's hope, he said to himself. He had embarrassed her even further.

'I don't know ... Nurul, I feel so inadequate most of the time.'

'We all do—most of the time—until we lose ourselves ...'

He lied. He had always known his strength. He was out to compete with the best of the best, into which fraternity he had been accepted.

At her recommendation, he bought a handmade set of silver jewellery for Sakina from a hippie stall. He didn't tell her that his wife wore only gold wrought by traditional goldsmiths. 'Gold is best,' Sakina Begum would say to him. 'What good is second-best? After all, I got *you* only by demanding the best.' There was a toy microscope and a doll for Muni and electronic calculators for his sons. He noticed her smile at his choices for his children. They discussed lunch and she said, 'Why not get something from a food truck and sit in the Yard, it's nice and sunny,' and they did that.

'Is this all right?' she asked. 'Or would you have preferred somewhere inside and have a beer or something? I'm sorry I didn't ask what you wished for lunch.'

'This is fine,' he said, holding up his can of Coke and the sandwich. 'And anyway, I don't drink.'

'Oh. I'm sorry. I thought ...'

'What? Come on, out with it!'

'Abe said ... he said once that you kept a bottle of Scotch in your office in London ... of course that doesn't mean—'

'Abe said that?' He turned red. 'Well ... once upon a time, but I gave that up.'

Where in Massachusetts did she come from? Salem, she said. Yes, one of her antecedents could have been party to the witch trials. That was the family gossip. As a child she had gone to the Protestant church every Sunday; she had stopped. And *his* family? she asked. What notoriety had they committed in the past? He told her they came from a secret society called thuggees—a name from which the English word *thug* was derived—who roamed the highways of India strangling travellers with knotted handkerchiefs and robbing them. 'Really?' she asked in alarm. He laughed. 'No, I tell that only to raise an expression like yours! Actually we belong to an Islamic mystical sect called the Shirazis, who came some centuries ago from Persia and settled in a little town called Pirmai. And have lived peacefully there ever since. Many invaders passed through the area but the town and the community survived. Only the Partition of India changed it, the Hindus and Sikhs all left.' There were ancient ruins outside the town, he said, on a rise above the river, where he would go and study during his exams in high school.

He became thoughtful.

'Tell me about the Partition of India—I've heard about it.'

A naive question, asked in all innocence. He shook his head. 'It's a big subject, better to read about it.'

'I'm sorry—again. I ask too many silly questions, don't I? I promise to leave you alone after this.'

He looked at her, blushing and wide-eyed, and caught himself. In the pale, glancing light on the Yard she was suddenly rather enchanting.

'Not at all. And no, don't—why don't you come to listen to me at MIT this afternoon?'

'Can I?'

'Of course—if you are interested in the subject. You'll learn another side of me.'

'What—what is the subject?'

'The scientific golden age of the Muslim world.'

'I'm interested. When?'

'In an hour. We should leave now.'

They got up, disposed of the trash and hastened to his hotel, where they left his packages and her backpack, and took a cab to MIT.

In an inexplicable way Nurul Islam felt lively, even youthful. As they climbed up the front steps of the institute, she barely keeping up with him, he found himself smiling. Now what is it? he asked himself. He looked up and saw two tentative-looking young men coming down to greet him. He introduced Hilary Chase to them.

*He was the third child growing up in their two-bedroom home in Pirmai, with two brothers and two sisters. Both parents took pride in his precocious abilities, never missing an opportunity to show him off. His mother, Halima Begum, taught him to read the complete Quran. He was six when he had mastered the Book by heart, a feat demonstrated in a special session at the mosque. Starting at that age, Nurul would accompany his father to the mosque for the Friday midday prayer, and afterwards, sitting on the pavement outside he would recite from the Book, taking requests from people, and receive gifts of money in appreciation. A local legend. Since early on he had formed a special attachment to his father, Ghulam Ali Shirazi. It was Ghulam Ali who attended to Nurul's early secular education, supplementing the rudimentary lessons of a small-town primary school with lessons from hired tutors. Until his death, he would proudly follow his son's successes. When he was older, the boy would assist his father in preparing his attars, grinding aromatic flowers and spices, adding solutions and essences, filtering the perfumes into little bottles for sale. When he was a famous physicist, he would fondly recall for his audiences a perfume he had named Bint al ajaib, or 'Wonder Woman.' He would mock-ruefully confess he had forgotten the formula for it.*

The Massachusetts Institute of Technology always filled Nurul Islam with a sense of wonder whenever he returned to it: squatted firmly beside the Charles, grey and compact, bustling with serious purpose—despite the sweet and quite contrary aroma of chocolate wafting down over it from the factory up the avenue. Here was a sense of purpose and industry fully displayed in everything you saw. The long, narrow corridors under the domes hummed with brainpower. When they spoke here, it was with excitement, always from some threshold of new discovery. When they joked, you could bet there was some intellect involved. Even when they philosophized, one could sense the gears moving, or—nowadays—the zeroes and ones constantly shifting registers. They could do with some serenity, Nurul had always thought.

The auditorium, the famous Room 10-250, was packed this afternoon, the faculty members seated in front. They would be judging him: What's happened to Nurul Islam? He's not that old. Is he already past his prime? On the other hand, this was a good time for the kind of lecture he had chosen to give today, young people in their counterculture rebellion were eagerly receptive to non-Western ideas and philosophies: Tao, Zen, Sufism, Hinduism, Islam, you name it, they were ready to listen. There were members of the public present too. The lecture, titled 'What Happened to the Islamic Golden Age?,' had received advance attention. A group of bearded men stood at the back, representing some mosque, Nurul guessed. His own invitation to speak at the Quincy mosque had been rescinded, no reason given.

'I will start with a man called al-Biruni,' Nurul began, having been lavishly introduced by the institute provost, Jerome Jerome. 'An itinerant scholar born in present-day Uzbekistan in the late tenth century, he wrote books on astronomy, mathematics, geography, anthropology, and physics. He commented on instrumentation, on the earth's rotation, noncircular orbits, and—contrary to Aristotle—the existence of the vacuum. Based on his calculation of the earth's radius, he predicted the existence of a continent between Asia and Europe—lo and behold: America! (A stir in the audience.) He knew Persian, Greek, Sanskrit and several other languages. And he spent ten years in India studying its culture, its society, and its science—a Muslim, yet a dispassionate observer of the world. Even today, his observations about India are valued, because there are hardly any other accounts from that period available. His book on India, my friends, is still in print nine hundred years later! Last night when I went out for my walk, I found a copy at Harvard Book Store. Find a scholar and scientist of that breadth anywhere in the world today.

'Then there was al-Tusi, who having switched his allegiance to the Mongols—who had conquered Persia and much else—founded under their auspices in Azerbaijan an institute of advanced studies. A tenth-century predecessor of the Institute at Princeton today, it drew scientists and scholars from all over. A coward, you may call him for switching his allegiance, but as we know, scholars will bow to any government that supports their research ...'

Laughter.

'Ibn al-Haytham, known to the Europeans as Alhazen, anticipated Fermat's Principle of Least Time by centuries and the principle of inertia, which became Newton's First Law of Motion six centuries later; Avicenna—or Ibn Sina—whose great book, the *Canon of Medicine*, was used for centuries even in Europe and India ...'

'Let me tell you about a certain philosophical novel called *Hayy bin Yakzan*, written in Arabic—which we can translate as 'Alive, Son of Awake'—by one Ibn Tufail in the thirteenth century. In this novel an infant on an island where there are no humans is fed and brought up by a doe, a female deer. That is the world the child knows. And then this mother dies, and the poor child wants to know, How could she be unresponsive, why is she so still? Motionless, not breathing. He cuts her open to investigate, and thus begins his discovery of the natural world—why things are a certain way, what rules govern them. Why a stone falls down and not up. The power of human observation and reason. The novel has profound philosophical consequences. I will not go into them. It has been called a precursor to *Robinson Crusoe*. For me it is a premodern postmodern novel, for the author gives two causes for the infant's presence on the island ...'

'Reason was valued. Observation was valued. What else is that but the credo of modern science? al-Biruni, a scientist above all else, wrote, "Science is good in itself ... its lure is everlasting and unbroken." When he was accused once of having used the Byzantine—therefore Christian—solar calendar for an instrument he was calibrating, he retorted, "The Byzantines bake bread, would you now proscribe baking bread?"'

Nurul Islam had warmed to his subject and had to be cautioned for time. Jerome Jerome gave him the slightest nod. Nurul Islam acknowledged. His new passion, he wrapped up, had begun as a mild curiosity about the history of physics, spurring an idle walk from his office to the British Library one rainy afternoon. What he discovered then and on the subsequent more urgent visits was a wealth of information, a knowledge hidden to most people but to which he could relate as a Muslim. And so he was led naturally to ask, What has happened since then?

'What I am saying is, first, that eminent scientists of the past have practised Islam. Their science preceded and presaged European science by a few centuries. But I am saying more. Islam itself encourages science. The Quran urges mankind to be curious about the Creation. The Prophet himself said, Go to China if you have to, to acquire knowledge.

'Why then, after such glorious achievements, were Muslims left behind, how did they become so backward? Take a look at the contents of all the current physics journals in the library, and you will be lucky to find one contribution by a Muslim. I learned about electricity in my hometown of Pirmai, in the Punjab, by the River Beas. But I did not know what electricity looked like, because we had no lights in Pirmai. I had to go to college in Lahore to discover electricity and the electromagnetic force. There I learned about another force, the nuclear force, which my teachers told me not to worry about, it belonged to Europe and America! How did this sorry state of affairs come about? Here in your cities like Cambridge and Boston buildings are lit up all night, while in my birthplace there is total darkness at night. I believe that this decline was due in good measure to the rise of fanaticism in Muslim lands, a belief that science was inimical to true faith in God; that if you believed in God and prayed five times a day and fasted during the holy month of Ramadan, then you did not have to worry about how the universe worked. Merciful Allah took care of it, why bother? There were other causes too for this retrogressive thinking, but wilful ignorance was a major one. So much so that the great Imam Ghazali was moved to write, already in 1100 AD, "A grievous crime indeed has been committed by a man who imagines that Islam is defended by the denial of the mathematical sciences, seeing that there is nothing in these sciences opposed to the truth of religion."'

Alas, there was such fanaticism still present today. There were Muslims who believed that theoretical science—speculation and imagination—was a sin. That to do fundamental physics was to worship another god. That science was Western idolatry, or a Zionist plot, or magic designed to confuse and exploit the rest of the world. In Pakistan recently someone suggested that the current energy crisis could be solved by tapping into the energies of djinns. (That sent a ripple of laughter through the hall.) But science, physics in particular, was a gift to mankind, it was a challenge to the human intellect and provided means through its applications to make our lives better.

'I believe science, in its broadest sense,' concluded Nurul Islam, 'can lead to a unification of cultures. We talk of the grand unification of forces; I say let those forces be the clashing different cultures and civilizations of the world. It is more important to unify them.'

Nurul Islam was a good speaker, if not a flamboyant one; he was a famous scientist; therefore in this bastion of science and technology he received a standing ovation. The questions that were asked were generous, and some comments by the Muslim students were earnest and sometimes emotional. He represented them. To his quote from the Quran extolling curiosity, there were two other quotes to reinforce it.

Just as the provost stood up to thank the speaker, an angry voice, identifiably South Asian, called out from the back. It belonged to a tall, broad-shouldered young man with abundant curly hair and an undisciplined beard. He wore a pink kurta over his jeans, and beads round his neck. 'My name is Qadir Khan,' he declared. His voice became louder as he went on. 'And I am a proud Muslim! I come from the backward country that you mentioned, the one that you have abandoned and maligned—'

'But, my young friend, I carry a Pakistani passport,' Nurul told him in his genial manner.

'You are British. You talk of Islam yet you do not practise it—you make fun of your birthplace—'

'My dear sir, on what evidence do you base this contention?'

'This … this … unification of cultures and religions you speak about is a smokescreen—a denial of the Holy Quran. If you are a Muslim then you know that the Quran is the last word and Muhammad is the last prophet—'

Qadir Khan was booed and shut up. In frustration he turned towards the back door to leave the auditorium, but not without a final word flung at Nurul, 'You speak of unification while sitting in the comfort of the West, when our brothers and sisters in India are being butchered by Hindu mobs—and the Palestinians—'

To an angry shout of 'Why don't you go help your brothers, then?' Qadir Khan shouted a reply, 'That's where I am going! Watch me!'

Nurul watched the broad pink back receding as the doors closed behind it.

There were apologies for the outrageous behaviour of the student, and the provost assured Nurul privately that disciplinary action would be taken; Mr Khan could well be on his way home sooner than he expected. Nurul said not to worry, it was nothing serious, only a young man excited and homesick. But actually, walking out of the crowded, noisy auditorium, he felt shell-shocked, disoriented, as though he were in a vacuum bubble and all the voices were outside it. He had not been attacked so viciously before. At Harvard, the previous day, there had been at least a semblance of form to the attack. It had been insidious, though … and now this. Young people from South Asia normally came in his presence to touch his feet, out of gratitude and respect. What could have made Qadir Khan so angry and contemptuous as to lose control of himself?

'I am sorry, you didn't deserve that,' Hilary said, coming over during the reception following the lecture, and he retorted, 'Who does?' and then immediately apologized, squeezing her arm. 'Sorry.'

She turned red. 'Oh. But don't worry about it ... you have a lot of admirers.' She smiled and made to leave as three anxious-looking young men came and surrounded him.

He didn't wish her goodbye, instead reminded her she should pick up her things from his room, why didn't she wait for him. They would go back together and perhaps have dinner.

She agreed, 'OK,' and wandered away.

But later at the hotel she declined dinner when she picked up her pack. 'You've had enough of this ignorant American girl, I'm sure,' she said with an embarrassed smile.

'Not at all,' he replied. And after a pause, 'I could do with company, after that ... that rocket.'

'Thank you.' Eyes flashing. 'How about Chinese—the Hong Kong on the Square—would you like that?'

'I'd love that.'

'How about meeting there in—'

'Forty-five minutes?'

She left, and he went and sat down on the chair. Careful, Nurul Islam. What?—she's just a girl. A girl?

She had changed into a jean skirt and a silk blouse. Better than the blue jeans everyone wore like a uniform, he thought. He wore a clean shirt, no tie, and his jacket. They sat in a window booth and when the food arrived she taught him how to use chopsticks.

'What did you think of that student who attacked you in your lecture?' she asked.

'Misguided youth,' he said. 'Not different, I dare say, from the young people in protest marches here—'

As she opened her mouth to object, he corrected himself, 'I know, protesting against government policies is different from calling someone an agent of imperialism and a heretic.'

'A heretic?'

'That's what people like that do, back home, and they can be dangerous.'

'My sister, Jill, is one of the protesters. She's the radical. I'm the straitlaced one, out of tune with my generation. I'll probably grow up to be an old maid!'

'You? Hardly. You're still young, bright, and attractive. If I may say so.'

'Thank you.' She smiled. 'Were you always straight—didn't you protest?'

'I did get into mischief, of course! All sorts. But for me learning was a privilege—as it is for many young people in that part of the world. Physics and mathematics thrilled me—I wanted to learn more and more … and to do it. I knew I could. Arriving in Cambridge—England—that's when my shell truly broke.'

She was gazing at him.

He told her how, freshly arrived, he caused a lot of amusement when he greeted his tutors and professors by bending to touch their feet the way he had been taught at home—show respect for elders and teachers. When he greeted Dirac thus, that night when he first saw him in the dining hall of St. John's, the great man asked mildly, 'Have you dropped something, young man?'

She broke out into a loud peal of laughter, which she stifled in embarrassment with a quick look around. He smiled.

They talked long, until the flickering lights signalled closure. It was, he later thought, a shattering experience, crashing into his composure, his confidence. And much later, he would add, into his life.

They had parted with a formal embrace that hovered on the edge of a hug. At the end of which they recoiled like two similar magnetic poles and with Goodnight and Goodnight, they walked away. She'd had enough of him and she was right, he thought. That embrace had been her full stop, the American way. And she had saved him.

The following morning he attended Abe Rosenfeld's class on advanced quantum mechanics, during which he and Abe fell into a discussion on recent interpretations of the formalism, and Einstein's objections to it, as the students sat gaping. Hilary Chase sat behind the class as the professor's assistant. They had greeted each other formally and he went on his way. It was for the best. He had dinner alone in his room.

The next morning she called. 'Would you like me to show you around Boston … Nurul? All the historic sites … if you have time …'

He waited, then said quickly, 'Why not? I have an interview at WBTN in a couple of hours.'

'I remember, you told me. I'll see you there then.'

*When he was a student at Cambridge University in England he wrote regularly to his father, in a formal Urdu, though Punjabi was used at home, was the language in which he had felt at ease for many years. He would tell his father about the lectures he attended, his professors' traits, his marks; and later what research he was doing. He wrote of the conditions in postwar England. 'This is the harshest winter on record. The ears freeze, the fingers freeze. The rooms are cold as ice. And I miss the sun. Back there we thought the English were lords, but conditions here are dire. All due to the recent war, they explain. Still, I enjoy the academic atmosphere, and the beautiful rose garden at my college, and the library is superb. To distract myself I read poetry and history. I've learnt much about the history of Islam. There are some Punjabi students here and we meet occasionally for gup-shup in our language and drink tea.' He asked if he should return home after his degree and join the civil service. Ghulam Ali replied, 'Stay put—what is home now? Nobody is sure.' There had been riots against 'heretic' sects in Lahore …*

*Gradually Nurul Islam began to feel as comfortable in English as he was in Punjabi; it was comforting not to have to repeat himself to the ladies in the market, to say the right greeting or reply to one without drawing a smile. It was an accomplishment, but he wondered if he was losing his grip on his native culture.*

JANE CURTIN: This is WBTN's *Crosstalk*, and I am Jane Curtin. With me this morning is renowned Pakistani British physicist Professor Nurul Islam, who is currently visiting Harvard University. Good morning, Professor Islam. Welcome to our show.

NURAL ISLAM: Good morning, Jane. Thank you for having me.

JC: It's a pleasure. I understand you were born in Pakistan but currently reside in London.

NI: Yes, I am a professor at Imperial College. You may have heard of it.

JC: Of course. You were a child prodigy, Professor Islam. Tell us what it was like to be a prodigy in a small town in Pakistan, where I understand you grew up. Could you find enough to stimulate you there, Professor?

NI: [laughs] Apparently I did. You see, I could keep myself occupied with mathematics, and the textbooks we studied were the same ones they used in England. Perhaps a little dated, but in the essentials they were the same. Physics is physics everywhere, maths is maths. In India and Pakistan we lagged behind in the most recent developments in science, but not too much.

JC: And now?

NI: That's still the case. In engineering, we are far behind. Space travel and satellites, electronics—they are a long way off. They require too many resources. Whereas in mathematics all you need is a pencil and a notebook—or even a scrap of paper!

JC: Just so. And using a pencil on paper, you wrote down your first mathematics result.

NI: Well, actually I was in first-year university. I improved upon an arithmetical theorem first proved by Ramanujan, an Indian mathematician.

JC: Another prodigy.

NI: As a matter of fact, yes. A great mathematician from South India.

JC: Now your father was a religious figure—he called the town—or village—to prayer at the mosque. Tell us what that entails. How many times a day did he have to do that?

NI: Actually, he did it occasionally—perhaps three or four times a week, when the regular imam was indisposed. There was a loudspeaker mounted on the outside wall of our mosque, where he would stand and call out—he would recite a formula, calling people to come and pray.

JC: And when he called, they would come.

NI: [laughs] Some. Not all people pray at the mosque all the time. The call is only a reminder. You could think of it as a town clock. People can and do pray wherever they are. Those who can, go to the mosque.

JC: You are a devout Muslim. You say your prayers every day?

NI: I try.

JC: How do you reconcile the two, Professor? From my understanding, most particle physicists are not religious. Surely your colleagues at Harvard or in London are not. How do you reconcile a belief in God with a belief in science—that everything can be explained by the rational mind?

NI: I don't, Jane. For me the two are separate, two different descriptions of our universe. They do not interfere with each other—at least in my mind they don't.

JC: You are a great admirer of Professor Dirac of Cambridge University in England, who is now more of a colleague, I understand.

NI: He is one of the greatest physicists of our times.

JC: Apparently, you've been quoted as saying that when you first saw him in Cambridge, as a young man fresh from Pakistan, it was—let me get this straight—as if—as if you had seen a manifestation of God!

NI: [laughs] I said that? Well, it was a profound, almost a mystical experience. To see in the flesh the man who wrote down the Dirac equation!

JC: Professor Islam, you are credited with many developments, the most important of which is the unification of two forces [pauses] … Professor Rosenfeld of Harvard came up with the same idea. Which of you got there first?

NI: I see you've heard some rumours. Jane, physics is not like the hundred-metre dash—although there are people who do think that way. Including physicists … and the media—forgive me—enjoy the idea of a race. But the reality is that a lot of people contribute to any new theory directly or indirectly. A lot of ideas are up there in the air. Physics is a culture. If you have an idea, you can almost be certain that someone has thought about it before. And then someone or the other gets to put the crown …

JC: Someone like you and Abe Rosenfeld. Some say a Nobel is on the way, surely. Is that just reward?

NI: A just reward is the satisfaction of getting something right, seeing the beauty on the page—and being acknowledged by one's peers. When you think about it, how many people in the world, for example those now walking outside on Boylston Street, know about the fundamental particles—let alone who won what and when?

JC: [laughs] I agree. I don't remember who won the prizes last year. The reward is the beauty of the creation. What are you working on now?

NI: I—and a few other people—are working on a greater unification—a unification of three forces. As you may know, there are four fundamental forces in nature—the electromagnetic, the weak, the strong, and the gravitational, and—you want me to go on?

JC: [laughs] Yes, please. I'll try to understand as much as I can, with my limited means!

NI: [laughs] Well. The electromagnetic force you know—it is what attracts a positive charge to a negative charge. What causes a shock when you touch a live wire. The weak force is one that changes a neutron into a proton, and vice versa. And we believe we now have one description for these two. It is what Abe Rosenfeld and I and many others have worked on. The strong force is what holds an atomic nucleus together—the attraction between protons and neutrons. It is responsible for what we call nuclear energy. Some of us are currently attempting to unify these three forces. Give them a single formulation. And when we've done that, there remains the gravitational force. Is that too much?

JC: Somewhat. I think I get the gist. And how far have you reached with unifying the three forces? If you can divulge that.

NI: Not very far. It's all very complicated mathematically. And incomplete. But we'll get there.

JC: A unified theory, wow. A theory of everything?

NI: If we include gravity, yes. A theory of how our universe is put together.

JC: A scientific alternative to God?

NI: So some say. Or a monument to God. A metaphor … Depends on how you think about God. This still is a burning question for philosophers of religion. (But God is also a very personal phenomenon, he could have said—'He is closer to you than your jugular vein,' as the Prophet Muhammad used to say. But Nurul did not want to get into that discussion. It was never easy to discuss God with agnostics or atheists … or with anyone.)

JC: And once you have unified everything, then what, Professor?

NI: There will always be questions to answer, puzzles to solve. Our world is a wonderfully complex place. God likes to play with us—to misquote Albert Einstein.

JC: And he said?

NI: God doesn't play with dice.

JC: I'm glad you admit that our world is wonderfully complex. Well, thank you very much, Professor Islam, and good luck with your research. Enjoy our city.

NI: Thank you, Jane. I intend to!

Hilary was waiting for him at reception, sipping absently from a glass of water. The radio was on here, tuned to the station. She looked lovely, the morning sun illuminating her brown hair, tied at the back. The long face, the large eyes striking. Beauty in its simplicity and elegance, Einstein's mantra. She caught him staring at her and smiled and got up, and they walked out through the glass outer doors.

'Well?' he asked. 'Did you hear the interview? How did it sound?'

'You did great, you seemed quite at ease. Obviously you have done these before. But … to be honest, Nurul, I'm not entirely sure about a theory of everything—whether it's possible …'

He laughed. 'I'm not sure either. We think that when the fundamental laws of physics are all known, we will explain everything about the universe. Can you explain human nature? Can you explain the miracle of love, for instance? … the attraction between two people?'

Some would say it's all in the brain. And the brain cells have DNA, which is made up of molecules and atoms, which are made up of electrons and protons and so on. And so we should be able to explain everything, including love and war, using the laws of physics. In principle. How far, really, could the explanations of physics go? He looked at her and smiled.

'No, I can't,' she said. 'I can't explain the miracle of love.'

'Something threw me off there, though. Quite unexpected. That question about Dirac—about the moment when I first laid eyes on him—I wonder how she came to know about that … how I felt … at that moment.'

'Oh. She spoke to me while they were fitting you up in the studio, Nurul. It just came out of me. Was that wrong of me—something I shouldn't have said?'

'They are smart, these media people.'

'Yes.'

It was a lovely autumn day, bright and warm, they could have been walking inside a painting. People were out in numbers. 'I thought we could take the T to Haymarket, have lunch there, then walk back to the Boston Common along the Freedom Trail—do you know about it?'

'Sounds fine.'

'OK, then.' She put her arm into his—at which he gave a small start, raising a smile on her face. On the way she repeated the story of the famous Boston Tea Party and about Paul Revere's midnight ride to warn the patriots that the British were coming.

'It's always puzzled me,' he said. 'Why would the Americans want independence from the mother country? They were the same people, after all.'

She responded, 'Now America is many peoples.'

'You're right.'

She appreciated that.

After a longish trek through the old city, they finally sat down on a bench in the Boston Common. It was a busy place. Very soon a tall blonde girl, wearing a crumpled saffron sari and a red dot on her forehead, came by to induct them into the movement of Krishna Consciousness. They declined the offer, and the proffered hard-bound colourful *Bhagavad Gita*, and the girl loped off to join her singing, tambourine-banging cohort. In the far distance a crowd had gathered to hear Noam Chomsky and Howard Zinn speak against America's involvement in Indochina, as a passerby informed them, leaving a flyer behind. Nurul had heard of Chomsky, who was a professor at MIT, and had even met him briefly after his lecture there; the other man he didn't know. Policemen were about, including a couple mounted on horses. Still, he thought, except for that rally in the distance, life seemed as normal as ever. Was it just America happily balancing extremes? Or he, in a sunny autumn daze? He took in the scene closer at hand: a couple of women pushing prams, two middle-aged men on lunch break throwing a baseball to each other.

Drawn into their own selves, they had not spoken for some time. Finally he turned to look at her, just when she turned and flashed her eyes at him. Their shared time together had so charged the air between them that the tension was barely bearable. Two magnets holding themselves apart, as he would observe to himself another day.

'Thank you, Hilary, for taking the time off—to give me this tour.'

'Do you have to say that?'

'Yes.'

Saying which, he abruptly stiffened.

'What is it?' she asked.

'I thought I recognized someone—across the street there. Staring at us.'

She followed his eyes but saw nothing in particular. 'Why would anyone care?' she murmured.

'Just my imagination,' he said.

'There's a song that goes like that—*just my imagination* ...' She laughed, then hummed the tune, nodding her head, and was almost a child, he observed.

There came the sound of applause from the rally in the distance, fists were raised. The mounted police remained unperturbed.

'Have you been drawn by politics, Nurul? The war in Indochina, nuclear disarmament, and so on?'

'No, I'm not political in the larger sense. Not involved, as such—that would be too distracting. My research comes first. But I do have causes!'

'And? What are they? I know of one of them!'

'Yes, I would like to tell the world about the contributions made to science by people of the Muslim faith. Here in the West, it is generally assumed that science began with the Greeks and proceeded in a straight line via Galileo and Newton on to Einstein. That is patently false, as I demonstrated in my lecture yesterday.'

'And the other cause?'

'I would like to bring the joy and thrill of pure science to the world's less privileged peoples—what is called the third world. I would like them to have opportunities to do field theory and abstract mathematics and physics ... They are missing out on an exciting human venture. Intellectual exploration. I want to share with them that joy and thrill ... see one of them stand shoulder to shoulder with an Einstein or a Dirac ... If I could find the money, I would start an institute of theoretical physics—in Lahore ... or Lagos or ...'

'Nairobi?'

He laughed. 'Yes.' And perhaps David Mason can head it.

She was staring at him. He opened his mouth to say more, then thought the better of it. They both fell silent.

What curiosity! he thought. Like she were probing a strange particle. But she was not offensive. Just ... curious.

'Does your religion mean so much to you, Nurul?' she asked.

He did not reply.

'Sorry. Do you actually pray, Nurul?' There was wonder, anxiety in her voice.

'Yes, I do, Hilary. I pray to Allah. But I am not a fanatic. It's what I grew up to believe and what I believe. That there's a God. And there's His Book. And there was the Prophet. And you? Is it only physics?'

'I go to church with my father when I go home … my mother's dead. I think I told you that already. But I don't think about church as such. It's more cultural, I suppose, my going. A sense of duty.'

'I see.'

A church is a sacred place, an awesome place, he thought, surely that must have rubbed off on her sensitive soul? She's hardly a cold rationalist …

'You must be very … moral,' she said.

'I can be tempted,' he replied after a moment, with a tremor in his voice, staring at those freckles, the bare shoulder, the brassiere between the buttons. Her wide eyes upon him, daring him. She was—

'Then please be …'

'Not yet.'

They leaned towards each other, stopped, then briefly kissed. A dry, frightened kiss.

Nurul Islam, you bastard. He mentally uttered some choice expletives to himself in Punjabi. *Bewakoof. Neech. Badmash.* But by this time she had moved closer and was leaning wholly on him, her head on his shoulder.

'I thought of you all that night,' she said simply. 'After the dinner. I couldn't help it. I didn't want to, but I did. And yesterday, I know you avoided me deliberately.'

You have to be young to be so bold, he thought.

'I thought of you too,' he said, finally. 'Couldn't help it,' he muttered. 'Though you seemed to have had enough of me—'

She laughed. 'For a while. I was uncertain … and frightened …'

'Frightened?'

'That attack by the student—the effect it had on you … I thought I'd better leave you alone.'

'I'm glad you didn't.'

'I want to know everything about you,' she said.

'Are you sure? You want to know more?' He laughed lightly. 'I'm too complicated.'

'We're all complicated.'

'True.'

'But I've lived a sheltered life, I know. I've missed out on a lot ... but that's fortunate, isn't it?'

He didn't reply, squeezed her arm.

*He frequently recalled this image of his father: a short, stocky, solitary figure waiting for him by the track at the dark railway stop of Pirmai, holding up a lamp. Wearing a white kurta-pajama which shone in the night light, and his grey Kullu shawl wrapped tightly around his shoulder. This was Nurul's sentimental memory, an emblematic scene. He had returned from Delhi, having booked passage there on a steamship from Bombay to Southampton. Meanwhile there had been riots between Hindus and Muslims in the area and a curfew had been declared.*

*'But, Abba, how can the violence reach here, in our town? We are friends with each other.'*

*'It is here, that's all,' his father replied curtly, his hand on Nurul's shoulder. 'Some say it's outsiders who are bringing it. Let's get home quickly.'*

*His teachers had been both Hindu and Muslim. On the day his matriculation results were released, Nurul had bicycled into the main street, which was called Ames Street then, to grab a newspaper, and the shopkeepers had all come out to cheer him, having already seen the results in the papers. 'Our Nurul' had obtained the best result in the whole of Punjab, ever. Our Nurul.*

*That harmony broken so easily, the world would never be the same.*

*'Anyone dead?' he asked his father.*

*'Two.'*

*'Who?'*

*'Doesn't matter. Let's go.'*

*They walked home in silence. On the way, Abba said, 'Good thing you are going away. Though Allah Himself knows we don't want you to go. But there will be more trouble.'*

*A few weeks later he took the boat to England. And missed first-hand the horrors of the Partition. But it did not leave him untouched.*

What have you done, Nurul Islam?

Thankfully there were no messages awaiting him, and he sank into the armchair in his room. At your age, behaving like a child, like a raw Punjabi lafanga, shame on you. He had travelled to so many places, nothing like this had happened before. Not even a temptation, when some among his colleagues carried on quick affairs lasting all of the three or four days of a large conference.

What was it about this slim, open-eyed young woman who smelled of fresh soap and light perfume? Dressed simply in jeans or a long skirt and a shirt. There was an honesty about her that simply drew him in. There was no motive or device in her—if he had told her to go away, she would have gone. He could sense on his hands the impressions of her touch, on his shoulder the weight of her head, recall the impression on his cheeks of the strands of her smooth brown hair; on his lips and moustache the indelible memory of that quick, hasty pressure in which the passion was in the implication, the first step taken. He was thoroughly compromised. He lifted his hand to his mouth, quickly dropped it. The smell of her hair. Oh God. Y'Allah.

There was no going back, was there. Did he want to go back? He had seen, experienced possibility; gone beyond the accepted bounds into unknown territory. But this was not a theory of physics, this was his life, and others'. Could base—was it base?—instinct—was it instinct?—could it be so overpowering as to brush aside the barrier of responsibility and commitment?

They had spent the entire afternoon together, oblivious of time, of place; there had been a visit to the Museum of Science, more revelations at the coffee shop (stares directed at them), a long walk with no fixed destination, and the ride back on the Red Line to Cambridge. He'd returned to his room, showered, rested, then they'd met for dinner at the Irish pub on the Square. He walked her to her place nearby, then a kiss, a peck, and he walked back to his hotel.

He had been in a dream. Walked into Wonderland, and for that long day left his world behind. They'd even shared a glass of champagne, as though to crown his sin. Just this once, she'd suggested, but don't feel pressured, and he'd agreed, just for this unique moment. Allah, look away.

My dear girl—Hilary—I'm sorry. What must you think of me? I don't know what overcame me—travel fatigue, I think, and the two rockets fired at me at my lectures—they affected me more than I thought was possible. I felt lonely and threatened. I was called a cheat and then a heretic—but so what? But now I'm truly sorry, I shouldn't have imposed on you … forced my company on you … As the older person and your teacher, so to speak, I should have acted more responsibly. Forgive me. Let's forget it, shall we? Let's be friends, and if you need any help, a recommendation letter or anything else … let me know.

Whom was he fooling? She was young but not a child. She was not an innocent Punjabi village girl, a Heer or a Layla. She was wise about the world, must have had boyfriends. She hadn't gone away after his lecture at MIT, she had waited for him. Another girl would have said, See you in the morning. She had flirted with him. And this morning she had called him up to show him around Boston. She had enjoyed his company, and he had liked her. Very much. Why? Why not? It's OK to like a woman, you're a man, but do you have to kiss her as well? And hold hands like a besotted teenager? And drink champagne with her to celebrate? You have a family. Wife, *three* children. Have you gone mad? Yes, I have.

And she? An American, another culture, no religion. That's what she said, anyway. This was not his league.

Now what?

I'm sorry, Hilary … Am I sorry? Perhaps she is sorry. Would that solve the problem neatly? Solve the problem. Renormalize, cut off the infinity. Because it was into an unknown infinity of a romance that he was heading.

He went to bed, lay on his back. As he fell asleep he explained to himself that with Hilary he had spoken to a kindred soul, felt a hand on his heart, as an Urdu poem described it. He had never confided in anyone like that, never felt so … understood? So spiritually close to someone. Allah, you claim to be always with me. Now what? Give it time, Allah says.

He woke up at four as usual, said the shahada, There is no God but Him, then his prayer, had a digestive with his coffee and stood awhile looking out the window. There was not a thought in his head. Harvard Square looked drained save for a single vehicle crawling on the road, out delivering newspapers or milk, he couldn't say. The dark entrance to the subway like the mouth of a wide cave. Soon this macabre stillness would fill with all the clamour of the world. Great intellects would mill around casually here and eventually wind up in … the stars? He turned and went to the couch, looked down at his notes on the table, all neatly stacked but in haphazard order, presumably by the room cleaner the previous day. He put them in order and picked up his pencil. He sharpened it.

It was some time later when the phone rang. Outside, dawn had struck. A bus ground its gears as it began its rounds for the day.

'Hello?'

'Nurul?' His heart skipped. It's starting. 'Is it too early? You said you always woke up early …'

'Yes … no, it's not too early.'

'Nurul? …'

'I'm sorry. How are you? It's early for you though, isn't it?'

'Yes, but I couldn't sleep.'

You shouldn't think too much in bed, he thought of saying, but that was too flippant. *She couldn't sleep because she's been thinking of yesterday and last night while you thought you slept it off. Have you slept it off?* Her voice sounded anxious but he could still hear that innocence, that freshness in it; it frightened him. He could imagine her long, fair face, the straight brown hair, the hazel eyes. Hazel?—what exactly is that? …

She was waiting.

'Would you like to come for breakfast?' he asked.

'Would you like me to?'

Caught. Howzzat? as they appeal in cricket. Out, says the umpire.

'Yes. Of course I would like you to.'

Of course, of course, of course.

Hilary, Hilary, Hilary. A lovely name, a new sound in his life.

Sakina Begum called.

'Where were you last night? I called but there was no reply.'

'I was out to dinner. You should have left a message, and I would have called you.'

'You could have called. Do I have to remind you?'

'No, my dear. But it's costly to call from here, especially from a hotel. We're not millionaires, and as I keep reminding you—'

'—You're not a carpet merchant, as you've told me many times.'

He laughed. 'How are you? How are things at home?'

'Muni was sick.'

'What happened? And how is she now?'

'She has a cold, slight fever. She'll be all right, I took her to Dr Khan.'

'Good.'

'That tap in the bathroom is still leaking. You'll have to give that Asif a talking-to.'

Asif was the plumber, short of work, which was why Nurul used him.

'I will, when I get back.' How important was this? He shouldn't get impatient. 'And how are you keeping?'

'Good. Listen—'

'Yes, my dear?'

'Won't you reconsider and give a speech at Maher's daughter's wedding?'

'I won't give a speech. I don't know the girl.'

'All right. But bring an electric blanket as a present.'

'It works at a different voltage here.'

'What difference does it make?'

'It makes a difference. You don't want your niece on fire on her wedding night, do you?'

'What a thing to say! Thoo-thoo.'

Khuda hafiz, Godbless, and they hung up.

Was this what she'd called for? That was unfair, she missed him. The question arose in his mind, not for the first time, though it hadn't for several years now, whether there had ever been love between them. But that was the wrong question. There was love, but it was woven out of mutual care and dependence, affection and respect. Their duties were cleanly defined, his those of a provider and protector, to give her a name and a home with children; hers of a mother and homemaker. She lent dignity to their home, a solidity. And he fulfilled her womanhood. There had never been between them the spontaneous passion, the romantic 'love' of the films, the *ishq* of the poets, let alone the kind of passion the kids exhibited so freely these days in the streets of London. Beatles and so on. Love, love me do. Having followed the traditional path of marriage, he had missed that feeling of the heart, and only the treasured memory of his teenage infatuation with his tutor's daughter, Sharmila, remained. His British colleagues had assured him, however, that their kind of love and his kind both converged to the same boring march to the drummer in the end.

He would never abandon Sakina Begum. How could he forget that shy look of the girl with the gold stud on her nose, the head covered, her barely disguised uncertainty as she stepped off the Southampton docks with him. Surely she too must have had her dreams of 'love' in her hometown. Pyaar. Ishq. Mohabbat. She had followed him abroad possessing only the rudiments of English, and learnt the cold hard ways of England, putting up with his occasional impatience—she would drop her fork, not used to eating with it, or forget to wear her gloves in the cold—and made him a home. She had to face the foreignness, the racism, being taken for a fool because of the way she spoke and dressed. He at least had his prestige and his work to hide behind, his travels that gave him the confidence to deal with crass racism. There had been the possibility of their going away to a sunnier America, where rooms were heated, warm water endless, and the pay better, but he had resisted, too used to English ways; London fog and tea and sausage rolls. Grumpy faces on the Tube. And there was the thought that in America they would be even farther away from their families.

He could squeeze Sakina Begum's arm with affection, give her a peck on the cheek that would turn her face red; he could never chase her in the rain in the manner of a Raj Kapoor … kiss her passionately, pinch or squeeze her bottom—now more ample and fleshier—lewdly the way his Punjabi blood sometimes demanded. Grab her … He could not even imagine her that way. They had their family, which bound them; and their years together, which bound them too. They had created a kind of love between them. But he could not talk to her about anything but family matters. Electric blanket. Maher's daughter's wedding. Dr Khan.

*When he first returned from Cambridge, after three years, preparations for his wedding were well underway. His father had informed him by letter that a bride had been chosen for him. He needed a wife so far away from home. She would make sure he ate well, remained healthy, and stayed away from bad habits. She was his father's elder brother's daughter, Sakina Begum. He remembered her vaguely as a little girl of the family, much younger than him, not worth much attention then. He was taken to meet her formally in a family visit after the betrothal was announced. She was small in figure but pretty, though slightly plump, as far as he could see past the long dress and the chador with which she would partially veil her face when spoken to. She had not been educated past primary school, but—she informed him—she knew most of the Quran. She read Urdu magazines and could cook rotis, and a mean nihari according to her mother.*

*The wedding was a joyous affair, if only in that it made the two families so happy. After the ceremonies, for a week Nurul coached his wife about customs in England and how she should behave; other women came by and complemented his instructions. Some joined the lessons and would practise with Sakina. How are you? I am very well, thank you. Mention not. Cheerio. And then Nurul and Sakina Begum left from Lahore for England.*

Hilary hurried into the dining room, looked around quickly, and came over. He had started on his coffee. She was wearing jeans and a white shirt, the hair gathered at the back, and the eyes looking puffed from lack of sleep. He half stood up, they both sat down.

'How formal.' She smiled and waited.

'I'm sorry, Hilary—'

'For what? Don't be, please,' she responded and leaned forward, placing her hands on the table, and looked into his face. 'For what? Yesterday?'

'I think I've trespassed—'

'Trespassed … why, why—what d'you mean?' She waited. 'You're assuming I don't have a will, that I'm a child … and that—' and she sat back and laughed lightly. 'Trespassed!'

They both laughed, he falsely because he wasn't certain, but that blocked the bitterness just in time.

'Things went a bit far, yesterday, didn't they?' he said at length.

'Yes. But far enough? Didn't you want it that way, Nurul? Maybe you've changed your mind. I understand that. Believe me. You have a position, and responsibilities.'

His breakfast came, toast with coffee, she ordered only coffee.

'If you want me to go away to my graduate student desk and leave you alone, I understand. Let's admit yesterday was a big mistake, and no hard feelings.'

He took a deep breath. 'Stay,' he said. 'I want you to stay.'

And come what may.

They agreed to meet later that afternoon.

Abe Rosenfeld was waiting for him in his office that morning, having just walked in after giving a class.

'I called up Alf Greiner this morning. He will do the algebra, for partial credit. And his student.'

'That's good.'

'I think we'll have it,' Abe said with quiet confidence. 'The preprints should be out within three months. I told Alf, no time to waste, rumours flying and so on.'

'I agree.'

Abe was staring at him.

'How did you get on with Hilary—you got your shopping done?'

'It turns out I got all my shopping done at Harvard Square.'

'What, you didn't get to Filene's? Some great bargains there—I bought some shirts over the weekend.'

Nurul laughed. 'No, not this time. And there's a shop in London where I buy my shirts now.'

'And pay much more on Jermyn Street, I'm sure.'

There was a time when Nurul, fresh from Pakistan, was the cheapskate, counting pounds and pennies, converting them into rupees to gauge the worth of a potential purchase. Gradually he had come around, buying quality and even the occasional snob value, but staying within his academic's budget, having learned where to shop from some of the wealthier members of the Pakistani and Indian communities, who would invite him to their functions as a celebrity.

Nurul had brought a batch of recent preprints from London, which he now placed on Abe's desk. Abe thanked him.

After a moment of contrived distraction, Abe turned to face him and said, 'Hilary's a good girl. Father's a doctor. She has a sister. Mother's dead.'

'We got along very well. She showed me around Boston and we had dinner together. Yes, she's a good girl. What do you think of her prospects?'

'Quite good, but she has to concentrate.'

Nurul left in a hurry, not to be seen flustered. Why was he telling me about her father? Will the man come at me with a shotgun? He went to the library and inspected a few recent journals.

Most scientists have done their life's work by forty ... Dirac, Nobel Prize already at thirty-one; Einstein, Nobel at forty-two for work done ten years before, General Relativity by thirty-six; Heisenberg, his Nobel at thirty-one ... If by the end of your student days you had not shaken up the world of science, made your great discovery or calculation, you may as well go plodding along till the end of your days, measuring out your life in mediocre research papers and average graduate students; but if you're special, you've peaked in your twenties, the greats already know you by name and reputation. And then it's a life of glory.

During his year at Princeton, still aged twenty, one day he bumped into Albert Einstein on the front steps of the Institute; they did their dance to walk past each other, before the older man stopped and introduced himself:

'Einstein.'

'Nurul Islam.'

'Islam? From Arabia?'

'No, sir. Pakistan. It was one country before, India.'

'India? Gandhi!'

For some reason they both laughed.

By the age of forty, surely even the brightest scientist knows his useful life is over, the analytic powers diminished, eyesight fading, memory starts to hiccup, and it's all pretense and impressing the young and advising governments and sitting on committees.

But the Prophet received his first message at forty, that was when his life began anew. He gave up his business and began to teach and lead ... and teaching a new way, a new method, he started a community of thousands, then millions.

A couple of years ago, when Nurul took his parents to Mecca, early that first morning when the desert sun had not yet risen to punish them, they found themselves standing together with hundreds of other Muslims before the Kaaba, the first mosque of God, built by Abraham and Ismael. He was just past forty and the experience had moved him profoundly. All the stories he had heard as a child, about the perfect man, God's friend Muhammad, his struggles, his compassion, his wisdom, came back to him. And Nurul Islam resolved to be as good and devout a man as he could. Soon after he returned to London, the Scotch bottle hidden in the bottom desk drawer in his office was dropped into the trash can.

And now here he was.

Sheikh Qadir Khan, upon release from detention in Guantanamo Bay, Cuba, in 2006, wrote up his memoir, *Confessions of a Former Jihadi*, which was published in India. He writes of his discipleship in Lahore as a young man during the 1970s, under Mowlana Abubakar Sufar, who had a virulent hatred of the West, matched only by his hatred of the heretics and blasphemers of Islam—the Shia, the Ahmadi, the Ismaili, the Shirazi. Mowlana Sufar's mission was to harass them until they renounced their beliefs, or to send them to perdition.

Two days following his outburst against Nurul Islam at MIT, Qadir Khan, not waiting to be disciplined by the Institute, packed his bags and caught a flight to Pakistan. He arrived in the capital, Islamabad, where he stayed with a friend at the University of Islamabad, then proceeded by bus to Lahore. Mowlana Sufar was waiting for him, seated as usual on the carpeted floor of his second-floor receiving room, leaning against a couple of bolsters at his back. From his dour face it appeared that he had not slept much. Perhaps he had been bothered by his toe, which the disciple noted was swollen from gout. There was no one else in the room.

Qadir Khan too had been a brilliant young student, and he too had had a hero. He was born in a village only a short bicycle ride away from Pirmai, and his idol had been none other than that prodigy from Pirmai, Nurul Islam, whom he had not actually seen but had often heard about. Qadir had followed his idol to Government College in Lahore in order to make a name for himself in the world of physics and mathematics. In Lahore the young man finally saw Nurul Islam, who was visiting the country—now independent Pakistan—from London. What impressed Qadir was that the great man remained a practising Muslim, and spoke of the glories of Islam in the past; what bothered him a little was that

Nurul Islam was no longer the reserved Punjabi boy from Pirmai. His stay abroad had changed his demeanour. His dressing, his mannerisms, and even the way he spoke English were different. One Friday Qadir heard on the radio a sermon by Mowlana Sufar, who had recently read in the papers that the famous physicist was on a visit to the country; Nurul Islam had met the nation's leader General Ayub Khan, who had glowingly praised him and held him up as an example for young people to follow. Pakistan was proud of Professor Islam, the general said. A boy from a village who had gone on to conquer the world of physics. A large photo of the professor and the general shaking hands accompanied the report. Sheikh Mowlana Sufar in his sermon first sputtered out that it should not be forgotten that the professor belonged to the heretical Shirazi sect. He went on to pooh-pooh the ideas of modern physics, which he called also heretical. 'What is this quantum physics, where God's creation is described as a field existing everywhere? And the atoms are cows in the field? What is this if not pantheism? And what is this Uncertainty Principle, or that German so-called theorem, where you can never know something? Allah knows everything. Allah knows everything. With Allah there is no uncertainty. In the Quran there is all knowledge, but no uncertainty. God is not blind or ignorant. He is not a gambler, praise be to Him.' The physics of what you cannot see, said Mowlana Sufar, is a corruption of young minds, which are needed for more practical matters. People like Nurul Islam were busy keeping Muslims backward by diverting their best minds into useless mathematical exercises. They might as well teach them to fritter away their lives doing crosswords or playing chess. Qadir Khan, convinced that Nurul Islam had been bought while out there in the West, became a disciple of Mowlana Sufar.

Admitted to MIT, Qadir Khan became frustrated when he could not quite match his former hero's easy genius and success. He had to work hard, like any other ordinary gifted student; and mathematical physics was very evidently not his métier, besides having been condemned by Mowlana Sufar. Following the mowlana's advice, he opted to specialize in the common-sense field of engineering, and specifically its nuclear branch. For his master's thesis, he devised a novel way of stabilizing nuclear centrifuges.

Every Sunday afternoon at four, Qadir and a small group of Muslims from the Boston area met in a room at MIT to discuss the problems now facing Islam in the world, such as the corruption of Muslim leaders, the domination of the United States and Russia, the increasing encroachment of Christianity in Muslim nations. They discussed jihad as a means. They debated more mundane matters, such as whether fasting during Ramadan could be excused or postponed on certain days, or whether it was halal to eat at restaurants where alcohol was served, or whether kosher meat could be considered halal in a pinch. Qadir would produce the answers to queries he had written out and sent to Mowlana Sufar. At the end of the session, money and books were collected for the Boston area's Muslim prison inmates.

On the day following Nurul Islam's lecture at MIT, Qadir Khan happened to tune in to WBTN's daytime program *Crosstalk* and heard the professor's interview there. He was outraged. But he also felt a soupçon of satisfaction, a vindication. The suave Nurul Islam calling Paul Dirac a manifestation of God! Curse on them both, Qadir Khan muttered to himself. The professor saying physics was an alternative to God! Blasphemy! Lanatullah alayhi. Allah curse him. What next? This, that—because after the radio interview, he had hung around the professor's hotel to find out what more the heretical physicist was up to, and he saw him emerge and meet with the same white woman who had accompanied him at MIT, and moreover the two of them had gone into a pub! More!—they came out of the pub and kissed. And this hypocrite was upheld as a model for Pakistan's young men and women?

It was this knowledge that Qadir Khan stored away in his brain when he took his flight back to Pakistan.

'Speak,' Mowlana said, after Qadir Khan had bowed, kissed the proffered hand, and sat down. 'What is on your mind?'

'Mowlana, I have left the university. I have committed to fight for the cause of Islam wherever it takes me.'

'Good. That is the most urgent task today. But you will not have to go anywhere for now.'

'In Boston—Cambridge—I ran into Professor Nurul Islam, the physicist—'

'Khrrr—' Mowlana Sufar emitted an angry guttural sound, a stifled oath. 'Don't besmirch the word Islam! He is a heretic.'

Qadir continued, 'He was visiting from London. He gave a lecture.'

'And what did he have to say?'

'In a radio interview afterwards, the next day, he said that the English physicist Dirac is like God.'

'Satan himself!'

'And he claimed physics is a substitute for Allah.'

'Curses, curses. Lanatullah …'

'I've brought a tape of the program for you. And an interview in a student newspaper—where he again brings up Dirac.'

'Drak, again! Who is this devil?'

'He should not be allowed to make such utterances, Mowlana!'

'He should not be allowed. I can pronounce a fatwa against him. But he has the respect of our government. I have it on good authority. The security people were here. They say he is an asset. He is needed …'

'And Mowlana … there is something else.'

'Yes? What?'

'I saw him with a white woman. I saw him kissing her.'

'Salah! A fornicator too! These young men go to the West and get seduced … and what do they become? A thousand curses upon him! Put that in his file.'

'Yes, Mowlana.'

'You know the girl?'

'I found out.'

'Hm. Pretty?'

'Ordinary. But they kissed. In public.'

The master nodded thoughtfully. 'One day … But for now he should not be molested.'

'Why, Mowlana? Why?'

'Why indeed. He is protected, that's why. He has the protective hand of the government on him. They may need him for their purpose … maybe to make the bomb …'

'Bomb!'

'Hm. Atom bomb. Hiroshima. For now we have to wait and keep an eye on him. Time will come.'

A girl had come, quickly placed a tray of food between them and hurried out. A spicy aroma arose, and the young man waited for his master, who concluded, 'Now come join me for a meal. Bheja! Brain curry. Brains is what we need in this country. The right kind. The Prophets have said you are blessed if you break bread in company. Hazrat Ibrahim never ate alone. Come, join me.'

The Pewter Pot, its name suggestive of old, colonial New England, had solid oak chairs and tables to match. Situated in the Square right where Mass Ave takes a bend and turns around, it was known for its varieties of oven-fresh muffins, and tea in old-style glazed teapots and coffee in large ceramic mugs. Sweet aromas filled the air as steaming mugs wended their way between tables. The dress code ranged from jeans to dresses, army jackets to sports jackets; snatches of conversation ranged from world revolution to mathematics to impending Christmas shopping.

Nurul, conspicuous in tweed jacket and wide moustache, was early and sitting at a table next to the back wall, facing the door. He was perusing a radical-sounding paper called the *Phoenix* when he heard her arrive and take the chair opposite him.

'Anything interesting?'

'They've a piece on my lecture, d'you believe it—and called me a member of the scientific-military complex!'

'They recognize you—how flattering!'

'Not so fast—listen: "Professor Nurul Islam of Imperial College, London, a Nobel prospect"—I never knew that—"spoke at MIT and was brought down from his lofty perch of quantum field theory by a compatriot, Qadir Kahn"—that's how they have it—"a graduate student who challenged him on the relevance of his abstract ideas to the people of the Third World."'

She smiled at him, her slender fingers joined delicately in front of her. 'You are famous. But irrelevant. Remember, no one over thirty is trusted by my generation.'

'And you are under?'

'Just.'

'And therefore you don't trust me, I see. Well, I don't trust myself either.'

'Don't you?' she grinned slyly.

'No. Especially when I'm waylaid by ... by ...'

'A temptress?'

'A brainy temptress. Now tell me what you did all day today.'

She had a lecture to attend in the morning, she said, and later went to the library to look up references. Then she went to her cubicle and started an assignment in particle physics, a knotty problem involving the summing of Feynman diagrams, and had a snack of yogurt and coffee.

He had been to the library too, he told her, funny he missed her. And he had met Abe earlier.

'He seems concerned about you,' he told her.

They ordered lunch, after which she said, rather casually, 'Abe's very protective.'

'You're lucky, then. You need a protector like him.'

'And you? Are you protective towards your students?'

'Not in the same way, I'm afraid. I do try to help them, though. But the English tend to be reserved, as you know. We are friends, and I go to the pub with them every Friday. I have fish and chips and Coke and they have beer and get progressively rowdy.'

She was beaming at him, with pleasure, which he found charming and affecting; a little immature, which surprised him, disconcerting him a bit. She was being possessive in her way, naively—but she was young. Under thirty, and he, beyond the pale for most of today's youngsters. Something had happened between them, it was real and momentous, not dismissible as ephemeral, a spark that happened when two lives accidentally crossed and would inevitably fade. It would not go away. They had to confront it. What did it, what should it mean to them?

She had turned serious.

'Yes?' she said.

'Your father's a doctor.'

'Yes. How did you find out?'

'Guess. What would he think ... and your mother—I'm sorry, I forget.'

She shook her head quickly and they became silent.

They had lunch. His was a meat stew with cornbread, unwise—he was not eating healthy in America. Hers, half a tuna sandwich.

Afterwards, over tea, he leaned forward and said, 'Let's go somewhere more private.'

She threw a quick look around the noisy room. 'This is fine, no one can hear us.'

'I don't want to shout about my affairs!' Wrong word. He turned red and they immediately left the restaurant. They crossed Mass Ave and entered the quiet Banks Street where she lived, on the second floor of an old brick house. They walked past the graduate residences and came to the river, rippling and sparkling merrily in the slanting rays of the autumn sun. A few picnickers relaxed on the grassy bank, couples like them, children ran around, watched by their mothers. Three crews were out rowing. A pleasure boat slowly made its way downstream. Across the river, a busy highway; in the distance, the Prudential Building all alight, from ground to top.

'How's this spot?' she asked.

'Perfect.'

They sat down on the grass, closer to each other than they normally would. But what was normal now? He had one leg drawn up, his hand on the raised knee, she was leaning back on two elbows, looking straight ahead, a dreamy look on her face.

After a moment's silence, he asked, 'What now? What are you thinking?' Tenderly he brushed some strands of hair from her face, on the way caressing her cheek with the tip of his thumb—and feeling rather juvenile.

She tilted her head, squinting her eyes against the sun behind him. 'My life's my own, Nurul. This is America. But you have a wife.'

'And children.'

'So?'

'So.'

She turned away towards the water, he could see her following the motion of a crew down the river.

'You've not told me what you think about me, Nurul.'

'I don't know what I think about you. I like those big searching eyes of yours and your hair, and your elegant bearing, your openness ... I know that I like being with you, and you give me the thrills, and I desperately want to hold you in my arms this moment.'

'Oh.'

'You didn't expect that.'

'No. Thank you,' she said. 'You also give me the thrills—and I also want to embrace you.'

I'm getting in deeper and deeper. We define the problem and ignore it; we show each other the obstacle and walk towards it heedlessly. Like uncaring neutrons. But neutrons do sooner or later hit an obstacle that stops them ... a concrete wall.

All they had achieved, meanwhile, was to edge their arms closer to each other. And yet in their mutual awareness they were in a close embrace.

'And my age? I'm forty-two, exactly,' and fifteen years older than her, as he had found out. 'You don't find that ... ?'

'Yes, but every relationship is a risk, isn't it? You don't know everything about the other person ...'

'True. There's a lot to think about, Hilary—and I know I'm acting my age here—which I should. Let's think about ... give it time ... and talk—write. If it's real, it won't go away, will it? Do you agree with me? We can't decide the whole—shebang, as you people call it—now, can we?'

She smiled. 'No, you're absolutely right. Let's take it slowly. But not too slowly.'

He put out his hand and she put hers in it. He stood and helped her up. As they walked back, hands now safely unclasped, she brought out a small photo of herself and gave it to him. 'It's what the university gives us each term, to give to our professors, so they can identify us.'

'You don't have to worry about that. But thank you. I don't have one of myself—'

'Oh?' She laughed. 'I'll find one, don't worry.'

That evening at the Rosenfelds', all four of Abe's senior students were present, including Hilary, and were engaged in a lively banter in the living room as Nurul arrived. Janis, Abe's wife, greeted Nurul warmly and called the two kids over—a boy and girl, ten and twelve—to say hello, then went upstairs to put them to bed. A radiologist at Mass General, she was petite of figure with short black hair, a cheerful, sharp-witted complement to her reserved husband. She looked attractive, wearing black slacks and a beige silk shirt. Abe, whose only change of attire appeared to be a loose, avuncular cardigan, served Nurul a ginger ale and they listened in on the young people excitedly discussing politics, with indulgence. Janis returned and dinner was served: salad, beef fondue, and a vegetable casserole; dessert was pumpkin pie. It would soon be Thanksgiving.

Over dessert and coffee, the young people sat around their guru on the carpet in front of the fireplace, taking this rare opportunity whose memory they would treasure over their lifetimes; they would have loved Nurul Islam to join them, but Janis said no, they couldn't hog both men. She took Nurul away and they sat together on the long sofa. She had met Sakina Begum during her stay in London with her husband and she inquired about her. They spoke about people she knew in London. And then she said, 'Let's walk out to the porch, Nurul. It's cool but nice outside.' She had something on her mind.

A brisk wind was blowing, and you could hear the branches swishing about on the trees. The street was empty, lights glowed dimly and mysteriously from the houses; a quarter moon cut sharply through wispy, listless clouds. 'It's quiet,' he said. 'It always surprises me, how deadly quiet a city can get.'

'Yes,' she replied after a pause, 'though if you listen carefully, you'll hear the Dudley bus on Harvard Square.' He heard a shuffling movement somewhere. 'It's raccoons,' she told him. The house was squat, red-bricked, with bay windows, leaded glass. The neighbourhood reminded him of London. He waited for her to speak her mind, having guessed by now her intention in bringing him out into the chill.

'I understand Hil's developed a crush on you,' Janis said. 'You should be careful, these girls can be impressionable. Who can blame them. Abe's had his share of groupies.'

'He has, has he? My, my.'

'Yes. He's managed to slip away, but I have to be firm. Men get flattered easily by adoring sweet young things.'

He brooded uncertainly awhile until she peeped into his face. 'Well, what do you have to say?'

'And if it's more than a simple crush, Janis? That can happen. Hilary's hardly a sweet young thing. A budding scientist.'

'Be serious, Nurul. She's young—'

'By fifteen years.'

'Well then. And you're married. You don't want a scandal, do you? Your world to come crashing down over your head? Look at what you've got. Look at what's coming to you. All the respect and accolades you ever dreamed of … And think of Sakina Begum—what will happen to her?'

'All right, Janis,' he said after some moments. 'Thanks, I appreciate that.'

Janis the sensible one. She could hit the nail on the head. On your head. He had not seen her in six years, and she could assume familiarity better than her husband could. There was a formal barrier between him and Abe, despite the friendship, a tendency to tread gingerly so as not to offend, that he did not have with Janis. They paused to listen—Abe playing the violin for his students.

'He doesn't often do that,' she brooded. 'What's on his mind, I wonder …' A moment later she whispered, 'Nurul, go to London and forget about her. And I'll work on her from this end.'

The guests all left together. Nurul walked with the four students part of the way, and when they reached Harvard Yard, he said goodnight to them and set off across it towards the lights of Mass Ave and his hotel beyond. It was dark and hard to see around him. Dry leaves rustled underfoot. On his right and left, dim lights from the shadowy student residences. A shout rose from somewhere and died as quickly. The raised silhouette of the university's founder.

Janis: 'I'll work on her.' How? Convince her to give up the infatuation … that would surely vanish his problem, open his eyes from a dream to the mundane reality of responsible behaviour. Home. Family. Stability. If Hilary acquiesced … was she the type you read about in novels, who twist men around their finger, bring them down from their pedestal and cast them aside, broken? And was all that they had spoken so tenderly to each other earlier—false? We'll see. Perhaps he'd been saved in time. We'll see. But I just can't believe she's that type … An image of her face came to him. Not her, she's not that type. He walked on, suddenly felt very alone and uncertain, there in the centre of the Yard, in a way he had not felt since he was a student. Time had passed swiftly. All the excitement of new research. The words of that article he had read earlier came back to him. 'The professor is a traitor to Islam and the people of Pakistan. Like the devil he weaves these abstract theories to mislead students back home …'

What nonsense. He was in the line of al-Biruni and Alhazen. And all those physicists of the past, whatever their faith, wherever they were … science has no religion, no nationality.

He had reached the edge of the Yard, where the darkness was now relieved by the penumbra of lights reaching out from the street; there were people on the sidewalks, and the bookstore, coffee shop, and pub were open and bustling.

He heard a shuffle of dry leaves behind him and turned, startled. Hilary came to a stop, breathing fast, apparently having run, and said, 'Weren't you going to say goodbye, Nurul?'

'Of course I was—'

She ran towards him and they embraced there in the darkness.

He reached the airport at just after noon, checked in, and sat down to wait for his flight. From his stuffed briefcase Nurul Islam drew out a student's research notes. The student, Patel, was working with him on his supersymmetry model. It was aesthetically elegant, but as yet mathematically patchy—put together with glue and string, his colleagues had teased. Patel seemed to have added some rigour to it. A pleasing result. Patel should go far, Nurul mused. Most students did not impress as easily. He had joined Imperial only a year ago, from Bombay. Nurul looked up briefly from the notes and saw the bank of pay phones gleaming against a wall not far away, and his train of thought was broken. He had the phone number of the office Hilary shared with five other colleagues. Perhaps he should call her; but to what end? They had decided to give 'it' time, meanwhile to keep in touch. Can I call you? she asked. He'd smiled. I'll call, he said. Please do. He had to work through his excitement, figure out what it meant. She had to work out hers, and face Janis. What were the options? It was something he might ask a student doing a problem. Should he simply have an affair on the side, so to speak? He wouldn't be able to bear the excitement and tension. It would be carrying on a dishonesty, and he couldn't do that. Meanwhile he needed his sacred space, this bubble inside which he worked and produced, in which neither woman existed, or could gain entry. A safe space, emotionally. A hermit's forest.

How far, how pure is the world of fundamental physics!—which we often claim in our arrogance can explain ourselves to ourselves, as flesh and blood and mind. Could we explain theoretically a conundrum such as mine? Where does the soul come into this? Where is God in this? Morality—right and wrong? Nowhere, Abe would say. Or rather, life emerged after the universe began with a big bang, and elementary particles arranged and grouped themselves, and gradually these groups evolved into even larger forms of life such as us, and morality was simply one of the rules of survival. He envied Abe Rosenfeld the certainty of his agnostic worldview. Everything was reason, system. Abe liked Spinoza, the philosopher. From first principles, a few axioms, Spinoza derived his whole system, including ethics. No God. But Janis was his anchor. How compatible they seemed. How comfortable.

Was he, Nurul Islam, naive, or stupidly delusional, losing his marbles? Was he actually in love? How silly. He hardly knew her. Attraction, yes. Fondness too. Hardly pure desire. Was this—as they called it nowadays—merely a mid-life crisis? A book on the subject was on the bestseller stand outside the airport coffee shop. Americans liked to give names to human conditions, expecting in the process to have understood them. He already had a love, his wife and family. A sublime feeling. Fondness. Care. Safety. He also loved physics, but in a different way. He enjoyed it, it consumed and defined him. He could not live without it. And he loved God, Allah. He couldn't explain this love, it was just there, he'd grown up with it; he spoke to Him, and He comforted him. He thought in his life there had occurred a few miracles, one of which was his admission to Cambridge University and his departure for England just in time to miss the havoc of India's Partition. Life had taken him on a path of success and fame. Now this new, intrusive feeling, this earthly infatuation. What was it? She was pretty, yes, to him she was. She was young, yes, and refreshing. Brilliant and naive, honest and simple. She was adorable. But it simply *was*, this new feeling, no amount of reasoning could explain it.

Or was it simply delusion and would pass? They had agreed to give it time.

His mind flitted briefly to the two ambushes, as he thought of them, upon his world of physics. The young Pakistani, and the older English Midlander.

A tall, fair man with a smart moustache, wearing a light suit, who could be Indian or Pakistani, came and sat down somewhat heavily next to him, sending Nurul a jolt. He placed his slim briefcase on his lap, his fine large hands upon it. 'Good afternoon,' Nurul said, acknowledging the man's gaze, and resumed his reading. There were other empty seats around, it was a little annoying that the man had chosen to sit right close to him.

'Professor Islam, it is an honour to be sitting next to you,' the man said, in a very proper English accent. To Nurul's startled expression, the man added, looking sheepish, 'I know about you, of course. I am from Pakistan. I was present at your lecture at MIT the other day. Unfortunate, that disturbance. Some of our people simply don't understand the niceties—'

'And you are?'

'Sorry, I am Major Iftikhar, Pakistan Air Force.'

'Well, Major, what a coincidence, then. Are you on official business?'

'I was, in Seattle, and on the way back I stopped over in Boston to meet a friend. And you, sir?'

'I came to give a lecture at Harvard. And there were some points to discuss on a theory that I and a man here have proposed.'

'A collaboration.'

'No, separately.'

'Any success—this discussion?'

'I would say so.'

'Well, I can tell you, Professor Islam—'

'Call me Nurul.'

'Nurul. Well, I can tell you, Nurul, that our entire country is proud of you. You know that. You may know that the president mentioned you in his convocation address at Lahore the other day. He called you a model for our young scientists, indeed a model for the nation in the greatness it can achieve.'

'Thank you, Major. But there are many good people in Pakistan, in science as well as in other fields.'

'Of course. Our country is blessed. But you're being modest.'

There was a silence between them, before the major spoke again.

'I understand that you advise the government from time to time.'

'Yes, I have advised them on nuclear energy and the science and mathematics syllabuses for schools.'

'I don't mind telling you, Nurul, that I was in Seattle to view an aviation show. From time to time the air force needs to purchase equipment. And often it needs expert advice.'

Nurul stared at the man. Major Iftikhar—what a military name—sat straight in his seat, his hair was combed back and his skin was smooth. What could he have in his briefcase that he held so tight? It was easy to imagine him in air force or army uniform. His black shoes were polished to perfection.

'Now that I have met you,' continued the major, 'I wonder if I can be so bold as to make a proposal—in fact to ask a favour. You see, your name has often come up in my circles, and now I'm sitting right next to you!'

'Go ahead,' said Nurul, who could guess what was coming next.

'Would you consider advising the military from time to time—on scientific matters? For suitable remuneration, of course.'

Nurul smiled. How much would the army pay? The major's suit looked exclusive.

'I hardly know anything about the capabilities of fighter jets and rockets, Major. And my own leanings are of a pacifist nature—don't you think we spend far too much on weaponry?'

The major gave a brief, good-natured laugh. 'Come now, Nurul. We are a country on alert, we have fought two wars with our enemy across the border. And we are fighting the guerrillas in the east. There could well be a third war. You can't be serious.'

'I guess not,' Nurul said, well aware of the seriousness of the insurgency in East Pakistan.

'In any case, the army does not buy only weapons. It buys paper and pencils too, and all kinds of equipment. It is a vast organization.'

'I would not be comfortable doing what you ask, Major. I am sure there are more competent people—engineers, businessmen—who would be more suitable.'

'But a name like yours as an advisor would add to our credibility. Think about it, Nurul. Perhaps there are some things for which only a few people are suitable.'

Major Iftikhar then got up and a little later returned with two cups of coffee and a donut. Nurul thanked him. The coffee had cream and sugar, as he preferred; the major's was black.

'I couldn't help noticing your pretty young companion at your lecture, Nurul. A student of yours?'

The major actually gave a wink, and Nurul glared at him.

'A student of Abe Rosenfeld, the physicist I was talking about. She took me shopping for my wife.'

Major Iftikhar nodded. They said nothing after that but boarded the plane together, and shook hands before they took their seats. Major Iftikhar went to sit in the front. He had a slight deformity in his right hand, which carried his thin briefcase.

We are a country on alert, he had said. Our enemy across the border. A border that need not have existed, Nurul thought. An enemy that was the same people. And this army major had gone shopping for weapons.

*The first time he returned from London, Pirmai had looked shockingly different. The Partition had metamorphosed it. He kept staring like a child from the taxi window, superimposing the town he had known upon the moulted evidence before his eyes. The sun was shining bright and hard. Ames Street was now Muhammad Ali Jinnah Road and recently paved; gone were Nathu Sweets, Pyarelal Emporium, Bahri Bicycles, where the family had shopped; in their place were Ali Abbas Brothers, Murtaza Stationery, Mian Lal Butchery. A few properties were still gutted and barely noticeable, having receded into silent history. The side streets he passed were newly paved. The mosque had been painted a beautiful light blue. Pirmai was a new and wealthier-looking place. But missing something of its former character.*

*'Was there a lot of violence?' Nurul asked his father one evening, when the two of them were out on a stroll. 'In the Allahabad locality,' Ghulam Ali acknowledged grimly. 'A stream of blood ran to the Beas … marauding gangs from outside, thirsting for Hindu blood.' On the other hand, as though in payback, trains from Amritsar dropped off Muslim corpses on the platform. 'Don't ask about Partition, son, it was God's miracle that you got away. For us, our blood turned black with fear and sorrow.' 'And now?' the son asked. 'How is it now?' 'With God's blessing, life is not bad,' the father replied. And indeed Nurul saw cricket played in the fields and alleys, betrothals in this season were marked by buntings and music, the odd circumcision procession wended down the streets accompanied by music; children ran about,*

*vegetable vendors called out bhindi, baingan, and the rest. But that naive innocence of before had gone. He recalled how the traders on the main street had come out to cheer him when the results of his final exam were announced in the newspapers. It had not mattered that he was a Muslim and had outscored Hindu boys.*

*One morning Nurul bicycled to every corner of the town, to look at the places he had known. After a long tour of the streets, he came to the old stone ruins where in their isolated stillness he would seek refuge to read and study, and dream about Sharmila. Here he had contemplated suicide when she married.*

*As he approached the place an overpowering stench rose to greet him. The area was littered with scraps of yellowed newspaper, tin boxes, metal pieces, broken sticks of furniture. There was a dump, a mound of refuse on one side. Crows circled raucously overhead, rats scurried about. Two stray dogs came trotting out from behind a broken wall, barking furiously. He contemplated the scene for a few minutes, then turned back with a sob, knowing that his old haunt, the ruins of a medieval fort and the setting of a folk romance, had become the scene of a massacre.*

*'And Rajan Sahab … and Sharmila, what happened to them?' he asked his parents back home, holding his breath. His mother was at the stove baking chappatis, Nurul sat on the ground with his father, waiting for the next round.*

*'They left,' his mother said.*

*'We didn't hear of them,' his father explained. 'There was a curfew. Still, one morning I stole out to their house to ask if I could do anything for them. There was nobody around. The place had been attacked and looted. They could have left before that, by train, or by car, or by foot in a caravan of refugees. We have not heard from them. Many people have simply not been heard from …›*

*'What's done is done,' said his mother. 'Let's not talk about it.'*

*Nurul exchanged a look with her. Had she turned so cold, or was this her way of coping? Shutting out. The terror and bloodshed, the guilt and the grief. There was some new furniture in the house, he noticed, a sturdy almirah and a finely carved small table with curved legs and ivory inlaid top that could have belonged to a set. From where?*

*Let's not talk about it. Forget it. But he could not forget, forget her.*

Sakina Begum's house would soon be filled with light. The man of the house was returning that day. She always woke early; this morning, the kids having gone off to school, she had taken pains to make everything seem as ideal as possible. This was her welcome for him, unstated but always understood. The bedsheets and tablecloth were all fresh. The floors and carpets had been vacuumed, the furniture dusted. Most important, his study at the back, away from anything else but the kitchen, was ready, awaiting him. However tired he was after his travels, he would always go and spend some time there. All by himself, in communion with his physics. That was Nurul Islam, world-famous and her husband. She had tidied his shelves, carefully wiped the book edges. She had even filled his pens with ink, put a new blotter in place, sharpened his pencils.

The kitchen was supplied with all the special items she needed, thanks to the Gujarati store down the corner. For dinner she would make samosas to start off, and biriyani, which he couldn't resist (she could imagine his face lighting up at the sight and the smell), and kheer for dessert. The doctor had recommended fat-free and light, but this was special.

She had known her husband since childhood; he claimed not to have noticed her, but she knew about him, had had him pointed out and heard his praises often enough when she was little. There goes Nurul Islam on his bicycle, do you see the books on his carrier? He is a hafiz to boot, and helps his father; he will go on to do great things. He would be pointed out as an example to her brothers, with words of caution: See how good he is, how he flogs the books. What do *you* plan to do, you loafers, with your lazy ways—make shoes? Cut hair and circumcise boys? Milk cows? He was handsome, with a strong face, curly black hair, and deep staring eyes, and wore a turban on special days. The day he broke the record and got the best matriculation result ever in the whole of Punjab, the news had spread through the town and people came out to congratulate each other as if it were Eid or Diwali, or India—still undivided—had beaten England in cricket; the mithai-wallah stood outside his shop to hand out sweets; boys, when school broke, came out chanting his name. In the late afternoon people went to Nurul Islam's house to congratulate and bless him, and a sheikh recited suras over him to ward off the jealous eye. Sakina was six and went with her family, and was asked to place a ten-rupee note in the boy's hand. The teacher, Mr Rajan, was there too, also receiving congratulations. From then onward she would hear the occasional remark at home, Sakina would be good for Nurul, do you hear that, Sakina? Even when he had gone away to England and she had her mind set on another lad in town, she would hear the remark, Our Sakina would be good for Nurul, do you hear, Sakina? Meanwhile she was removed from school after grade six, at which point she learned to cook and knit and helped her mother in the house.

And then one day they said to her, He is returning home, you shall marry Nurul Islam. It was ordained and so it will happen.

Nurul arrived at his home in Harrow that morning, having taken a taxi from Victoria. Sakina Begum opened the door for him, and before he could put down his bag and briefcase, she put a laddu in his mouth and cracked her knuckles at the sides of her head. He put a hand on hers.

As was his custom, he came inside and unconsciously glanced left and right, then up the stairs. The children. Then he went and dropped down on the sofa and Sakina brought him a cup of tea. He looked at her.

'How are you, my dear?'

'It is good to have you back. Did you accomplish what you wished to?'

'More or less. Abe and Janis send their regards.'

'Oh. And you gave my regards to them, I hope? Did you?'

'Of course.'

He agreed he should rest awhile; but he didn't go to bed, he went to his study, put his briefcase down, and sat down on the chair. He glanced at the mail, then sat back and fell asleep. The radio from next door was dimly audible through the walls. A comedy program.

She watched him from the doorway. Since the days of her engagement, when he was not even back in Pirmai, she had been told by her mother and father that he was her god; it was not only Hindus who believed this of a husband. But this was a special god. She should do everything to keep him happy, for he was destined to bring glory to the family and the community, and to Islam itself. Had she kept that promise? She had kept him contented. He adored his three children, especially the little one. And his work brought him joy. All that—barring a few doubts—was her own happiness.

When he woke up and had had his shower and said his prayer, she made an omelette for the two of them, which they ate with parantha and chai. He enjoyed it. His meagre diet was a struggle against himself, and on some days seemed like a slap to Sakina's cooking; but a part of her, not clearly articulated, perhaps felt a bit of relief that he wished to control his instincts. She couldn't help feeling surprised every time she observed him thus, at how—despite having gained some weight—he had maintained himself. He looked robust and supple. She had let herself go a little, it was a struggle to keep looking trim and fashionable beyond her own inclinations. Moreover in this climate, in this culture, it was difficult to know how to dress, what was drab and what smart. She rarely travelled with him, except on a few occasions, such as to Italy once and America another time at a big conference, when she had spent time with Indian and Pakistani wives, and it had been nice. And she preferred not to go to his office parties, though she did sometimes, because she was familiar with a few people whom he had previously brought home for dinner and she could speak with them. It was never easy to meet strange men, the first thing they wanted to do was shake hands. Don't do the adab, he had instructed her, it looks like a salute, just join your hands in an Indian pranam.

He had brought down his gifts, and now presented her with hers. She looked at it and smiled.

'Do you like it?'

'Yes. Gold would have been nice, but this is nice too,' she replied.

'You have enough gold as it is; this one is handcrafted, it's truly American.'

Her jewellery was all handcrafted too, by traditional goldsmiths, and came in fancy green-and-gold boxes. His gift had been wrapped in a piece of roughly torn newsprint, she was surprised at the crudeness. She could guess that he had bought it from a street vendor. She was disappointed.

'Did you bring a wedding present?' she asked.

'I didn't have time. But let's go to the shops this afternoon and buy something nice.'

That pleased her.

It was damp outside, for which the two of them were properly dressed, she wrapped in a shawl, and he wearing a dashing maroon scarf. He greeted the neighbours they passed and they responded in kind, with cheerful waves and greetings. Everyone on the street knew the professor. At the corner store he inquired when the amroodh, the guavas, would arrive. Wait for January, he was told by Mr Shah, formerly of Kenya, and he could get both Indian and Pakistani varieties. At Debenhams at the local shopping complex they bought a set of kitchen knives as a wedding present, then they sat down for tea. She recalled how, when they were just newly married, he had taken her to Oxford Street and how she had been dazzled by the brilliantly lit stores that seemed endless and sold everything. They couldn't afford much then, but they had tea and he had bought her a cake and instructed her how to eat it with a fork. He had been a little embarrassed. They lived in Earl's Court then and she recalled one evening, returning from a meal at Wimpy, how a man had whipped her with a handkerchief as he passed, and called out a racial slur. Her Punjabi husband, with choice expletives, was ready to fight and she had to hold him back. Which of his many admirers would know a detail like that?

She stared at him.

'What?' he asked. 'Something the matter?'

'Did you buy that scarf in America? I haven't seen it before.'

'Yes, I bought myself a present there.'

She felt only the slightest doubt of his goodwill, that it must have cost more than the present he had bought her. But she dismissed it; after all, he needed things too. And would she herself have thought of such an elegant present for him? She put her hand out to feel its material.

They returned home by taxi. On the way, he told her he would give a short address at her niece Salima's wedding reception. She put her head on his shoulder.

The children returned from school and went to greet him in the sitting room, the little one running all the way into his arms and onto his knee, and received their presents. Father and daughter began to examine her toy microscope on the carpet in the sitting room and the boys to play with the calculators. Mother watched with satisfaction. Soon they had dinner. The family was together again.

After dinner and dessert the boys went to their room to study. Sakina went to the sitting room and watched television. He did not join her immediately; a little edgy and preoccupied, having done no work all day, he wandered off to his study. Only Muni could disturb him there, and she duly made that claim by arriving to sit quietly on his lap, before going up to bed after caressing his cheek and giving it a peck. There was a letter for him on the desk, which he now opened. He gave a start. Its message was similar to one he had received some months previously and dismissed with contempt. 'You are a fraud, sir. Proof: Abe Rosenfeld, preprint, March 20, 1969; Nurul Islam, lecture at the Oslo Symposium, May 8, 1969.' Like the other, it had been written on an electric typewriter. The stamp said Italy, the postmark said Rome. The other one had been from London. There was a cohort of these devils at work, it seemed. Why did it matter to them? He thought of the Midlander at his talk at Harvard. Abe had found out his name: Duncan Harvey. Nurul placed the letter and envelope in a folder together with the previous one.

After perusing briefly the notes for his class the next day, he went up to see the boys. They were at their desks and he joined them, sitting on one of the beds. They discussed school, then he told them about Boston and Cambridge. Harvard would be a good place to go to, he said. Cambridge, England, of course, should be the first choice. The subject of their quarrel came up: who would get to use the new cricket bat and who would use the old one. He proposed that the one who scored the most runs in his next match should get first choice. They all knew it would be Rahim; not only was he older, he was also a good batsman. Mirza put on a sulk, but smiled. Later they would buy a new one, his father told him. Then he went next door to Muni's room. She was waiting for him, lying on her back, eyes wide open. She flashed a big, shy smile at him. The imp, she knew what hold she had over him. He went and kissed her goodnight and she closed her eyes in a moment. Such delicate life, he thought. So precious.

He joined Sakina downstairs and they watched an episode of *The Avengers*. It was followed by the news, which concluded with a report on the Pakistan army's recent atrocities during the war in East Pakistan. 'Such madness,' he muttered.

'I don't understand it,' she said. 'Allah be thanked our families are not affected.'

He agreed. 'Yes, Allah be thanked, they live far from there.'

According to the news report, the war was reaching a climax and there was the possibility of India intervening. Major Iftikhar came to mind.

She proceeded upstairs and he ambled off to his study, saying, 'I'll be up soon, dear.' He knew exactly when on her way up she paused to watch him. In the study, he turned on the Quran recitation on his tape recorder and began a letter to his father, but could not complete it. He listened to the tape for a few minutes, then turned it off, making a gesture of piety, switched off the lights, and went upstairs. He undressed and joined his wife in bed. They embraced, but did not make love. That cumbersome activity had ceased for some time now.

To his thought, put to her humorously sometimes, that she would have been happier with a businessman husband—a carpet merchant or grain broker—she might have agreed, though to his face she had denied that possibility. But she knew she would have preferred a simpler, less gifted man; that would have been better for them both. And with a large family around her, in surroundings she knew well, she would not have been lonely. She would have had no apprehension about talking to people, speaking like the others, dressing like them. Stepping out of the house and taking a bus. And the weather ... She had heard of course that the young genius, her prospective husband, had fallen for a Hindu girl when he was young. A bright girl with a mind to match his. Almost. Someone who played chess with him. But Sharmila went and married someone else, and that was that. The boy pined for her, imagined himself the legendary lover Ranjha, and resigned himself to his fate. And Sharmila disappeared during the Partition.

Lying beside her, Nurul recalled a letter he had received from his father three years back. Following the customary greeting and blessing, it went on, 'I would like to inform you, my son, that yesterday I got married again. I now have two wives. Your younger mother is the widow of the Urdu teacher at our high school. Her name is Hanna Bibi. You should know that your mother is happy with the arrangement, I asked her permission first, as is proper by our faith, and it relieves her of some of the burden of running the household ...'

Second and even third marriages happened among many peoples, including Muslims, for whom the practice was sanctioned by the Holy Book. When Nurul visited home a year later, his mother behaved as though that was the only life she had known. She seemed happy.

But when he discussed his father's new domestic arrangement with Sakina, she had said with a confident smile, 'I would not like it.'

'Of course you wouldn't,' he said and gave her a brief squeeze. 'We live in London.'

The scarf he'd worn today was a gift from Hilary, he was conscious of its touch all the time he wore it. She had bought it for him that day of their outing in Boston, when she showed him around the city. And he had bought for her a pair of earrings ... more expensive than the gift he got Sakina, but that was not intentional.

What had he gotten into? he asked himself once more, trying to be objective. Why this outbreak of irrationality, utter silliness? This was a historic age of scientific discovery, an age of lasers and space travel, protein synthesis and organ transplants, new elements and new materials, superconductivity and supersonic travel, nuclear fusion, black holes, and, in his own field, the grand unification of forces and particles. There were young whizzes already on the scene with some fearsome ideas and abstract mathematics, but he had hopes that one of his supersymmetry brainwaves might be 'it.' The Nobel Prize. Vanity aside, this was work that illustrated the beauty of creation, the work of Allah. He could not forget, of course, that he was the only living Muslim scientist of note. That was a matter of pride but also a burden. He would be judged.

And now this.

'Dear Hilary ...'

To Nurul Islam the Partition of India was a tragic occurrence, with all the illogic of political ambition and communal hatred behind it. It destroyed millions of lives and left an evil shadow in its wake. Two wars had soon followed between the two nations, the new India and Pakistan, which remained on permanent alert, as he had been reminded by Pakistani Major Iftikhar at Boston's Logan Airport. Did the architects of the Partition not realize they were creating two havens for fanatics to brew their hatreds? The absurdity of Partition was reflected in the fact that two people of different languages and very distinct cultures—Bengalis and Punjabis—separated by a few thousand miles of Indian territory, became part of a single country, Pakistan, purely on the basis of the faith they practised. As for his own family's fortunes, as Nurul once mused, if the bureaucrat Sir Cyril's pencil had wavered a little to the west while he was drawing the boundary, he, Nurul Islam, would now be an Indian. With what consequences? Lives had hung in the balance of that pencil. His mother had once proclaimed, 'If our ancestors had settled fifty kos to the east, who knows what would have happened to us now?'

It was January 1972. Pakistan had recently, only the previous month, lost a thoughtless military campaign against its own people (though Bengalis) in the east, into which India had sent troops. As a result, East Pakistan became independent Bangladesh and some ninety thousand Pakistani troops languished as India's prisoners of war. It was after this humiliating defeat that the new president of Pakistan, Beyram Teymuri, made an unequivocal resolution about his country's future: to that end he called an urgent secret meeting of the nation's top scientists. The meeting was held in the western city of Quetta, and Nurul Islam had been invited.

When he was called by Pakistan's High Commissioner in London and informed that the president had invited him for this meeting, Nurul had to excuse himself from his lecture duties for a week and postpone a seminar he was to give at Manchester so he could go. It was inconvenient, but 'secret' and 'urgent' placed a compulsion on the invitation. This was almost an order. What could be the reason for it? Education or industrial policy or something similar would not warrant such an order. Was this pure politics—elections round the corner, rounding top scientists to one side? At Lahore Airport he was met by a military adjutant, taken past immigration and customs gates without inspection, then straight to a government guest house, where already a few other science brains of the country had been put up. They all knew him and came to pay respects. Here he found out, much to his astonishment, that they were all bound for Quetta early the next morning.

'What's this fellow like—Nurul Islam? Pukka Punjabi, you say?' asked Beyram Teymuri.

'Yes. Ancestry is partly Persian, though. More important, as you know, is that he is from the Shirazi Sufi sect.'

The president threw a glance at General Owaisi.

Beyram Teymuri was sunk in an ornate sofa in the receiving room of the residence of the chief minister of the province. He was a man of above-average height, and slightly paunchy, though pictures from student days showed a slim, dashing young man in blazer and ducks, who played cricket and tennis. The skin on his face was rough, a wispy grey halo crowned his bald head. He came from aristocratic stock, his ancestors having been viziers of nawabs in pre-independence India.

'Yes, but what's he like?' Beyram Teymuri persisted, crossing his legs, joining his hands behind his neck, and leaning back.

'A genial fellow, very likeable. A devout Muslim, though. He's made himself a spokesman for—'

'I've been told.' The president turned thoughtful. 'Our most eminent scientist,' he mused. 'Does he have to wear his religion on his sleeve? We all believe in Islam—the religion based on which this country was founded. But faith should be like a wife, you have one, that's all. And you show her when required. You don't carry her around all the time.'

'Well …'

'I thought these physicist fellows were more the atheist or agnostic types, you know, they claim to explain everything rationally, what's the need for God, and so on? I knew a couple of them at Oxford.'

'Our man is an exception. Of course, he comes from a small town, and belongs to a small sect. They are followers of the Sufi philosopher Ibn Arabi—whom, as you know, the orthodox in our country consider a heretic. His father said the azan at the local mosque—in Pirmai. Boy was a genius, best matriculation result in Punjab, it has not been topped on either side since Partition.'

'How marvellous. And a Shirazi. Can't he keep it to himself? Can't they keep it to themselves, these Shirazis and others who rushed into this country at independence, instead of openly advertising their deviancy and rousing the fanatics? I wonder which side's more fanatic sometimes …'

The general did not correct the president to say that Pirmai was on this side of the border, and it was the Teymuris who had packed bags and fled to the new country. Such details didn't matter and history was what you made it to be, anyway.

The president poured himself a Scotch from the decanter in front of him and sat back again. 'Send our genius in,' he said wearily.

'Come in, Professor Islam. Have a seat.'

'Adab, President Sahab. It is a pleasure to meet you,' Nurul said.

'Dispense with the Urdu, yaar. This is official business. Let's stick to English, or we'll be reciting Ghalib and Mir endlessly and accomplish nothing.'

Nurul laughed, and said in English, in an accented voice that seemed momentarily to startle the president, 'All right, sir. Let it be English, then.'

'Professor, I've heard a great deal about you. Naturally. We are filled with admiration … what can one say. You are a model of achievement, a beacon to our science students. A blessing to our nation.'

'With God's assistance. I've been lucky—which may be the same thing.'

'That's fine,' replied Teymuri. 'We give thanks to Him'—he glanced upwards—'in His own time, meanwhile we can take pride in your accomplishments, which I understand are considerable. Mind you, it's beyond my comprehension—I was shown one of your famous publications, and I confess it looked to me like ant trails going all over the page. I'm an Oxford man myself, you Cambridge chaps always beat us when it came to numbers … and instruments.'

You Oxonians are good at making speeches, you mean, Nurul thought. 'President?' he inquired.

'What do you think of nuclear energy?' asked Beyram Teymuri. 'That's the subject of this small and extraordinary conference that I have called here in Quetta. I thought I should meet you privately first, hence this meeting. It's a privilege. And I must apologize for the inconvenience—the secrecy and so on—but to come to my point, what do you think of nuclear energy, Nurul Sahab?'

'I am a firm believer. It would solve our country's energy problems and bring us into the modern age. So many of our people still don't have electricity. But you must know that I have advised the government on these matters.'

'Yes, and you've done salutary work with our Atomic Energy Agency and helped us procure the Canadian reactor. And advised the Institute of …'

'Nuclear Science and Technology, sir. PINSTECH, as they call it.'

'Yes. The Taj Mahal of Pakistan, is that what they say?'

'The site is very beautiful, sir …'

'Designed by an American. My point, however, is, what do you think of the *military* use of nuclear energy?'

Nurul's heart took a jolt. He picked up the cup of tea which had been placed before him. Sweet and creamy, desi-style without his asking, though he didn't mind. The president had received his in a silver teapot, with sugar cubes and milk separate. His eyes met the president's. Why do I agree to these games? For the sake of my country, to do from afar what good I can. Or perhaps it's vanity?

'You mean an atom bomb, sir?' He used the layman's term.

'Precisely. To cut to the bone. A weapon like the Americans used on Hiroshima and Nagasaki—and which six other nations already have, including Israel, and India will soon have.'

So it's true. We are to embark on a road to folly, spending millions on a weapon which dare not be used, while millions in this country live in dire poverty. Nurul Islam had already heard from his friend Zaffar Khan, an old classmate from Lahore who was also present at this conference, that the nuclear bomb was the main—no, the only—purpose of this Quetta meeting.

He was aware that the majority of the population of Pakistan, especially the scientists, would support a Pakistani nuclear weapon. It was a status symbol, like an airline. It would solve their bruised ego after the humiliation the country had just suffered in the east. Why should only the Western powers, our former colonizers, have it? Now China had it too, and India would have it soon—despite the death in a plane crash of Homi Bhabha, their chief nuclear scientist; he had openly declared his enthusiasm for it. But Nurul knew he did not have the heart to endorse it, give his blessing to something with the potential for such massive destruction. How could anyone who had seen pictures of Hiroshima victims speak so blithely about nuclear bombs? But then perhaps he had become too alienated from his roots and was not used anymore to seeing real suffering? But that's how he was. The only argument he knew that made sense to him for possessing nuclear weapons was that of mutual deterrence: if you have it, and I have it, neither of us dares use it. Unless there's a madman among us who doesn't care. And the horrors of the subcontinent's Partition, let alone the recent war in the east, had amply demonstrated that there was no dearth of madness on either side.

'I think, sir,' Nurul began, in answer to the president's question, 'and can I be frank, sir?'

'Please. I expect nothing but. Go ahead.'

'I think, sir, that the world already has too many nuclear weapons. We should be calling for their total ban. Worldwide. We should set an example. It has been calculated that there is a total destructive capability on our planet equal to thousands of Hiroshima bombs ... there exists a real possibility of the total annihilation of human life on earth.'

'Surely the good Lord would save us from that fate, professor,' the president said, with a forced smile. 'He needs human beings to worship him, after all ...' In spite of the quip, he looked ruffled, stunned, Nurul thought. But where do you begin your honest warnings if not at home?

Teymuri had recovered and his pitch was higher as he continued.

'*We*, Nurul Sahab? Who is *we? We* have been humiliated by the war in the east, where we lost half our country; thousands of our finest jawans were captured by the Indian army, and to bring them home I have to go through a Versailles of our own, agree to the most humiliating conditions that will be demanded by that Nehru's crowing daughter. This would not have happened if we had been properly armed. Professor! We are a smaller country than our enemy, and for our survival we need the atom bomb!'

'We will have bombs, sir, and they'll have their bombs—and who wins then?'

'I see that you know your Gandhi.' There was the mildest hint of sarcasm in that. Teymuri went on, 'The point is that *we should not lose*. If nobody wins, that is precisely what we want. If we had the bomb, we would not have lost the east. Professor—have you considered this, you who speak all the time, and rightfully so, of the achievements of Islamic science in the past—consider this: the Christian world has nuclear capability, the communist world has the capability, the Jews and the Chinese and the Hindus have the capability. Where is the Islamic deterrent? Where is the Islamic bomb? We who once led the world in science and other achievements?'

Which is what the president, his bald pate gleaming dully, exhorted to the gathering of twenty-two chosen scientists an hour later in the brightly lit room which had been set aside for this meeting. The large fireplace sent off heat against the January cold. As was customary, tea had been served, with two digestives for each delegate. Outside the large windows it was bright and sunny and the grounds were being swept. The president had paused for effect, and now he continued in a more even tone, 'I want you to give us that bomb. Make this nation proud once again.'

An uneasy murmur erupted around the long table. The men—they were all men—exchanged looks. What's he saying? Is this for real? Do we have the capability? The money? How and where?

'How long will it take?' persisted the leader, ignoring the sceptical looks.

'Ten years, at least, sir,' ventured a senior scientist.

'Yes, that seems reasonable, if not too optimistic,' agreed another one.

'Too long. We will get you everything you need. Money, facilities, staff. In two days I fly to Saudi Arabia to talk to the oil sheikhs. Money will be no problem for an Islamic bomb, I assure you.'

'We can do it in five,' a young scientist from Islamabad piped up.

'I want it in three,' declared the president, and they knew he was serious.

Amidst all this, at his place at the table close to the president's, Nurul Islam was well aware that his own somewhat muted reactions were under scrutiny. Teymuri had pointedly not asked for his opinion here, and that had sent out a signal: our genius professor has reservations. But around the table general disbelief had turned into excitement and hope. Finally, the government was paying attention to their needs. The program would give a long-awaited boost to their impoverished departments, with money, equipment, and staff, and to the status of science in the country. If they failed, they would still come out winners. But to make and successfully test a nuclear bomb would be a major achievement, putting them among the ranks of Fermi and Oppenheimer of Los Alamos fame; it would be an accomplishment to make the nation hold its head up among other nations. Teymuri was promising unlimited funding. It all seemed irresistible if you did not keep in mind the evil object under discussion, a monstrosity with the capability of causing the death or mutilation of hundreds of thousands at a go. But other nations had it, as Teymuri said, their arch-enemy next door, India, would soon have it, and one nation had already used it.

Bringing the session to an end, the country's leader said, 'Three years! Go to it, boys! Pakistan zindabad!' and in the resulting echo of Long Live Pakistan! he stood up and headed for his helicopter.

As soon as he had left, General Owaisi got up and spoke about secrecy. Not a word to colleague, family, or friend. All present would sign a secrecy oath before leaving. Funding would come under the banner of 'Better science education for our future.'

A lavish buffet had been set up outside, towards which the delegates headed with undue haste.

'I'm not sure I can be part of this, my friend,' Nurul said to Zaffar as they sat down at one of the small tables with their plates. 'It will do us no good in the end. It is utter folly! We should, instead, call for a total nuclear weapons ban in our region.'

'I don't think much is expected of you, Nurul. Or of me. I had a meeting earlier this morning with Owaisi and expressed my reservations. As soon as we gave our opinions on the matter, we cut ourselves out. And we've made a powerful enemy in Teymuri.'

'He's only a politician. They come and go.'

'Don't forget the family. After him his son. What can a man from Pirmai, and now London, know about the affairs of Pakistan?'

Nurul chuckled at Zaffar's last quip. 'Yes, when I left, there was no Pakistan. I departed from Bombay.'

Groups of scientists had formed to discuss their next moves and possible collaborations. Select members of the defence bureaucracy were going around answering questions. Army security hung about. There was excitement and urgency and even disbelief that such a serendipity had come their way, and they would be able to do world-class science at last.

'You'd better tread carefully around this, Nurul. Don't breathe another word about your reservations. Or in no time you'll be branded a traitor. And you are a Shirazi heretic, don't forget.'

'Yes ... already half a traitor, you mean.'

'Don't give them an excuse. The switch can be turned on any time, and there will be riots. Remember '53? You were not here, I was. Go along for the time being.'

In 1953, massive riots, no, a pogrom, had erupted against the Ahmadiyya sect in Lahore and other cities, instigated by a fundamentalist party. Other small sects were also attacked, and there were several anxious days as Nurul and Sakina awaited news from home, fearing the possibility that the violence would spread to Pirmai.

Having signed their secrecy oaths, Nurul and Zaffar left for their hotel and met later for dinner, after which they sat together late into the night in the lounge, drinking tea and discussing recent events in politics and science.

He was flown back to Lahore the next morning. He had spared a day for this city that he had known and loved so well as a young man. If you've not seen Lahore, you've not seen the world, it was said. Having checked into his hotel, he called for a tonga to take him into town. A cool, wintry breeze blew against his face as the old-fashioned horse-driven conveyance clip-clopped past old sites and new developments. A sinking feeling of time having passed. Gulberg, the location of his hotel, was a modern, expensive suburb, with wide roads, fancy shops, and classy restaurants. It could be any place where there was money. Slowly now the old city arrived, first signalled by the noise, then the air, and they were absorbed into its bustle of people and traffic. He got off at Government College, where he had received his start as an undergraduate. They had offered him a job when he finished with accolades at Cambridge, but with the understanding that he would have to step back from the scientific frontier where he currently was, to become an ordinary science lecturer at a third-world college. A modest but important job, and he would be required to coach badminton as well. Did he want the job? No, thanks, he replied, he would stay where he was for the time being. Now he walked the grounds and the corridors, smiling past excited, busy, chattering students, peeped into classrooms where he had studied, gave free rein to his nostalgia for his carefree years. His happiest years? Perhaps, but happiness matures too. When he wandered into the library he found it as haphazardly stocked as before, and still behind the times. As he sat reminiscing over a cup of tea and a samosa at the outdoor canteen, he happily eavesdropped on an animated conversation by some young engineers on the subject of space exploration. So much potential, he mused. At noon, finally, having introduced himself to the astonished, exhilarated physics head, he gave an impromptu lecture to a full house on another recent pet subject: the value of fundamental—not fundamentalist, he quipped—science, even though it seemed practically useless. If it had been valued in his time he might have returned, he told his audience. And he floated an idea: Why not think of a Pakistani institute of fundamental science that would attract scientists from all over the world? Such an institute would be a peacemaker. Science for peace instead of war.

Towards the end of his lecture he saw a student get up and hastily depart. Reaching the door, the young man turned and threw a stare towards the front. Nurul's surprise would not have registered with his audience, and he continued speaking, knowing that the fellow was the same one who had heckled him at MIT the previous year. He must have joined here after that incident, expelled by the institute or having left by his own decision.

Thereafter there was a luncheon with students and faculty at a quickly arranged buffet on the lawn. Food had always been a priority at any gathering in this country, he mused happily to himself; the custom revealed a ground level of generosity and decorum. He was surrounded all the time. Among the young people he sensed a lot of pessimism and uncertainty. There seemed little hope for the future, except in those who had prospects of getting away. They wouldn't know yet that money was on its way. These young men and few women would be offered jobs building and testing centrifuges, studying nuclear reactions, building cooling systems and nuclear shields, modelling bomb damage on crowded cities … The college principal came to shake his hand, as did members of the faculty. When he had the chance, Nurul inquired from the physics head about the young man who had left during his lecture. Students were consulted and the answer soon came by relay. The man was called Qadir Khan, a disciple of Mowlana Sufar, a radical preacher who could be heard every Friday on the radio railing against blasphemy, immorality, heresy, etcetera, whatever suited him that particular day. He had a special abhorrence for quantum physics, which he called idolatry. And the young man himself? He was a satisfactory student, but a rabble-rouser. There were a few of them around, and you simply ignored them or they would start a riot outside your house.

It was midafternoon when Nurul arrived back at the hotel, where his father, Ghulam Ali, was already waiting for him, sitting in the reception hall, looking humble and out of place on a plush red sofa. Nurul made sure he had a room for the night.

Nurul had declined several dinner invitations so he could spend the evening with his father. They toured the old city, where Ghulam Ali did some shopping, and they went to pray at a small mosque and afterwards had dinner nearby. They returned to the hotel in a taxi and, ordering a tea tray from the kitchen, sat outside in the dark in the garden. Ghulam Ali had brought news of the family. Nurul's two brothers were in Karachi, and his youngest sister was with her husband in Houston—illegally, Nurul guessed. She was always calling on her mother to visit her, but Halima Begum's arthritis made travelling difficult; moreover there were grandchildren. Hanna Begum, his father's new wife, had a child of her own, a boy whom they called Little Nurul.

Nurul had noticed how his father had aged. There was a slowness of movement—even though he feigned his fitness by appearing not to exert; there was the unavoidable shot of undisguised pain somewhere, the spots on the face and the loose skin … and the resignation in some of his observations. It pained the son to watch his father thus, to accept the fact that this, or the next, could be their last time together. He felt guilty he could not see his mother this time. He had to rush away to teach, and there was the lecture at Manchester he had postponed, then the conference in Florida … Were they important? Should he have stayed behind, never have left India (as it was then), lived a simple, uncomplicated life so he would be here in Pakistan now to hold the large family together, take over the reins from his father … look after his parents in old age?

'I sometimes wonder if a civil service job wouldn't have been better, after all,' Nurul said. 'A job with the railways was possible, remember, Abba? Can chasing formulas be a life's purpose? In vain pursuit of glory, I seem to have joined a circus.'

He was of course voicing the opposite of what he had lectured earlier at the college. And what he sometimes said when asked, that physics reflected the glory of God. But why did *he* have to do it? Nurul Islam of Pirmai, of the small Shirazi sect, simple people who desired nothing more than to live in peace and worship their God.

His father looked at him a long time, until Nurul turned and met his eyes.

'What's ailing you, son?'

What to say? He had shared many a thought with his father over the years, as a boy and an adult, even subjects his father would not have an inkling about. He had explained in his letters how he had renormalized the meson field; his work on massive neutrinos, his correspondence with the great Pauli, bumping into Einstein in Princeton … And then all his excitement at discovering the achievements of the Muslim scientists of the past, and his mission to spread the thrill of fundamental research to the young men and women of the poorest countries.

'You were born for one thing only, Nurul, and it found you. Allah found you. Out there in backward Pirmai, He found you. Like He sent Jibreel to Muhammad in the cave, peace on him. You were lucky and you have achieved great things with that opportunity. Don't be ungrateful for the gift. Perhaps it is not chasing formulas'—*phaarmula* is how he pronounced it, his son smiled—'but spreading the message of science to the unfortunate that is your true mission. But your chasing after phaarmula has helped you in that.'

Nurul thought long on that. He was not a prophet. The angel Gabriel had commanded Prophet Muhammad, Read in the name of God, and the Prophet had read, and the world changed. He, Nurul Islam, was a simple boy from Pirmai with all the human weaknesses.

'You're right, father. But a gift is also a burden—of responsibility.'

'What's really ailing you, my son?'

'Life at the top … of one's field … Abba, causes a lot of uncertainty and competitiveness—*hassad*. There is a word in English, *hubris*—'

'Hoobris …'

'It means a certain kind of pride, a feeling of infallibility …'

'*Abhimaan*, we call it.'

'More than that, Abba.'

'And what about this hoobris?'

'I sometimes think I have it.'

'You must fight it.'

They became silent again. A quarter moon was out that night, a proper crescent, Nurul observed: a sign? He looked away towards the screech of insects in the bushes in the distance. From the hotel lobby behind them came the crash of a falling tray. The air was smoky from the mosquito coil in the grass at their feet. Both men wore kurta-pajama, Ghulam Ali also his turban. His beard was now full and came down to his chest. It had been dyed with henna for many years. He had become heavier. He let out a fart in the traditional manner and looked towards his son to explain himself. Nurul had in mind his too-easy confidence, his enjoyment when students and peers fawned upon him, his pleasure at being quicker—faults at which he often caught himself. It was like playing a sport, he explained to himself—when you're playing it, all you want is to win and crow over a great shot. He said,

'You know that unification theory I worked on ...'

'Let me see, light and weak, you explained.' And he repeated that phrase, as he had perhaps done before, 'Light and weak ...'

'Many people have worked on it ...'

'So?'

'Sometimes you have an idea and you are unaware from where—or from whom—you might have got it—or the gist of it ... I had this idea for a long time, worked on it with my friend David Mason. I've told you about him. We moved on, set it aside. And then Rosenfeld published his result, and a few months later I brought out my notes from a lecture I had given earlier at Imperial to my students ... and I presented the theory at a conference in Oslo.'

His father said nothing, looked down at his feet, waiting.

'Suppose I forgot,' Nurul continued, 'and came to this discovery only second- or third-hand ... others were there first and they don't get the credit that I do ...'

He told his father about the letters he'd been receiving, three so far. He did not want controversy and he did not know how far his accusers would go. He didn't know what Rosenfeld actually thought. Or Feynman, or Dirac.

'You let them go as far as they want, don't respond to them. You have the genius, nobody can take that away from you. And you have Allah's blessing ... As you said, nobody knows where the ideas crop up from. How do you know, or how does he know where he—Rosenfeld—might have absorbed his ideas? And you are a great scientist, not a student. At that level, son ... others might not get the credit, but you are there. Don't spurn a gift, my son.'

They started walking around the lawn. Ghulam Ali, tightening the shawl around his shoulders, wanted to know all about his English-born grandchildren, for whom he had brought burfi and laddus. It would be Nurul who would eat them, though he did not say so. And Nurul reported to his father on his family's news, which he had already done in letters. They went back inside the hotel to their adjoining rooms.

'I am leaving very early in the morning, Father, so I might not see you …'

'Try knocking once, anyway.'

They embraced, Nurul touched his father's feet, and Ghulam Ali blessed his son, 'Live long and Allah grant you peace and happiness.'

And then, as Nurul turned his key to open his door, he blurted out, 'Abba, one more thing … I have fallen in love …'

His father stared at him, his hand poised to open his own door, as though his son had suddenly gone mad. 'Love? What love?'

'With another woman. An American woman.'

'Let's go inside,' Ghulam Ali said, and the two of them went inside Nurul's room and sat on the bed side by side. Ghulam Ali took his son's larger hand into his, as though Nurul were a kid, and Nurul told him about Hilary Chase.

'It is natural,' said Ghulam Ali. 'A younger woman, a beautiful one, a different woman. But it wears out, you must know that.'

'But I am in love, Father. I've never had this feeling before … as a mature man. As a youth once, yes … Respect, yes, for my wife. And affection. And care. A different kind of love. But this is a new thing, it's taken me over.'

'You have a family, Nurul. A loving family. Think very carefully about this. Give it a lot of time. Over here, it's different. There, it is different.' Saying which, Ghulam Ali got up, put his hand on his son's head and went to the door. He paused there, then turned around and said, 'Fornication is sin, you also know that.'

The room was luxurious, naturally. Housekeeping had turned down the bed and done his laundry; they had placed a basket of fruits with crackers on the table, with a note of good wishes from the manager. He wished he had offered the fruits to his father; he would tell the desk when he checked out to give the basket to him. He opened the packet of crackers and nibbled on one. He briefly looked over some notes he'd brought with him.

The calculations in them were tedious, crawling over from page to page, which was why a student was doing them, not the professor. The symmetries they were working on were beautiful, but the work involved was messy; this aspect of science was like the kitchen of a great house, hiding all the waste and tedious labour that's not seen upstairs, and is in fact often kept a secret. Like the great chefs, physicists and mathematicians preferred not to show the hard details of their work. He himself had revelled in such calculations when young, took pride in his mathematical stamina, producing pages of intricate stuff. Nowadays he applied himself to some calculations merely to keep fit, as he thought of it. It was an easy trap to fall into, to let the students labour on all the details of a theory. You could miss something vital then.

He put the calculations back into his briefcase, closed it, then lifted his feet and got inside his mosquito net, carefully tucking it in under the mattress on all the sides.

That night he had a terrible dream.

He was in a sweat and trembling, having just presented his results to a gathering of some five hundred senior physicists on the renormalization of the meson field. His claim was big, the meson field theory was solved. He had done it. But Feynman's hand was the first to go up, full of confidence, in that arrogant manner of his, and Nurul knew he was in trouble. Feynman, in an old grey sweater—an affectation—spoke out from his front-row seat, 'Dr Islam, I commend you on your talk, in which you make a bold claim. I wish for all our sakes that you were right—but I detect at least one sign error in your presentation—'

'An odd number of them,' spoke a thin voice with a chortle. Dirac!

'In either case, then your calculation blows up in your face.'

'There's no mistake,' spluttered Nurul. 'I've checked … many times …›

And Feynman, awaiting just this chance to show off, jumped up from his seat, loped off to the board, and showed where the mistake occurred. Nurul tore at his hair in despair. 'And I checked so many times.' He sobbed.

And then all those eminent scientists stood up as one and started dancing around in a circle, singing,

*oompa roompa dippety doo*
*your sign is wrong and so are you!*

Then Feynman, still at the board, holding the chalk, addressed him: 'It's all right, kid, it happens to the best of us.'

And the chorus of eminent scientists sang in approval,

*plus is minus, minus plus*
*and it happens to the best of us!*
*oompa roompa dippety doo*
*your sign is wrong and so are you!*

'Ja,' said Einstein, at the back of the circle, ice cream cone still in his hand, 'the best of us!'

And I'm not one of the best? Nurul Islam woke up, still sweating.

'She's a lovely woman,' Janis Rosenfeld said, 'a little shy, but then she's from Pakistan—imagine living among those Brits!' She was speaking of Sakina Begum, whom she'd got to know a little when she spent a month in London with her husband some years ago.

'How did you find London when you were there?' Hilary Chase asked, changing the subject.

The two women had come for a late lunch at the Coffee Connection on Mount Auburn Street, a large, bustling place serving coffee from all over the world, roasted, ground, and brewed on site; the sandwiches were fresh too, Hilary said.

'Amazing,' Janis said, of London. 'Exciting! You can keep walking and walking and never stop. London never ceases. And the museums, and all that history! So much to see that you've only read about! At times quaint and foreign to us, but quite incredibly wonderful. I have some pictures of Abe from that time, one of him standing next to a guard at the Buckingham Palace gates—you know, the red uniform and those crazy black hats! He hates me to show it! I bet one day they'll fetch thousands ...'

'I'd love to see them!'

They said not a word for a while, then Janis said, 'You know, getting back to Begum—'

'Sakina Begum.'

'Yes. Lovely woman.'

'You know her well?'

'I got to know her a little during our stay there, and saw her maybe a couple of times later. But you know what I want to talk to you about.'

'I guessed.'

Janis had taken her hand across the table. Hilary wondered if Abe was behind this. But she had known Janis for several years now, and Janis had been kind to her. The waitress came around and Janis quickly withdrew her hand, and the two of them ordered. They decided to share a club sandwich and have coffee from Sumatra.

'It's none of my business, Hil, but then I suppose it is. I know them better and am older than you, I hate to admit … but like a big sister?'

'Go on.'

'Hil, they are lovely people, but they are different. I love Nurul, you know that. But this infatuation … can I call it that?'

Hilary nodded. 'You could, I suppose. Could it be anything else? After all, can we explain why we fall in love?'

Janis stared at her for a moment.

'Love. I'll tell you how Nurul explained love to me once. He said you marry a girl by arrangement. For the sake of the family and everyone else. Gradually you get to know her as a person, all the strengths and foibles, body and soul, and you've fallen in love. An enduring form of love. Annealed. Perhaps he is right, but you know which girl he was talking about. Sakina Begum.'

'That's not what he said to me … He said he had fallen in love only once, as a teenager. And when the girl married someone else, he wanted to kill himself.'

'Romeo and Juliet.'

'Perhaps …'

'And what do you think there is between the two of you? Pardon me for talking to you so frankly, I will stop if you want me to.'

'No, I don't mind. I could do with a devil's advocate, I know that. But you know, Janis, I've been infatuated before, but never this way. This is different, mature … he is so … so *different.* So empathic. It feels so absolutely natural, being with him. I like being with him.'

'So it's true love.'

Hilary had turned red and her eyes sparkled; she looked away. Janis waited, watching the young woman on the verge of tears, then she said, 'I thought it might be the glamour of a brilliant scientist … or the exotic. Something new. An escape. He has a charming personality and he's good looking … he has that flamboyant moustache, for one thing.'

They burst into laughter, a release valve.

'He even has English manners.'

'Yes, he does.'

'But you know he's a devout Muslim?'

'Yes, of course. I'm reading up on Islam, actually.'

It's hopeless, of course, Janis said to herself, much as I expected. You can't win against youth, and it has all the time in the world for mistakes; so it thinks. Look at them in the streets and in the communes. Passionate politics and easy sex. Not this good girl, she holds her own. But he's of a different world, and he's charmed her out of America, for the time being.

'Well, try it out,' she said finally, 'it could be love, as you say. I envy you. But you could ruin two lives—and one of them that of a very gifted man.'

'Don't say that, Janis. It can't be so bad.'

'Let's hope not; but be sure of what you do.'

They went on to other matters: the upcoming elections and the war in Vietnam; would Nixon be re-elected, and how soon would the troops return home. Here too the two women differed, the older one believing in a strong America, the younger one in a less interfering America.

For all her talk of that special feeling she shared with him, all the confidence she displayed to Janis, she could not come to terms with Nurul's letter, which he had written to her the day he returned to London. She had opened it with great excitement, expecting she did not know what, but its neutral, matter-of-fact tone broke her heart. 'Dear Hilary, a short note to thank you for spending your time with me in Boston. You made shopping so much easier! Sakina liked her authentic American gift. The tour of Boston was memorable ...' And so on, a few lines more of what he appreciated. Not her. Of course he had to be discreet, she understood that—but then she didn't. Didn't he trust her, did he expect her to wave his letter about and read it to everyone, or to blackmail him in the future? How could this relationship—or the promise of it—be real under the circumstances? She saw—or imagined—hints of his real feelings behind his thanks for the time she spent with him. Still. It burned her up. This was not what love was supposed to be like, it could not be so muted or calculated, they were not on opposite sides of the Berlin Wall, after all. But then perhaps that's what it was, his marriage was the iron curtain behind which he lived. There must be an escape. You could ruin two lives, Janis said. Nurul was not one to abandon his wife. Hilary didn't want that either. Then what? A secret liaison? How?

She had tried to analyze what she felt for him. Janis had called it infatuation, but it was stronger than that, and deeper. It was love, she was convinced. She had been captured by that frankness; that honesty and open-heartedness; the humour and the missing sense of the ironical. There was no pretense in him, no arrogance and showing off that other famous physicists displayed. He never took her for granted. All that, she thought, made him what he was to her. But then how to go on from there?

She took a week off to visit her father in Salem, became a daughter of the house again. She shopped and cooked and stocked up his supplies, she tidied up his study. She picked with him the family photos he should display, which to put away. Together they spent an afternoon cleaning up the backyard for the winter, another morning cleaning the garden in front. She got his car tires changed. At his suggestion, she went out with the guy who ran the mechanic shop, whom she had known in high school; he had always been good with his hands, and they'd all thought he'd go for engineering. He was separated.

When she returned to Cambridge, she learned from her office mates that there had been two foreign calls for her during her absence; they were from London, was the guess, because an English operator had come on the line the second time. It was a man who had called. She wondered what her colleagues knew of her situation; perhaps they guessed, word spreads around, and she had not behaved normally. There were those questioning looks, the covert smiles: a call from *London*? It had to be Nurul, she thought. It *must* be Nurul. The next few days she stayed close to the phone, anxious, rehearsing what she would say when it rang for her. But it didn't. And then, late one night the phone rang in her apartment. She was in bed, and she knew at once it was he. She jumped out of bed and beat her roommate to it.

'Yes,' she replied to his query, 'it's me … Hilary … it's late, but never mind, I was awake … well, sleeping lightly … Yes, yes, I received it.' Then in a lower voice, 'I was disappointed, Nurul—truly disappointed—' She almost sobbed. 'Such a *formal* letter? Such a … such a … Was I so mistaken?'

'No, you were not mistaken. I'm sorry if the tone hurt you, Hilary. I thought you would understand—the letter was mined with all sorts of hints.'

'This is hardly the time for hints … Don't you trust me to be discreet? Don't I have a reputation to worry about too?' She paused, breathless. 'Are you afraid I might blackmail you?'

'I'm sorry. I rang a couple of times before, at your office. And then I had to rush off to an urgent meeting in Pakistan …'

'Hush-hush.'

'Yes.'

'Are you helping them make a bomb?'

She wasn't serious, of course. 'No,' he replied.

'Well … Nurul? What were those mined hints that I failed to appreciate? You can spell them out now, you know.'

She was happy, the constriction in her chest was gone, she felt warm.

'I'd like to see you,' he said.

'How? I mean how is it possible?'

'I thought about that. There's this meeting in Rome …'

'And you're going to be there? I can't afford to come, Nurul. Meetings cost money.'

'Borrow the money—from your father. Tell Abe you're using your own money, he doesn't have to fork up funds. Surely you can convince him it's for the good of your career?'

'Let me think about it. But are you sure, Nurul—are you sure you want to do this? Do you care enough, about me … ?'

'I thought it was for me to ask you, if you were sure. Yes, I am sure. And I know I am in a difficult situation. An impossible situation. But still, Hilary … I am …'

'You are … ?'

He waited a moment before saying slowly, 'I can't help it, Hilary, I'll say it. I'm in love.'

She drew a deep breath. Like with Sharmila? She must have voiced this thought amidst the clamour in her head, for he answered,

'Yes. Like with her.'

She told him she would work on Abe, then they hung up.

She was walking on air. London must have called again, her friends observed. She went to inspect the poster outside the physics office announcing the Rome conference on particles and symmetry, and then went and knocked on Abe Rosenfeld's door.

'What do you think of the Rome conference—on particles and symmetry?' she asked.

He looked at her. 'All talk, and a chance to see Rome on grant money. There's nothing new to report,' he said.

'Oh. I thought I should go.'

'Not worth it. When something better comes along, I'll let you know. Hopefully you'll have something to report then.'

A mild rebuke. She turned around and left. She would have to work on him. There was more to life than physics.

*'Let's play chess!' Nurul said to Sharmila one Saturday afternoon after his lesson with her father. He had heard that she had a chess set. He did not own one because his father disapproved of chess: shatranj, the game of degenerates, he said, for which kingdoms had been lost.*

*'Do you know how?' she asked, eyebrows raised, derisively.*

*'Yes!'*

*He would beat her, and she would be impressed, he thought. He grinned at her. Her green nylon dupatta with little gold stars had fallen to her shoulders. The kameez was a dark green, the salwar white. Today she had two braids instead of one, and she had just taken a bath. The long, mocking face; the light down on her cheeks ...*

*She brought out her chessboard, an old one with red and white squares belonging to her father, barely holding together at the fold, and placed it on the floor. She took black and he white, and they arranged their pieces. She brought out an orange and peeled it for them to share.*

*They played, and he fought hard, to the bitter end, and lost.*

*'You have to learn the opening moves,' she said to him. 'Not just the first three or four—at least ten. You know why you lost?'*

*'Why?'*

*'You wasted two moves in the beginning to protect your queen, which you brought out too soon. In that time I got ready for you, and I stayed ahead of you throughout.'*

*He never beat her, even though she introduced him to the proper openings; for one thing, he was too much in love with her. He would watch her ponder, her chin on her girly hand, the plastic bracelets on her wrist, and shift position; he would watch the faint shade of facial hair above her lips, and the loose strands curling at her ears; he would watch her dupatta inevitably fall to her shoulder. Even the sight of her white feet and toes excited him.*

*'What are you staring at?'*

*'Nothing.'*

*'Concentrate.'*

*'I don't want to—no, no, I do want to continue playing.'*

*'Then play, Nurul Islam. Play.'*

*And lose.*

*Oh she knew, she knew he was in love with her.*

A cloud had slipped over to cast a shadow upon Sakina Begum's placid world. A letter from her younger sister Zubeda arrived containing, amidst all the news about herself and how they were all getting along, advice that she should be sure to keep herself desirable for her husband, because men keep on having needs. No sooner was this curious advice registered than her mother wrote, asking her, did she keep her husband contented in all matters? And Sakina wondered, What was up? He had recently visited Pakistan; had he complained about her? 'Did you meet the rest of the family?' she had asked. 'Only Abba,' he replied, 'there was no time.' What had he said to his Abba? The thought entered her mind that he might have seen a woman there, to possibly bring her to London as his second wife; but she dismissed it, he was far too sophisticated and far too busy. What kind of men had more than one wife in London, anyway? Some low-class fellows, who had no shame in asking for welfare support for two families. And wasn't he happy, with two sons, a darling daughter, a doting wife, and all the prestige? Still, she tried to up the contentment level. She took opportunities to cook the best dishes, brought sweets home; she dressed up a little more and went and bought a new perfume called Seduction. That was rather embarrassing, at the shop. They had always slept snuggled up close, and once recently he got roused and they made love. It was awkward and embarrassed them both. She'd always found it awkward. She could not do the tramp or the seductress. She did not have the body, the personality. That night she cried a little.

But there were other things she could do. They went out to a concert of sitar music and a couple of Hindi films, and he was truly happy to be out. They invited two couples for a dinner, an English and a Pakistani, the husbands both academics, and there was the lively inevitable discussion on religion and politics. They took the three kids out to the V&A, where they also had a tea. The Indian High Commissioner invited them for dinner at her house. But it was an ordeal finding an appropriate sari for Sakina to wear, and so they declined. Social life in London was a stress. And that came from not having your own family close to you. And not having married, as he would tease her, a carpet merchant.

She could tell that he was bothered after returning from Pakistan. It was his meeting with the president. What did Mr Teymuri want? Nurul wouldn't say except, only once, 'The man is mad.'

She was worried. 'Listen,' she told him. 'All this work and travelling, constant beating your head against formulas and turning your brain into mincemeat is not good for you. You should take it easy, relax, you're not young anymore.'

He glared at her.

'What are you saying? The Prophet, God bless him, received his first message at age forty. And he travelled and fought battles and had children after that.'

'That was then, when men were stronger, not soft like today. And he was the Prophet!' She quickly bowed her head and made the pious gesture.

'We live longer now. Forty now is like thirty then—or twenty-five.'

But it was not the same for women, she thought. Maybe in the future, but not now.

Her cousin's son had come to London to study engineering. When they invited him home, he humbly asked for Nurul Uncle's help in getting admission to the University of London. A simple thing. Aftab was twenty-one and had been in one of the army brigades that was sent to East Pakistan; he was one of the thousands made prisoners of war and had been released only six months before. That caught Nurul's ire. His eyes flashed, his cheeks turned red, and he looked fearsome. First he wanted to know why Aftab couldn't study engineering in Pakistan. To the boy's spluttering answers, the uncle asked, 'Did you stand by and watch while your army buddies went about raping and burning? Or were the reports untrue? We saw them on TV, we read about them in the papers!'

Sakina had to intervene. 'He's a good boy! I know him, he would not do anything like that. And he didn't go of his own accord! He's lucky he's alive!'

The reports they had watched about the atrocities of the war were truly sickening. But Nurul eventually helped the boy get admission to a good polytechnic.

'Tell me, Muni's father, what's happening to you?'

What calmed him, finally, was when Eid came and he was asked to lead the prayer at the Central London mosque that morning in front of hundreds of Muslims. He proudly wore his kurta and turban, perfumed himself, and took along their two sons with him, both also in elegant kurtas. The mosque had sent a car for him. Afterwards, she heard, men had crowded around him to shake his hand, young men came and touched his feet to receive his blessings. He even made up with the Pakistan High Commissioner, whose invitation to a musical recital at his home Nurul had turned down soon after his return from that disappointing meeting in Quetta with the country's president. Sakina Begum never understood what had happened between them, but another invitation duly came, to an exclusive dinner, and they went.

Rahim was fourteen and Mirza twelve, good British Muslim boys. Pakistani too, to some degree. When 'he'—she still couldn't think of him as 'Nurul'—was at home, he always paid attention to their school work. In maths and science they could not aspire to be geniuses, though he kept them on their toes; in English he would declaim to them with passion the romantic poetry he remembered, amusing them, for he was rarely so disarmed. They understood conversational Urdu and Punjabi but spoke them haltingly. When he recited for them Ghalib or some other Urdu poetry, and explained it, she knew he was holding them close to his heart. Mirza wanted to be a lawyer; Rahim didn't know. And Muni, whom he liked to cuddle, his darling Mu-mu. Even as she sat on his lap, he made sure she remembered her $(x-y)^3$. It was their play, she would recite the formula, then he would give her two numbers, an $x$ and a $y$ to substitute in the equation.

But often he was not at home. He was travelling to conferences, speaking about his work on explaining the unity of God's Universe. He had tried to explain it.

'Imagine, jaan'—my darling—'trying to explain everything that exists … from the stars to this cup in my hand … how they are put together. That's what we are trying to do in physics nowadays. It may be possible, in a sense.'

'But isn't "Everything there is" Allah Himself?'

He stared at her with a smile and she felt a glow of pride. She was not so naive. And she was his wife, after all.

'Some people believe that. But there is a difference. We pray to Allah, and we praise Him and His Prophet.'

'But can't that "Everything" be praised too?'

'Yes, but you don't have to kneel to it or fear its wrath. If you understand the fundamental laws of physics, then you understand how the universe works, and—Abe and his like will say—there is no need for a God.'

'But Allah can change these laws,' she said. 'Then what?'

'That, my dear, was the quarrel between Ghazali and Ibn Rushd—or Averroes, as he is also called—a thousand years ago.'

'What did Imam Ghazali say?'

'If you want miracles, then Allah has to interfere. If you put a match to a candle, it will catch flame only if the Great and Merciful wills it.'

'What do *you* think?'

He smiled. 'I don't know.'

'Too much thinking about these matters is not good. It is pride itself.'

'Like Azazel's pride, you mean,' he teased. 'And look what happened to him.'

She smiled.

It had been her job to teach the kids the Quran. This wasn't her husband's demand, it was what her mother-in-law had instructed her to do. You have to teach it daily and patiently, remember, each child has its own aptitude and pace. Nurul would then sometimes ask one or the other of them to recite some verse; or he would turn on a recording of a recital. He himself knew the Book by heart, having learnt it as a child. At times, sitting with company, to illustrate a point he would astound them by reciting a surah impromptu. And he a scientist. Wasn't he an atheist? No. Didn't he have doubts? Everyone had doubts.

Not she, Sakina Begum. She had never had doubts about Him; but then she never asked questions about His creation. She did not need fervour either in her worship, and she certainly could not recite from the Book by heart, nor did she need to listen to tapes of recitals. It was a man's job to tussle with God; it was a woman's job to tussle with man. But not their Muni, she would be a bright star. Like Marie Curie, a great scientist, he would say. Or Madam Wu of Columbia University, who had confirmed parity violation and won the Nobel Prize. But Sakina Begum wasn't so sure about that. She wanted Muni to grow up a normal woman. There was some virtue in being normal.

He enjoyed watching comedy on telly—Charlie Chaplin, Buster Keaton—during which he would double up laughing, letting himself go entirely. The children upstairs could always tell when he was watching a favourite comedy. Sometimes Muni would slither down the stairs and with her big black eyes watch him possessively through the rails, from halfway. He could never tire of watching these shows, while Sakina could not help feeling a certain anxiety: she was never sure whether her anxiety was for him, that he was suddenly going mad, or for herself, for he became such a different person from the one she knew.

She had no one to talk to, to express these or other anxieties. Here in London you dared not show any cracks in your exterior. And whenever she went back home to Pakistan, she was treated as an honoured and fortunate guest, an 'England-returned,' who lived well and brought a suitcase full of presents, toys, clothes, chocolates; what concerns could she have? But the sisters and cousins and aunts in Pirmai, in their casual salwar kameez and with their easy manners, could simply walk over to each other's houses during the day and have tea and gossip. Sakina had to be careful what she ate and drank there, her Urdu was dated and sprinkled with English, the heat bothered her … she was simply out of touch. A 'faariner.' Pardesi. Everywhere.

'My dear, why don't you finish your schooling?' he had suggested once. 'It will be good for you. You can even find a job then.'

It seemed a good idea and expressed his concern for her. She was bored, Muni was not born yet. They decided on a correspondence school, and soon the lessons started coming from the British Correspondence College, exclusively for Mrs Sakina Begum Islam, in handsome blue booklets with the college coat of arms on them. She was excited. The college brochure promised a bright future ahead, and related success stories of people just like her. But the lessons were hard and she simply couldn't cope. The pile of unworked blue booklets kept growing. Nurul had volunteered to help, but he would be tired in the evenings, and often preoccupied with his own work. Or he was away at conferences. She gave up on the BCC. But there was another, surer way to teach herself: helping the boys day in, day out with their lessons, becoming a child with them and reading their textbooks and doing homework with them, she gradually realized that she was educating herself as surely as though she were at school. And of course merely running a household in London was a learning experience in itself—going to the shops and the post office, dealing with the milkman and the postman, the plumber and the electrician. But she could not get rid of her accent; if she tried, it was as though she were acting a role. It didn't bother her when the children laughed at a mispronunciation, when Nurul—if he were present—would smile gently at her and demand of the one who had laughed loudest to say something in Urdu or Punjabi or repeat after him a line from Faiz or Ghalib or Bulleh Shah. But she thought she could hold a conversation at his department parties, or among educated Pakistanis. Once she had been introduced to Lord Russell, who was often in the news, and they had chatted and he had invited her to join him in a protest march against the bomb. She was flattered but declined.

And then, like a gold star for her achievement, Muni was born.

Nurul Islam was angry with a student. Sitting behind his desk, having been distracted by something evidently trivial, he gave the young man the full benefit of his glare.

'Sir, I did the calculation as you suggested, and it doesn't work,' said Mushtaq Mohammad, standing awkwardly before the professor. He was a small, underfed-looking fellow. With the temerity to have the name of a famous cricketer, the professor thought. He had placed a sheaf of handwritten notes on the desk, which Nurul had not deigned to look at.

'What do you mean, "it doesn't work"? Make it work, it has to work, the three quarks must combine into a baryon. It's as simple as that. It has to work.'

'I did exactly as you said, sir.'

'Exactly as I said. That was only a suggestion, sir, a thought. You're supposed to put some original ideas into the problem and make it work. Some mirch-masala. Some salt. Don't do *exactly* as I said. Just do it any way! I am not here to do calculations for you!'

Not very kind, but what to do. Most of his students knew that the professor only threw off suggestions, sometimes wide off the mark; it was for them to do something with them, prove him wrong or advance them to some level, or whatever, and then they would discuss. Mushtaq was close to tears. He seemed to be in his mid-twenties. By his age Nurul Islam had had an invitation from the Institute for Advanced Study in Princeton. And why did students from India and Pakistan desire to study only under him?

'Sit down. Let's at least see what you've done,' Nurul told him grudgingly.

'Can I come back in ten minutes, sir? I'll go outside and say my prayer.'

Nurul drew a long breath. 'You might as well say it here. We can say it together.'

The two stood side by side and said their prayer. Then they sat down, on either side of the desk. Nurul stared at Mushtaq. Something about the student's gesture to end the prayer had drawn his attention. It drew from him an inordinate amount of empathy.

'Where are you from?'

'From Pakistan, sir. Dilawari.'

'What are your plans when you finish?'

'I want to go back and teach college, sir.'

'Just teach? Then why come all the way here—' How did he get admission, anyway, he evidently was not among the best. Exaggerated grades, he guessed. Influence. Bribery. All those were possible in that country.

'I wanted the chance, sir, to learn from the very best, from a great man like you ...'

'And you are a Shirazi?' Nurul asked softly. 'The way you ... when you finished the prayer.'

'Yes, sir!' A shy, grateful smile.

'And the family's from ... ?'

'From Gurdaspur in India. We came at Partition, sir.'

'And arrived safely. No casualties, I hope?'

Mushtaq did not respond to that. It should not make a difference who he was, but Nurul's heart had softened. He advised the young man to take a step back from his current program and enrol in two introductory courses, one in mathematical physics, the other in intermediate quantum mechanics, and he would talk to the registrar and the lecturers concerned to make that possible. And he should work very hard to catch up. And come to him if he had problems. He then sent Mushtaq on his way.

Such a long way to go. When will we produce our Einsteins, our Diracs?

But who are *we*, as President Teymuri had asked him in Quetta? The memory of that meeting still irked. That cocky Teymuri. What talent did you need to become a politician, and decide unilaterally to embark on a nuclear weapons program? A talent to talk bombast and manipulate power and people, and to start a war. That afternoon in Quetta, after the president flew off, Nurul had been given a wide berth by the senior scientists who were present. Of course he was given his due respect; but the man of the hour was Dr Arif Khan, the materials scientist who had spent time with the Atomic Energy Agency in Vienna, now head of Project Babur, as the bomb project was named. Nurul had felt slighted, a bit envious, but of course that was simple vanity: he had neither the expertise nor the inclination to work on Project Babur. For the others present there, it was a lifetime's chance. There could be no bigger project than making the bomb.

He could not discuss the nature of the secret meeting with his father when they met. But he knew what Abba's response would be, if told that a single bomb could destroy an entire city with its hundreds of thousands of people. Generations born deformed from the radiation. Their sect was a peaceful one, which was why it got picked on. Abba would have advised him, Stay away from it, son. Don't wash your hands in blood.

Pakistan's nuclear option was an open topic among its elite. Of the Pakistanis Nurul met in London, the majority opinion was that their country needed a bomb; an Islamic bomb. Only then would the country survive. A bomb gave you a deterrent, an immunity; more than anything else, it brought 'us' prestige—after all, how many nations of the world had the capacity to develop their own bomb? The people of Pakistan would have to make sacrifices to make it possible. If need be, we'll eat grass, but we'll have our own nuclear bomb, as Teymuri had so graphically put it.

Who would eat grass? Not Teymuri. Not these wallahs in London.

And what was an Islamic bomb? One in which the uranium atoms uttered 'Subhanallah!' as they split, and the neutrons and gamma rays went along their happy paths praising God as they entered into human cells and destroyed them? A bomb with Quranic verses imprinted on it? The Hiroshima bomb, he had read, had a pinup of an American actress on the outside casing. *Ecce homo*.

Back to the unification problem. The beauty of symmetry. The human body was symmetric outside, but inside it was not. Why didn't people have two hearts, one on the right and one on the left, or on either the left side or the right side, with equal probability? After all, when you tossed a coin, there was equal chance of getting either a head or a tail. But the heart was on the left side only (except in the case of that Ian Fleming villain Dr No). At some point nature, evolution, God decided, Let's put the heart on the left side, not the right. His friend Higgs in Edinburgh would call this choice a case of broken symmetry. And then came the abstract symmetries—conceptualized from our recognition of ordinary symmetries, like rotation. We define some mathematical operations, under which the laws of nature don't change. And behold, magic! Such awesome beauty—you wish you could shout it out to the world—Hey, look, do you see this, it tells us why protons and neutrons are almost alike! And why they are not. Gell-Mann did that. He stipulated a symmetry for protons and neutrons and predicted the existence of quarks and strange particles. Smart guy, Gell-Mann, though he couldn't help showing off that he was a renaissance man, read James Joyce and listened to Bach. Still, that was a revolution. Which he, Nurul Islam—and a dozen others—wished to extend to describe all the particles, from one supersymmetry. Why did the electron and the proton have the same charge but masses that differed by a factor of two thousand? Why were there four different forces in nature? Why didn't the proton decay like the neutron? All these questions would be answered by one single symmetry, and one universal force.

God may or may not play with dice, but he surely likes symmetry. And I'll play the game of symmetries with him.

It is said there are seventy thousand veils separating God and his worshippers, so profound is He; as you push aside each veil there is revealed something new. Allah never fully reveals Himself. But on the night of Miraj, when the Prophet, peace on him, ascended from al-Aqsa to the seventh heaven on the winged horse Buraq, God revealed Himself in stages to Muhammad. Peace upon him again. Each profoundly beautiful symmetry of physics can only be one of those revelations, as we ride our Buraq up the hill of discovery.

From that esoteric thought to Mr Beyram Teymuri and his bomb. Because Pakistan had been humiliated in a foolish, arrogant war and lost half its territory across the subcontinent that was not even connected to it by land or speaking the same language. It now called itself Bangladesh.

India should not have been divided in such a ridiculous manner in the first place. But he would not say that in public.

There was a brisk double knock on the door and the figure of Pete Sorensen of Lund University stood grinning there.

'Nurul!'

'Pete Sorensen, you son of a gun!'

They shook hands. Sorensen pulled him closer and they embraced. Then the wispy-haired Swede sat down, crossed his long, stilt-like legs. He was more legs and head than anything else.

'Well,' he said. 'Look what I brought for you.' Digging into his battered briefcase, he brought out a bundle of preprints from North America describing some current research and passed them over to Nurul. 'All the news that's fit to print!'

'And how are you, my friend?'

'I'm well, as you see for yourself. And you?'

'Couldn't be better. And what news do you bring from across the pond?' Nurul asked, as with a quick flourish of the hand he spread out the preprints and peered at their titles. 'Gell-Mann up to anything?—have you heard?'

'Murray's always up to something. But there are young guns emerging that you should keep an eye on. You're on your way to becoming a dinosaur!'

'Hm.'

Sorensen himself was an experimental physicist, now returning to Sweden via London. He was scheduled to give a talk in a couple of hours. Since they had met long ago in Rochester, New York, Sorensen had been Nurul's contact with the experimental universe. From Pete, Nurul would get the lowdown on how close they were to a breakthrough in Chicago, or Berkeley, or Darmstadt.

'Any talk about the Nobel?'

He shouldn't think about prizes, he knew and often preached that; the best prize of all was the opportunity to do what he loved and the joy it brought, but the Nobel was one gift he could give to his mother and father, to his country, and of course to his small beleaguered Shirazi sect that always had to justify itself to the Islamic world.

'Bohr and Mottelson are next in line, I hear, for their work on nuclear models. If not this year, then the next. They are in the right place too.' He eyed Nurul for a while. 'There is talk you were in Cambridge, Mass—how did that go?'

If there was a hint of something in the question, Nurul ignored it. Why was there *talk*? 'Great,' he answered. 'Abe and I had some good discussions on renormalizing Lesser Unification … Sorry—I should have asked—would you like some water right now, before your lecture? I can have some sent. I presume you don't want tea.'

'I could do with a real drink before my lecture,' Pete Sorensen said, looking around as though Nurul ran a bar in his office, before adding, 'I don't suppose you—'

Nurul paused, then said, 'I can oblige you there. I've given up, but a visitor brought a gift recently from Edinburgh. What else can you bring from Scotland …' He opened his bottom drawer, took out a glass and a bottle of single malt. 'At your service.' He poured the drink.

There came a mildly amused look on Sorensen's face. 'Rosenfeld once told me about Nurul Islam's secret elixir, available only to the chosen few! And you?' he asked hesitantly. 'Will you join me, or … ?'

'I can make the odd exception,' Nurul said, and nonchalantly took out another glass and poured a small shot for himself. They raised their glasses and drank.

'Something the matter?' Sorensen asked, Nurul having turned suddenly silent.

Nurul shook his head and raised his glass again at Sorensen. A few fluid ounces of alcohol for a friend, and only on occasion. God was not so unforgiving. There were bigger villains to catch.

In the seminar room there were some twenty people present. It was a lazy afternoon, and this was a specialist talk. Sorensen brought out his transparencies and began. There was nothing new that he said, just a report on recent experiments to verify the predictions of the Islam-Rosenfeld theory, and proposals for a new accelerator to detect heavy particles. Tea was served in the common room.

Earlier in the week Nurul had received a postcard from Hilary at the department address, telling him she had registered for the Rome conference—Abe had given his blessings after all, and her father would pay the expenses. It was a cheerful note, with a familiar tone, and signed 'with affection.' Unable to resist, Nurul had called her right away at her study, only for another graduate student to pick up the phone and answer, 'She's not here. Can I take a message? Who shall I say called?' Nurul sensed mischief in that query, but what could he do. 'Nurul,' he answered curtly. 'Tell her Dr Nurul called.'

Perhaps he should have used another name. Dr Isham?—what a joke, even to think like a teenager. The word would now slowly—rapidly—spread, how could it not. Did you hear ... Nurul Islam has something going on ... a graduate student ... of course he's married, and he's a teetotaller Muslim to boot ... These big-time professors always have their groupies in every port ...

After Rome, what?

*One Sunday morning in Cambridge, soon after his marriage, there was a knock on the door of his flat. At first Nurul didn't recognize the man at the door, small and dark in an oversize black coat. It was a shock to realize who he was—Raj Mohan, a lecturer at the private college in Pirmai. He had been a good-looking man with slicked hair, always wore a jacket and a bright shirt with wide collars. He would be seen daily breezing down the main road on his bicycle on his way to the college. Self-assured and proud, it was him whom Sharmila married and thus broke the teenage Nurul's heart. You could see the smirk on his face when he walked around town, proud of his catch. A smirk that dimmed a little when Nurul's matriculation results were announced. 'Pure fluke,' Raj Mohan had said. Now he stood outside Nurul and Sakina's door, a man who looked like he'd been through life's wash too many times and was wrung out.*

*'Nurul Islam? Raj Mohan ... from Pirmai—you remember me—'*

*'Of course! Come in, sir.'*

*'I'm sorry if I'm—'*

*'Not at all, not at all!'*

*And there he sat, Raj Mohan, his hands between his knees, looking lost. Shrivelled ... the image would always remain in Nurul's mind: sunken eyes, cheekbones jutting, hair unwashed. He had removed his coat and wore a jacket underneath. He said he was not hungry, but Sakina Begum fried him scrambled eggs, which he ate. They chatted hesitantly. What was he doing? Still at the college, he said. But he had taken a year off to look for his wife. He understood that Nurul Islam had gotten married in Pakistan.*

*'What happened to Sharmila?' Nurul asked.*

*In anticipation of the Partition, people had begun to leave areas where they were a minority group and felt insecure. Mr Rajan, Sharmila's father, had at first refused to leave his home. What could possibly happen to him? he argued; he was a teacher, everyone knew him, Hindu, Sikh, and Muslim. He had taught them or their children. Incidents of violence in Pirmai had always been minimal. Soon, however, there came terrible stories of lootings, rapes, and killings, and trains dropping off dead bodies at railway stations. Sharmila finally convinced her father to go: once the violence had ended and sanity returned, people would be able to come back to their homes, on this side of the border or the other, and families would be together again. People wouldn't abandon their ancestral homes and villages forever. Mr Rajan acquiesced and agreed to join a caravan of private cars and taxis bound for Delhi; Sharmila and Raj had matters to settle and promised to follow soon. Meanwhile she went to spend the night with her father before his departure. It could be days and weeks before they met again.*

*'I should not have let her go by herself,' Raj Mohan stated simply. His hands dropped to his side. 'What kind of husband would do that at such a time?'*

*What did she mean to Nurul now? The girl who had shown off by playing her sitar or beating him at chess, who knew—with a smile—how much he admired her. He was passionate about her, but he was two years younger, still in school, and she was already in college. That she was a Hindu never entered his mind. Then suddenly she got married, and he nursed a broken heart for months. He went to college in Lahore, then abroad, and became successful; he was now married and his life's work lay before him. It was exciting. He was out to make a name. What could she possibly mean to him, except as a memory, a happy and sad memory, someone who met with a tragic fate? But Sharmila had a place in his heart, her fate had only lodged her in more deeply. She was his romantic memory—'Play, Nurul Islam! Watch your openings!' The long white fingers that picked up a piece. Checkmate. He drew a deep breath. 'What happened?' he asked.*

*'She didn't come back, I couldn't find her.' Raj's voice lost control and he broke down.*

*The area in which her father lived had been attacked in the night. Some residents had run off to the ruins, others were killed in their homes. And then, a massacre at the ruins. Raj Mohan couldn't find his wife, dead or alive.*

*'The killers were not from our town,' he said, as though to assuage the pain.*

*He went to the ruins and examined the carnage. Men, women, and children, lying there stinking among the rubble and rubbish. He found Mr Rajan's body, but not Sharmila. Not even a scrap of clothing. He took the teacher's body to the temple, where it was washed and taken for cremation. Over the months he wrote many letters, to Indian and Pakistani newspapers, to authorities on both sides who were in charge of locating lost people. Nothing.*

*The three of them sat silent in the living area of the little apartment in Cambridge. Outside, the wind blew and whistled fiercely down the street, the windows rattled. They all must have entertained the same gruesome thought, all knew what had happened to thousands of women during that period of madness.*

*Raj Mohan left as quietly as he had appeared. Suddenly he was no longer there and Nurul and Sakina Begum were left alone in the apartment. They did not discuss the subject, though there was nothing else to think about.*

*But that night Nurul Islam lost his faith. Prayers and devotions, injunctions and rules, the example of the Prophet, all these that had been a part of his life system, none of these had any meaning for him now. Where was the place of religious belief amidst the mindless horrors of the world? Where human feasted on human? Where was God? Europe too had many stories of war's brutality and loss, there was disillusion all around. At Cambridge he had friends among whom were Punjabis—Hindus, Muslims, Sikhs; they would drink, they would curse at the politicians of their land, they would eat what was forbidden …*

*He had come around afterwards, embraced again the faith that had been his comfort and anchor throughout his life. Reacting to butchers was to allow them to lead you.*

*Years later when he asked his father about Raj Mohan, he learnt that the man had hanged himself in his home.*

'What bothers you today?' she asked him quietly, coming to stand in front of him.

He had been sitting in the dark in the sitting room, brooding. Even Muni knew to leave him alone—when she approached, he had slowly shaken his head. No. This is me, in the darkness, I have to cope. A part of me has died and there's this feeling inside me of emptiness, of guilt and redemption denied. Someone's left a great wound inside me and the only person to blame is myself.

'David Mason died,' he said flatly.

'Oh.' Her hand flew to her mouth, her eyes widened. She quickly went to leave.

'He killed himself. The news came to the department. I just can't believe it ...'

No brother, no sibling came as close. They had fallen apart, *he* had fallen away, but that shouldn't matter, so Nurul had always believed. Surely time would heal whatever misunderstanding there was. You had to wait. Their bond wouldn't just break. They would pick up where they left off.

They had collaborated in Cambridge, then in London, where Nurul first came, a hotshot young professor, followed by David—Nurul had insisted on his appointment. Together they had obtained some exciting results on the weak force. Then David went away suddenly to America, family in tow. Didn't stay in touch, didn't reply. He was heard of from Baltimore, then Syracuse, before taking up a post in Kenya.

'You will go to the funeral?' she asked from the doorway. 'I could come.'

'I don't think Una would want me to. She didn't even call me, it was from John at the department that I heard the news ...›

She said nothing, simply went back to the kitchen.

Could she sense his grief, his pain; the sudden emptiness inside him, with the knowledge of a presence now gone, a quarrel that forever would go unresolved? The guilt—he felt it, though he was never completely sure of his fault. He glanced towards the kitchen. He could have done with a little babying, a hand over his head, someone to say, It's all right, jaan, don't be sad; these things happen, we have to go on. Rather unusually, when he had needed her most, she had simply left. Deal with it.

David had been the quiet sort, resilient and punctilious. The two of them approached a problem from opposite ends: Nurul came up with flashes of insight, half of them dead ends; David on the other hand posed a problem, then went about methodically to seek a solution. All his work was written out neatly, with the conclusion at the end, positive or negative. Mason's Theorem was now a staple of field theory textbooks, simple and elegant, and it had been missed by the preening giants of physics.

One day, late at night in his office, at the end of a long calculation, they'd quarrelled. Nurul had proposed they announce the result in a short letter that would be published in a matter of weeks, he could write it up. David wanted to wait for the next stage and then publish the complete result. 'You're too ambitious, too hasty!' David had accused, after some back and forth. Nurul protested that their world was not such as to await David's pleasure. *Too ambitious?* Surely for them both? He in turn had accused David of not having the guts to come forward and stand by his calculation. This was just a bit short of calling him a coward. David retorted long-windedly that perhaps his overweening ambition could be attributed to the fact that he was of a colonized people whose past achievements had long been obscured and whose present ones were non-existent. Nurul Islam, 'a new Muslim genius,' after how many centuries? Nurul called him a closet racist. David countered that he harboured an inferiority complex common to his race. Nurul reminded him that it was at his insistence that David was at Imperial, after all. The arrows flew, tipped with choice poison.

A dirty quarrel, no holds barred. All this, had it been simply waiting to hatch, and now it had? It drained them, they apologized profusely to each other afterwards, went home in cabs. The next day was as usual, there was no mention of the quarrel; at the end of the day they went for a drink at the pub, Nurul making it one of those rare occasions when he allowed himself a Scotch. For David's sake. And they apologized again, Nurul more than his friend. David asked Nurul to go ahead and write up the letter, Nurul said no, David was right, they should do more work first. Both agreed that their quarrel had brought them closer. It was a good thing in the end. A friendship needed argument to steel it.

But something had changed. Words had been spoken that could not be taken back. They could not be the same with each other, were a little too careful in their dealings, a little too ready to yield. They had hurt each other; and that residual pain, the memory of those wounds they had mutually and recklessly inflicted remained, however much muted or suppressed. Accusations echoing in the brain, creating doubt and insecurity. Nurul thought he had received more than he gave. He had attacked his friend's personal weakness, his lack of confidence, but David had instinctively drawn deep from the English reserves of racial prejudice to mock Nurul's background. His race and religion.

They never again did any work jointly.

Nurul knew that David believed he had not received enough credit for their work together. He was right. Nurul got invited to many fora, he spoke enthusiastically about conjectures and results; he prefaced his talks with quotes from Persian and Urdu and from his life's experiences. He stood up and pronounced, and took the jibes with the glory. In all of what Nurul presented, David always received his due, but he was only occasionally present in person, and usually quiet.

It was just the way we were, I talked and he was quiet. He waited, always waited for the next step, the complete theory. And I received the attention. Even his famous theorem, I pushed him to publish the first part quickly. I shouldn't have reminded him about that, or my small contribution to its proof. He called me envious. My nature, my exotic background caught attention, in a field where American bravado always grabbed attention, and the quiet, unassuming Englishman got ignored. If he had spoken to me, if we had discussed this situation … could I have helped him? We were close. We were friends. The times we spent together as families, in each other's homes, met for Christmas and Eid.

David had been the magician at the boys' party one year. It was hurtful, his decision to go away without notice, without consultation. When he had gone, twice Nurul had him invited to speak at a conference, and he had turned the offers down. After that Nurul wrote a short note to him. 'I thought we resolved our issues, David, at least we were honest with each other. Friendships don't just die, we agreed. Is it our different cultures or upbringing? Where I come from we simply say what's on our minds.' No reply. If anything, Nurul suspected he had offended David even further. If his friend had been a fellow Punjabi, in no time they would have carried on as before, arms around each other's shoulders. Yaar, what matter, life goes on. But he was an Englishman, whose depths Nurul could not even begin to fathom.

'What could have made him turn away so completely like that?' he said out loud.

Friendship is trust, David. If you did not trust me, you could not have been my friend. But do I trust myself? Perhaps he knew me better …

And the so-called Islam-Rosenfeld Model—the final straw? Nurul was certain that in Oslo he had acknowledged David's contribution, their earlier work of some years before. But David Mason's name did not appear in the proceedings of the symposium or in the excitement that followed. Did Nurul Islam simply fool himself into believing he had credited David? Was he simply callous and greedy for glory and got carried away, not insisting that Mason be credited along with Islam? But so many people had contributed to the formulation over the years.

However much credit he gave to David subsequently, it was his and Abe Rosenfeld's names that became associated with the theory. David remained a footnote.

'You did not say your prayer today,' Sakina reminded him, coming into the room and sitting down with her cup of tea. 'Shall I bring you another chai?'

He briefly glared at her and she looked away. It was one of those inexplicables in their relationship how, normally so gentle and understanding, she could manage to intrude into some profound moment of his thoughts, some pain or ecstasy, with something mundane and irrelevant. And why was she so cold today? And why was he picking on her, even in his mind? Were his prayers mundane and irrelevant? He had felt too dirty and tainted to pray; now, reminded, he got up and went to his office past the kitchen, with its aroma of steaming daal and fried bhindi, and went through the motions of prayer.

There were calls of condolences that evening for the death of his friend and collaborator. And a request to write an obituary for the *Guardian*. After dinner and dessert, having read to Muni and put her to bed, he went to the boys' room and sat down to his Thursday night ritual, hearing Mirza's recitation of a Quran excerpt; he couldn't pay attention, and the boy had finished before Nurul realized it. He paused and told them that Uncle David had died in Kenya. Did they remember Uncle David, and Aunt Una, and Susan? There was an awkward silence. Nurul sat on Mirza's bed, under a poster of the Rolling Stones, Mirza sat at his desk, and Rahim on his own bed, leaning against the wall.

'What was he doing in Kenya?' Rahim asked.

'He was teaching,' Nurul replied. 'He was a brilliant scientist, but he preferred to teach where there's a dearth of good teachers.'

'I remember Susan.'

'I don't,' said his younger brother.

'You should. She babysat us. Did you speak with Aunt Una, Dad?'

'I will, as soon as I go downstairs.'

'Wish them well for us.'

Nurul went back downstairs and sat down in his study. Sakina was in the sitting room watching the news. With some trepidation Nurul picked up the phone and rang the Masons' number in Nairobi. It took a while before he got a through-line and Una answered. He felt a stab at hearing the familiar voice, and imagined the pain it must carry. How close they had all been, and how clean and unstated the break was.

'Una … How are you. This is Nurul. I am grief-stricken, I heard the news from John Hemmings and I don't know what to say—please accept my heartfelt …'

'Thank you, Nurul. It's been a shock. I appreciate your calling.'

'Thank you. We had our differences, Una, and I wished we could have brought them out in the open … he was my dear, dear friend. You both were.'

'I know—'

She choked and he could tell she was crying. 'Why did he do it?' she wailed. 'To us!'

'Take it easy, Una,' he told her and waited, until she said finally, 'I'll be all right … Thank you for calling, Nurul.'

'I've been asked to write an obituary for the *Guardian*. Do you wish me to say anything in particular … or hold back on something?'

'I know you'll do your best, Nurul.'

'I will. He was a brilliant physicist and mathematician. That's why the *Guardian* wants an obituary. Why did you go to Kenya? How did he find Kenya? I understand he taught at the university there.'

'He thought he'd do something useful. He liked it. We both liked it. Everyone liked him. I taught at a school here … You know, he was offered a post at Cambridge, but he thought it was not enough … too little too late.'

It was always the same, he knew, younger and lesser minds come and feel threatened, and from their positions of newfound power keep the really brilliant minds away.

'It's been good here … ,' she added. 'Which is why it's so shocking … what was it that I didn't know? I have to think about it, Nurul.'

'Look after yourself. Sakina and the boys send their good wishes. We're thinking of you.'

*Why did he do it?* Her words echoed in his brain. He gave a shudder. Oh David, you were cruel. Cold as ever.

David Mason

The World Lost A Brilliant Mathematical Physicist

Dr David Mason is known for several major breakthroughs in mathematical physics, including what came to be called the Mason Theorem, and his was one of the earliest proposed unifications of the electromagnetic and weak forces.

Born in Milltown, Yorkshire, in 1932, Mason attended Belfield Secondary School, where he distinguished himself early by his precocity. Says his former physics teacher, Peter Harris, 'By the time he finished his O Levels, it was he who was teaching me physics and maths.' While still sixteen he was admitted to the University of Bristol as an undergraduate, where he caught the eye of the renowned emigré physicist Rudolf Peierls, who recommended him to Cambridge. Among his mentors at Cambridge were the astrophysicist Fred Hoyle and Nobel laureate Paul Dirac. After a lectureship at Cambridge, David Mason took up a position in the department of theoretical physics at Imperial College London.

Dissatisfied with the gamesmanship into which he believed his field had entered, Mason left Imperial College and after a stint in the United States took up a professorship at the University of Nairobi, Kenya. A former student and colleague there, Francis Ogwell, said, 'He was awe-inspiring, but not always easy to understand. He would do a problem one way, then another, then show you the shortest and most elegant way. He never patronised you, always assumed you were as capable as he. But he was a genius.'

Mason published chess problems under the name Lucretius. He was also a professional-level squash player. He leaves behind his wife, Una, and daughter, Susan.

*'Mr Islam—'*

*'Call me Nurul, please.'*

*'Nurul, would you like to join Una and me at the pub?'*

*They were on the pavement outside St John's, Una stood a few feet away, perhaps so as not to embarrass him. David Mason was tall and lanky, with a long granitic face, wearing a blazer; she was only half a head shorter, a schoolteacher with short brown hair.*

*'I'm sorry, I don't consume alcohol,' Nurul replied.*

*'Then'—David threw a glance behind him at his wife—'why don't we get fish and chips and eat in our flat.'*

*'Are you sure, Mr Mason?'*

*'David. Of course I'm sure. And we can continue our discussion there.'*

*It was the most forthcoming Nurul would ever see the quiet and reserved David Mason.*

*'Thank you, I will be most happy to join you.' Nurul Islam put his right hand over his left breast in a gesture of gratitude.*

*'Do you experience chest pains, Mr Islam?' Una asked, having come forward.*

*They would break out into peals and guffaws every time they recalled this moment, years later. Nurul, and for that matter Una, was never sure if she had meant to be funny or had asked her question out of serious concern for him. But this was how their friendship began. That conversation was repeated in many editions.*

*They walked to the Masons' home, David and Nurul talking of Dirac fields with and without masses, and the violation of parity, how exciting it all was and how many discoveries there remained to be made, and Nobel Prizes to be won, until Una interjected. 'Now, now, if you insist on talking shop, I'm stopping right here at the pub. And try and be modest, there must be some things you boys can't do.'*

*At their home, over tea, Nurul admitted that yes, he missed his home and was lonely, even though there were people from India and Pakistan in Cambridge; he explained to his hosts that he would go home and bring back a wife chosen for him by his family. He did not mind. What was love?—it was something that could develop if there was commitment between a man and a woman. He came from a backward place called Pirmai in Pakistan. David told him he also came from a backward place, called Milltown, in Yorkshire. Una was from Leeds. Nurul extolled the glories of Lahore, and said he looked forward to seeing London properly.*

*When Sakina arrived, it was Una who took her around and showed her the rudiments of surviving in England, even taught her acceptable English pronunciations. And when Nurul was away, the Masons looked after her, and the boys played with their only child, Susan.*

While her husband sat in his study and spoke to Una Mason on the phone, Sakina Begum sat before the television pretending to watch the news. She was crying. She asked herself the same question Una had asked, Why would he do it to us? What unhappiness had he harboured, gathered over the years?

David had always seemed a calm, self-contained man, a considerate individual with a quiet sense of humour. Sakina had known him more than her husband imagined, and she had not enlightened Nurul about this relationship, kept it as something of her own. He had come over one afternoon when Nurul was away to give a lecture. It was a Saturday during the Christmas season, a cheerful time, but quiet at home. Muni was at a friend's house and the boys were at a match. David rang the bell, and stood at the door, tall and loose-limbed, his woollen overcoat hanging on him as on a hanger, holding a large bag of goodies.

'Something to cheer you up for the season. I thought I'd look in on you, how are you doing?'

'I am very well, thank you.' She was delighted and invited him in.

'Una sends her regards,' he said, taking the sofa in the sitting room.

There was an amused smile on his long stone face and he had kept his coat on—she had forgotten to take it from him—and looked awkward leaning forward on the couch. He had a large dome of a forehead and his hair, always combed back, had thinned. They sat in silence for a moment, then she went to the kitchen and brought back two cups of tea.

'Done your Christmas shopping already, I suppose?'

'Yes, before Nurul left we bought the children's presents. And he will bring some things from there, I'm sure.'

'Vienna.'

'Yes, Vienna.'

'Chocolates,' he said, and they fell quiet for a moment, then he asked, 'Would you like to go out and take a look at the shops? At all the colour and cheer this time of the year? Oxford Street should be enjoyable. We'll just walk around and look.'

She beamed, paused, then blurted out, 'Yes! I would enjoy that.'

He stood up, helped her with her coat, and they walked to the Tube station. The train was crowded and they had to stand. They stepped out at Oxford Circus directly into a pedestrian throng, which they happily joined, she first delighting in the Father Christmas at the Tube entrance, recalling how at Muni's nursery school Nurul had once played the role; on their way they paused to listen to a group of young carol-singers, peeped into a dazzling toy store, chiming, buzzing, rattling, and hissing with marvellous temptations for children, and stood to take in the fairy-tale beautiful displays of the shop windows. She felt grateful to be in London at such magical moments, when all the other travails seemed worth it. After every stop outside a display window, they would join the crowds again. At Selfridges, she got tempted by a beautiful cake, but he said there was one already in the bag of goodies he'd brought, and so she picked cashews and dry fruit. They had tea there.

They met a few other times this way, he simply showing up at the door when Nurul was off somewhere. 'You are my guardian angel!' she told him, 'you arrive just when you are needed!' 'Like the genie of the lamp … all you have to do is wish!' He was her secret, something she could mull over in her privacy. They were in a new phase in her and Nurul's relationship with David and Una, they hardly got together now. There were always the children to blame. She told him about her life in Pirmai, as the fourth of six children. Yes, she missed it, but she realized that she had changed and found it hard to fit in there. Everything had changed there too. After two weeks during her last visit, she had the urge to return home—yes, London. Since the age of eight she remembered being told to prepare to marry Nurul Islam. Yes, he had been a legend. And when the time came, she married him.

'What?' she asked, eyes flashing, as he stared benignly at her.

'You're a brave woman.'

'I had no choice. Nobody has a choice. And it's not as if he's a devil!'

'I didn't mean that … And if there had been a choice?'

'That doesn't mean anything. That's in … another universe—isn't that what you physicists talk about?'

He broke into a laugh, then said, 'Alternative universes, yes, in our fantasies.'

'And you? You had a choice?'

'Yes. I met Una at university, in Bristol.'

He was the oldest of three children. His father was a veterinarian, birthing cows and sheep and mending horses. Not wealthy, unlike city vets; his clients were small farmers who couldn't pay half the time. He was bad-tempered, too, and David liked nothing better than to stay in his room reading … or solving chess problems, he added sheepishly. The first chance he had, after A levels, he left home.

He made her try different English foods during their outings. The first time they went out she ate steak-and-kidney pie; another time, bangers and beans, at a pub. The bangers turned out to be pork, he had forgotten, and he apologized profusely, his face red.

'It's all right,' she assured him, 'really.'

'But it's forbidden to you.'

'It hasn't changed me, has it? Do you see horns growing out of my head?' She gestured with her hands on her head. 'I think … in a different place, some of these—forbiddings,' she giggled and blushed, 'these forbiddings should be relaxed.'

'But you still wear the scarf,' he motioned, making a circle around his own head.

'Not all—'

'Not all forbiddings can be relaxed.'

They laughed. What she had meant to say was, she didn't cover her head all the time.

He was fond of Nurul. 'It was a most fortunate thing—meeting him—and through him, you. Nurul was so original and *new*—you know what I mean? At Cambridge, nobody could understand how his mind worked, leaping at answers; they just knew he was a genius.'

Once he said, 'Do you know about the fox and the hedgehog? The fox sees many things and it leaps from place to place; the hedgehog stays close to one place but observes in detail …'

She was silent for a while, then said, 'And you are the hedgehog and Nurul the fox?'

'Doesn't that make sense? He has many brilliant ideas, but I like to prove one thing at a time, completely, and only then move on. I am more a mathematician. We worked well together.'

'Worked?'

'Well ... yes ... different paths now, you know.'

That was when he told her he was moving with his family to America. She was shocked beyond words, put her hand to her chest, then her mouth. He hadn't told Nurul yet, or anyone else in his department.

Why was he going away? she asked. Why leave everything behind—friends, London, steak-and-kidney pie ... ? Why such a drastic step? 'Why leave *us*? Who will come to rescue me, who will be my genie?'

That hit him, and he paused before he said, 'I'm sorry. I feel I should. And Una concurs. I have an offer to spend a year in America. After that, we'll decide. I thought I would go to East Africa eventually. There are positions opening there, and our government pays the salary. I could be more useful over there ... teaching boys and girls who are less privileged ... the hidden wonders of our universe.' He grinned sheepishly. 'Isn't that what Nurul wants to do too?'

'But not by going away.' She was almost in tears.

'Yes. He can't hide. He's like the sun ...'

'And all the brilliant work you two have done together? All the Islam-Mason work for so many years? Different paths now?'

What did she know of that work? Nothing, except how exciting it had been for them. In the throes of some new idea, they couldn't stop talking about it.

'I'm afraid I'm not cut out for it any longer. It's too much competition and seeking after glory and prizes. I thought I was like that at one time. Now I know I'm not. At the end of the day, what does it matter who did it first? As Nurul says sometimes, we all contribute.'

She said nothing.

'Remember the hedgehog?' He smiled.

'Like a hedgehog you hide into yourself for protection.'

He didn't reply.

There was more to this hedgehog-fox business. He promised to stay in touch, but past the first few notes to Nurul, with best regards to her, he stopped; Nurul tried hard to convince him to return, but to no avail. Something was broken. It had pained her. And Nurul too. Now finally he had taken his own life. He had spent time with her over several months, speaking his mind, revealing himself. What did he see in her? She had fantasized sometimes ... in an *alternative*—she spoke it carefully—*world* ... Only once did she tell her husband about these outings with David Mason.

As she prepared to go upstairs, she saw through the kitchen that Nurul was slumped in his chair, fallen asleep. A Quran recital was playing on the tape recording, the rich, mournful disembodied voice of God in the night that she recognized as Surah an-Nisa, The Women.

She went and touched his shoulder, waking him with a start, and together they went to bed.

As he was about to leave through the front door the next morning, holding Muni's hand, the phone rang. 'It's for you,' Sakina announced, and he went inside to his study to answer it on the extension. 'One minute, Muni, don't go anywhere.'

'Hello, Dr Islam, this is Major Iftikhar,' the voice at the other end said on the phone. 'I wonder if you remember me?'

'Major—I'm afraid not, sir, enlighten me. I was about to leave the house just now.'

'We met in Boston at the airport—'

'Yes, yes. Of course, I recall now. What ...'

There had been something underhanded about the military man with the rich, chocolatey voice and polite manners, Nurul recalled. He had been generous enough to bring him a cup of coffee at Boston airport, but he had left him a little uneasy.

'I would like to come and see you, Professor Islam,' Major Iftikhar said, and continued after a significant pause, '... on a government matter. It's important, it's about your visit to Pakistan some eight weeks ago.'

They agreed that Major Iftikhar would come that evening after dinner and share tea with the Islams.

It was precisely seven when the major arrived at the door, wearing a black wool blazer, and walked in with a cane. He gave a quick look around and greeted Sakina in the traditional manner, saying, 'Adab, Begum,' and Nurul with a firm handshake, a press of the arm, and a warm 'Nice to see you again, Professor.' He sat down in the living room, and when the boys, who were in the kitchen, were called to meet him, he exclaimed brightly, 'Ah, the boys, how are you, young men? I am Major Iftikhar.' The boys, impressed and delighted, responded to him and left. The three adults had tea, after which Sakina disappeared and Nurul and the major were left to talk in private.

'Bad business, about your people,' Major Iftikhar said, referring to a recent attack on a Shirazi mosque in Karachi. 'I am sorry.'

'Yes, Muslims against Muslims, you wonder what Partition was about,' responded Nurul. There was not much more to say, and he had said this often enough.

'Indeed.'

'This is what I would have liked to ask Mr Jinnah, Was Partition worth it? Couldn't he have foreseen this kind of outcome?'

'But unfortunately, Mr Jinnah is dead,' the major promptly replied with a twinkle in the eyes.

'Yes. Well, Major—you had something to say to me.'

'Only this, Professor—and this is not to be divulged, I beg you—after lengthy consultations, it has been decided not to go ahead with the weapons program—the bomb …' His voice had dropped significantly, and he continued in the same manner, 'That's what Mr Teymuri himself has asked me to convey to you.'

'Really?' Nurul couldn't help looking towards the doorway, which was empty. Sakina could be heard in the kitchen. The boys were back upstairs, where Muni was protesting about something. 'Mr Teymuri was extremely keen about it, Project Babur and so on. "We'll eat grass" and all that—he was passionate—what changed his mind?'

'Project Babur is on hold. Some research will be done at PINSTECH, that's about it. The costs alone would kill us. So atoms for peace it will be, and your leadership on the atomic energy commission remains vital. Mr Teymuri is concerned however that you do not speak about what transpired in Quetta. Anything you say on the subject would only create unwanted publicity and a diplomatic crisis. The fact that it was considered at all would be enough to bring repercussions. Even a war.'

'Our neighbours, are they going ahead with their project?'

'It has been suggested that South Asia be made a nuclear-free zone. The option is being discussed by our two countries.'

'You can assure Mr Teymuri then that I will not speak about the matter. And I am delighted by his decision. It is wise and prudent. We have more urgent priorities to attend to in our nation.'

'Agreed.'

Sakina peeped in to offer more tea, and stayed with them, their official business over. It seemed to Nurul that the major was not such a bad sort after all, and he was flattered that the president had sent a special emissary to speak with him … not that he was a nobody himself. It would be a good idea, he thought, to float his scheme for an institute of fundamental research in Pakistan that would provide a research haven for scientists from the developing world. That might bring India and Pakistan together. India, after all, was big on non-alignment, staying neutral between the East and the West. David's death had somehow made this idea seem more urgent. He and David had spoken about it.

'I must go,' said the major, standing up. 'But first—' He brought out from his briefcase a package, which he unwrapped to reveal a book. 'Compliments of Mr Teymuri.'

It was a collection of poems by Faiz Ahmed Faiz, handsomely bound in green leather and embossed in red and gold, and signed by both the poet and Beyram Teymuri.

'Wah,' Nurul exclaimed, utterly moved. 'You have made my day, Major.' He ran his hand over the texture of the cover, dipped inside the pages. 'Thank you, and thank the president, please.'

'With pleasure,' replied Major Iftikhar warmly. 'You are our shining star, Professor Islam.' He now turned to Sakina. 'And for Begum …' He put his hand in his briefcase and brought out a case sheathed in deep purple. He opened it: a stunning silver set consisting of a necklace and earrings with rubies.

A taxi was called, and Major Iftikhar departed. As he left, he put in Nurul's hand a brochure. 'Have a look at this,' he said.

'The president himself sent us these gifts?' Sakina asked, her eyes glowing.

'He's only a politician,' Nurul said nonchalantly.

'Well, I could see how impressed you were by your present!'

'It was Faiz,' he replied mischievously. 'That's what impressed me. A book signed by Faiz himself.'

He was flattered, of course, and the gold emboss on the green cover was beautiful. He glanced at the brochure given him by the major. It was for an engineering company, something called Universal Technologies. He set it aside. He wondered if he should have sent a message to Mr Teymuri, a request that outbreaks of religious violence against the Shirazis and other sects be controlled more forcefully by the government. The major's visit had been too quick, and the message, not to say the gifts, had disarmed him. He had to keep his wits about him the next time.

*Like all Urdu speakers he was passionate about poetry. As the editor-in-chief of his college magazine,* Gulistaan, *and editor of its English partner, Lotus, he had allowed himself to publish a few of his own pieces, some poems, observations on college life, including a report of a chess tournament, and two stories. The subject of the stories he would later find embarrassingly romantic, and the language Victorian, with characters saying such things as 'Alack!' But there was a dark truth to them too. In one story a boy and girl who lived across the street from each other fell in love. The only problem, besides the fact that such free love was forbidden, was that he was a Muslim and she a Sikh. When the romance was discovered, she became a virtual prisoner, rarely allowed to leave her home, and that only with her mother and a brother beside her. She was not allowed the corrupting influence of storybooks, and found in her hands only the Sunday newspaper's puzzles page. And so the two connived to communicate with each other through composing and sending to the paper clever chess problems. He was the black king and she the white queen; each illustration of a problem's starting position—the queen behind a phalanx of pawns or guarded by a rook and a knight, the woefully helpless king positioned at a side—conveyed a tender or a desperate love message. The final message, after several months of pining, was from her: the white queen beside its king, bishops on either side, pawns in front, and the black king in checkmate position. The girl was married off. In his other story, a young Pakistani scientist and avowed atheist visits the shrine of Baba Ganjshakar in Lahore and there has a vision in which he is 'shewn' the existence of God. He goes home inspired, and writes down an equation—for which he wins the Nobel Prize.*

*The author of course did not produce an equation in his story, but he had an idea of what sort it would be. At the time Paul Dirac's γ-matrices were coming out of his ears, as he put it. The equation would therefore be, in his mind, a beautifully simple relationship, a brilliant epiphany subsuming everything, and evoked by a Sufi's ecstatic song or in the poet Amir Khusrau's cry,* man kunto maula ... *of whomever I am Lord.*

*But it got him into trouble, this mystical formula of his story. He got called up into the principal's office, where next to Dr Omar sat a mullah, Mowlana Qayum, with a rich salt-and-pepper beard and wearing a green turban.*

*'Nurul Islam, this story you published in Lotus—"The Formula"—is quite inappropriate,' said Dr Omar, leaning with his elbow on his table, an open copy of the magazine in front of him.*

*'Quite inappropriate,' echoed Mowlana Qayum, scratching his beard.*

*'But sir—Mowlana—I don't understand. Is it the language ...'*

*'My son,' said Mowlana Qayum, 'don't pretend. You know what is the problem.'*

*'No, ji,' Nurul replied. 'I don't know. It is a simple story ...'*

*'It is blasphemy, my child. Painting pictures of Allah is blasphemy, even if it is through phaarmulas.'*

*Nurul could have argued that he had not actually written the formula, merely suggested its possibility. And wasn't every formula, everything in the universe for that matter, part of the picture of Allah? Fortunately for him he did not tread those waters. He capitulated.*

*'You are right, ji. I did not realize that. Forgive me.'*

*'He's a good boy,' Dr Omar said approvingly, the problem resolved. 'Our best.'*

*'I know that,' said the mowlana. 'That is why it is important that he not deviate. Bless you, child. Now go.'*

*Nurul left, he would recall, red-faced, his heart thumping violently in his chest. Something as simple as his story, a fantastic tale if anything, scribbled off quickly, had been misinterpreted as … blasphemy! He was only reprimanded, nothing more, he was the pride of the college. 'Our best.' But if he were someone else and not 'our best'?*

*He stopped writing stories, they were too risky. He wrote Urdu poems instead. Every young man was a poet, anyone in a sentimental mood penned away a sad lyric. On Saturday afternoons the boys would gather under a tree in the college grounds, and anyone who wanted to would come forward and recite his poetry. It was a free-for-all and not to be taken too seriously; the poet would repeat every flourish, often with a wave of the arms, and the audience would echo it with relish, then immediately exclaim its praises, 'Wah!' 'What cruel lines you've wrought! What arrows you've shot!' 'What's Ghalib, in comparison, what's Faiz?' 'Yaar, what's Shakespeare?'*

*Harmless, really.*

In the Chases' living room in Salem, Massachusetts was an oil painting of the HMS *Yardley*, which had brought John Chase, a doctor, to America at Boston Harbor in 1766. It was a history the current Dr John Chase was rather proud of, in his mild way, though his wife, Harriet, had always claimed that her Quaker ancestors were in Maryland well before; unlike him, she couldn't provide details of that history. One or the other of the Chase sons had always been a doctor; but now John Chase, a widower, had no son but two daughters, neither of them studying the profession, to their father's—mild—disappointment. Harriet had died of cancer four years before. He would not forget that day, the hour. It was July, midafternoon and sunny outside. Inside their house, his wife lay in the family room; she called their two daughters to her, separately, and in a barely audible voice spoke to each. Then they all gathered and, with John sitting beside her and holding both her hands, the three of them witnessed Harriet breathe her last. Five months later, their younger daughter, Jill, a sophomore at university, left home. On the morning of the day after Christmas he and Hilary had come down to the kitchen to find a note on the table: 'I am dropping out.' What that implied exactly, John Chase didn't know. He knew that 'dropping out' among the young was a new phenomenon, it was their protest against what they called the establishment and the middle-class American way of life. He had had arguments with Jill about America fighting the war in Vietnam, but what was so special about a father and child disagreeing about politics? He was a patriotic man and although he had served in WWII, he was a pacifist, as both his daughters knew. But he was unwilling to lay the blame for the war only on one—the American—side. He did not impose his views on his daughters. Now for some undeclared reason Jill had left home, and

Hilary took on the task of keeping in touch with her younger sister. From her, John Chase learned that Jill had lived in a commune in Providence, travelled by road with a boyfriend to California, and—this, with much pain—she'd had an abortion.

But Jill had come home this past November, stayed until Christmas Day, and made it a point to look after her father, giving no clue as to what had caused this sudden upsurge of filial attention nor revealing anything about her recent life. When Hilary arrived on the eve, looking the happiest anyone had ever seen her recently, Jill announced, 'She's in love.' Hilary blushed, and Jill said, 'I guess I have no right to ask you who your guy is.'

'That's right,' Hilary said.

On Christmas morning they were sitting with their coffees in the living room before the tree, which Jill had decorated extravagantly in a somewhat hippie-ish style. Making small talk about the weather forecast and so on, they were waiting for Jill to depart. She wore a denim skirt and a red shirt, with a yellow bandanna round her head, and her backpack, plastered with peace and Om symbols, was ready and waiting for her at the door. A car beeped outside, and putting on her oversize army-navy jacket, she left with quick goodbye embraces. She did not meet her father's eyes.

Hilary and her father stood watching through the leaded windows as the battered red Chrysler drove away, then took to their chairs and sat silent for some moments. John had already started the fire earlier, and outside it was snowing. Hilary looked at her father and it made her sad. Alone in the house and two daughters to worry about, one of them at an undisclosed address. He had many friends, but no one very close, except his accountant, who had died recently. A local church group made it a point to check up on him. Hilary went and put on some Bach and returned.

'You have something to ask, Dad?'

'I'm happy to see you … so happy, is what I would like to say.'

'Thanks, Dad.'

'Well, I'm not going to presume to give you advice, my generation being out of touch and—'

'Go on, Dad. What d'you want to say?'

'Just this—not advice but a declaration—I'm always here for you. I won't judge you or anything. Just don't run away from me.'

'Oh, Dad …' She went over and hugged him.

When Hilary told him she was specializing in theoretical physics at college, he did not give it much thought. Theoretical physics was good because he could not imagine her surrounded by instrumentation in a lab or at one of those giant accelerators he had read about in *Physics Today*, a magazine which she regularly forwarded to him. But when she told him she was going on in her field to do her Ph.D. with a professor called Abe Rosenfeld as her advisor, he started to be concerned. First, was she good enough for all that abstraction, or would she end up humiliating herself? What kind of career would this concentration give her, a woman? She had already told him that jobs were becoming scarce in the field. The boom that followed the space race against the Soviets was over. Wouldn't she be better off as a doctor in Salem, where he could set her up as a partner first, and then she could be on her own, and the pressures would not be too great?

One afternoon he had called up Professor Rosenfeld, and having sworn him to secrecy, expressed his concerns. Abe Rosenfeld assured him that Hilary was one of his brighter students; she should not have too much of a problem finding a job, if she was willing to relocate; he would help her. Moreover being a woman would be an advantage, because there were so few women in the field. Even the federal government had a need for female scientists in administration—but that would be a last resort. John Chase was comforted. He felt proud.

When Hilary called and asked to borrow money to go attend a conference in Rome, her father said, Of course. And why speak of borrowing, she was simply taking from her inheritance. But why Rome, why that far—was it important? Yes, she said, it's important. He sent her a check. And then he called her supervisor, Abe Rosenfeld, to thank him for keeping an eye on his daughter, and to ask him about the conference. Abe Rosenfeld told John Chase that the Rome conference was not his idea; professionally it would not be very useful. But Hilary was keen to go, and getting away to Europe for a few days would do her good. She seemed distracted lately, but nothing to worry about.

To which John Chase replied, 'I understand there's a young man in her life now. That's gratifying to know. She must be going with him to Rome.'

He expected a paternalistic rejoinder. What he heard turned him cold.

'I wouldn't say he's young, John. But she seems very keen on him.'

'What—do you know him? Is he also a scientist? Who is he?'

'Yes, he's a scientist, but you will have to ask your daughter about him. Let me assure you, he's a gentleman, your daughter will come to no harm—besides what love does to young people … She could make a worse decision in these times. And John …'

'Yes, Abe?'

'You've not heard any of this from me.'

John Chase convinced himself not to worry. Hilary was twenty-seven; she was a budding physicist, working under an eminent man in the field. He was proud of his daughter. She had always been a serious student … which made her a little naive, he'd always thought. Someone who had her inquisitive eyes on the night sky should also take time to look at the ground in front of her. Jill was a different matter. He worried about his younger daughter but not in the same way. When Jill took a ride with a strange man, she knew what she was doing. But Hilary? John did not know her as well, though it was she who spent more time with him.

She called him from the airport to tell him to look after himself, which gave him the opportunity to tell her to do the same for herself.

'Call me from there,' he said.

'I'll try, Dad. And don't worry.'

'You're the first one in the family to visit Europe, you know. My war experience doesn't count.'

'Are you sure, Dad?' she said, with the slightest hint of teasing.

He would sometimes talk about his stint in France and Germany, but the weeks or months he'd spent in England seemed to be a closed subject, the merest mention of which would turn her mother pensive and irritable. This was a subject Hilary and Jill had spoken about in private. There seemed to have been a woman he'd left behind.

'Bye, Hilary. Watch out for those Italian men now.'

'Bye, Dad. I will.'

She went and sat down to wait for her flight. The thought of Rome was exciting; this was an adventure into a dream or fantasy. Movieland. The Italian men; she smiled. Like who, Marcello Mastroianni? But to actually stand on the steps where Caesar was assassinated, at the site where the legions marched, the grounds where the gladiators fought … Would there be time to see everything? Was she keen to see the Vatican? Not too much. Tours had been promised to the conference participants, she should be sure to take them. But she would be with Nurul—or would she? Wouldn't he be busy meeting with colleagues, senior members of their order for whom she did not yet exist? This journey was just so she could be with him, he'd better have time for her. This meeting was for commitment. A life decision. What would it be like to see him again? Hear his voice again? See the smile and the dimple on his cheeks as he narrated a story? She recalled that night at the Yard when they embraced. An impulse, a simple infatuation? She recalled Janis's warning. Janis could be right, and she could be making the biggest mistake of her life. She could get hurt, and hurt two other people in the process. Why not let things be, why get into this complication? Suppose she went back, right now, forgot about Rome, forgot about Nurul Islam—when you gave a thought to it, what a foreign name!—suppose she took the Red Line back and into her simple life of a physicist … write an earth-shaking thesis on her topic and find a job at a prestigious university. Wasn't that easy and sensible, the wise thing to do?

A life without any risk, is that a life lived?

After high school she had taken the safe route, unlike some of her classmates, not to say the many more from her generation, who had *engaged*, as they liked to say, gone away to protest against the established order and change the world. Now, was this escapade to meet a man her own way to be different, take a risk? A Muslim, an older man, a foreigner with a moustache? She audibly stifled a laugh at the thought. How cynical. Instinctively she reached down into her bag for reassurance: what should she read—her guide to Rome? her guide to Islam (the religion, not the man, him she had to discover for herself)? or Schrödinger's lecture on the origins of life?

She knew so little about the religion, it frightened her; what she had read seemed to her so counterintuitive. Did he actually pray five times a day, facing east? Did he fast for a month every year, and did his mother and the womenfolk in his family go about draped in black veils? Did they stone people to death … for adultery? Shudder. Did his ancestors go around in hordes carrying swords, by which they converted the people they conquered to Islam? How could he come from such a background and be that brilliant and suave man she had met? That kind and considerate man?

Abe had not raised a fuss about her going to the Rome conference. 'What the heck,' he said, standing by the board in his office, having written down some expressions on it, 'there's no harm, go and have a good time in Rome.'

'Thanks, Abe.'

He did give her the long eye, though.

She had had to find someone to take over her two lab classes, and postpone her monthly report to Abe's group about her progress. She had been lax and distracted the past few weeks.

'When you return, you could give us a report on the proceedings,' he said, then added softly, 'Maybe the department can pay for a portion of the trip.'

'Thanks, Abe.'

'Don't have too much fun now,' he said with a smile as she left.

She nodded.

*When Nurul Islam was nine his father took him to the funeral of a relative. It was a young woman, Zakia, who had been found with her throat slit at the town outskirts, near the ruins. At the funeral, the dead woman lay on a bier on the ground, her body draped in a white shroud. Her long face was pale as marble, a strip of her brown hair was visible at the forehead. She was apparently a sinner, but her murder was a crime and a few policemen, including a British commander, were present at the edge of the crowd. Nurul was asked to say the prayer, and in his white kurta-pajama and his cap, holding his hands before him he had said the Fateha, the opening verse of the Quran. He tried to look away from the body but his sight would shift back unwittingly. Several times he faltered in his recitation, which was the simplest possible, and his father came to his rescue. Finally, the body was taken to be buried, his father walking along with other relatives to accompany the bier, and Nurul had followed behind. All the women waited in the compound, weeping.*

*The young woman had committed sin with a man; this he heard from overhearing his parents. The man was a local official and married. A week after the funeral the girl's father and two brothers were arrested for her murder. It took a year before they were released by the court.*

*Nurul always wondered why his father had taken him to that funeral; he had been to others, including that of his grandmother, who lived with his uncle. But this one had been special, attended by a large number, and he had been asked to recite the Fateha. One day when he was older, he had asked his father,*

*'Abba, that funeral of the young woman, Zakia—do you remember—I always wondered why you took me there and why you had me recite the Fateha.'*

*His father paused, recollecting, before he replied, 'It was an important event. A disturbing one. I don't recall exactly, but it must have been so that you would witness it, Nurul. And you do remember it, after all.'*

*Nurul did not say more, but his father had guessed that it bothered him still. It was a horrific event, a seduction of a young woman followed by her murder. And people said she should have known better, she had waylaid the man, girls are older than their years and the source of sin; and it's been this way since ages. An example has to be set. Honour has to be preserved.*

*He had been at her funeral and remembered it, the pale, long, tender face with the ring of brown hair; all the watching congregation. His grandmother's funeral on the other hand was only a vague memory.*

Humming softly to himself, Nurul Islam entered his office with a cup of tea in one hand and a biscuit in the other. A cheerful beginning to the day, a Saturday, and absolute stillness in the house and outside on the street at that early hour. He sat down, glanced at the work pad before him, looked away, let that brief sight awaken his brain to where he had left off the previous day. Perhaps this is my final entry into the fray, he mused. Greater Unification. But with that feeling of satisfaction came a certain qualm, like a bitter almond edge to an exceptional pudding. He had seen it on the horizon. Dozens of physicists were working away developing the concept; brilliant young minds, groomed at the best universities, trained in the most abstract mathematics, poised at the blocks ready to dash off into glory and leave the older guys panting behind. He could sense being passed. Did he have the energy to keep up? He had to retire sooner or later. Abe Rosenfeld had sat back a little, mentoring proteges and sitting on committees. What would he, Nurul Islam, do if he retired from active research? Encourage younger physicists, that's what, especially those from the so-called third world. Be less impatient. Write a book on the Muslim scientists of the past, their vital contributions. Then there was his dream of a global physics institute. Perhaps it would be housed in both India and Pakistan. Forget the bomb. Open that pernicious border, for this cause, at least.

It was four in the morning and he should be working, preparing the lecture for Rome. Back home in Pirmai the azan would be called at this hour, *La ilaha illallah, Allahu Akbar! Come and pray …* Now and again his father would be asked to render this early-morning reminder to the faithful. Sleeping on his mat, his brothers and sisters in a row next to him, Nurul would listen to his abba washing, getting dressed, then silently making his way to the mosque, the soft flapping of his slippers receding and fading into silence. At the mosque he would wash again, his feet and hands and face; he would gargle. Then he would go to his post, stand before the loudspeaker, put a hand above his ear, and recite. It was quiet and chilly, and into this silence went the cry from his father's throat, a single line of sound rising to the stars, affirming a Muslim's truth: There is only one God, and he is Allah and he is Great. Nurul would be listening.

In his office, he brought out his small rug, spread it out on the floor, put on his skullcap and quickly said his prayer. There. He had not forgotten. He sat down at his desk again. From upstairs came the sound of snoring, a familiar rhythm and timbre, a music as familiar to him as her voice. It turned on when she'd tired herself out during the day.

The idea of Greater Unification was to simplify the plethora of particles which had been discovered in the last couple of decades. There seemed no end to them, there must be a way to put them all in one theoretical bag. The problem was that there were two kinds of particles in the universe, the fermions, none of which liked to stay in the same place as any other of them, and the bosons, which did not mind sitting on top of each other. You might think of the first group as the aloof northern Europeans and the second as the Asians. They had all emerged from Africa and then migrated and diverged into their different varieties of human. How did we emerge from Africa into this plethora of races? What was needed now was a single description for all particles, to say that they are essentially the same—they all came from Africa, so to speak. Race as symmetry-breaking. And the Higgs bosons, the missiles that went flying as the races and nations started diverging.

When he had given this analogy to a conference in Berkeley the previous year, it was received with a lot of humorous appreciation, but there were some who were offended. He had to ask one physicist, 'Jim, do you object to being descended from an African?' That was unfair, who wants to be called a racist? The problem was also that his analogy conflicted with the Creation story of the Bible and the Quran. And there were scientists who, if they did not take the Creation story literally, did not take it lightly either.

And he, Nurul Islam? He had learned to keep the two apart. Moreover, as far as his faith was concerned, the stories of the scriptures did not interest him—let others do the interpreting and worrying. He was interested in God, the Prophet, the Book, and his duties.

He wrote down his lecture points for the Rome conference, for which he would depart the next morning, anticipated some questions and answered them on the paper. Finally he stopped.

He heard Sakina waking up. How delighted she had been with that present from Teymuri. Now she might think that marrying her cousin Nurul Islam had not been such a bad thing after all! But he had started wondering about Major Iftikhar's visit. All that talk of atomic energy for peace and a nuclear-free South Asia, could it be true? Or was it just a smokescreen? Why would the major come to see him at home merely to tell him that? And the presents, were they a bribe? For what?—so he wouldn't speak out against Project Babur? He wouldn't, not for now. Did they think they could use him like that, the naive scientist? That Beyram Teymuri was a wily fellow, Nurul had seen that. He must think of me as a brilliant fool, easily seduced by flattery and gifts. Should he return the presents? The beautiful Faiz?—like hell, as the Americans said. And Sakina would guard that ruby set with her life. She had daughters-in-law to think of. A daughter to marry. Muni. Some young man would come and take her away.

It had rained at night, but looking out his door through the window in front he saw it was clear now and getting brighter. The yellow of the first daffodils in the distance. Rome should be nice and warm, if it didn't drizzle. He heard Sakina coming down the stairs and called out to her. She replied on her way to the kitchen. He felt a pang of guilt. Cancel this trip, don't go. Say you're sick. But I have to do it, she will be waiting.

Hearing Nurul humming a ghazal as he came down the stairs, Sakina Begum noted to herself not for the first time that though he was devoted to his home and family, his mood always took a lift on the eve of a trip. She briefly wondered how necessary this one was, but then they all were, that was his nature. He would not be left out. If only he had been more ordinary. But she did enjoy his celebrity, and what more proof of that than a gorgeous gift from the president of Pakistan? Mr Teymuri was from a princely family, the set was from his private collection, she was certain. She had spent a long time looking at it; it turned her breathless. What had she done to deserve it? Become the wife of Pakistan's celebrated scientist. She would have to store it in a bank vault, it would come in handy when the children got married. How would she divide it? Perhaps Muni should get it all, then it would for certain remain in the family. Something to discuss with her husband.

She got out of bed at six and said her prayer. After which she came down, picked up the newspaper and milk from the door, and—having answered 'Yes, I'm up!' to her husband—she made two cups of tea, delivered one to him, and sat down in the living room. How the week had flown; another one awaited with its demands. Her preoccupations around the house filled her hours as much as Nurul's calculations and his lectures did his. An upcoming visit by Mirza's class to some museum for which a permission had to be signed; Rahim's disappointing school cricket match last weekend with his new bat; Muni's visit to the dentist would have to be postponed because Nurul would be away—and what to cook for the kids in his absence? She'd had a long chat with a wistful Mr Shah at the grocery store about his life in Kenya, after which she had come away with a gift of two old but good mangoes that she would use to make lassi. Her niece Salima's wedding had gone brilliantly well, Nurul had given a thoughtful speech, and they had given the couple the expensive set of kitchen knives they had bought together as a present. Having fleetingly gone over everything she could recall, finally she converged upon what occupied the centre of her mind: David Mason's death and a recent phone call she had received, which had left her bothered.

Why was that lorry rumbling outside, and this being early Saturday morning? She went to the kitchen to prepare breakfast. Parantha today.

'Is that Susan?' Sakina Begum asked hesitantly. 'This is Mrs Islam—your Auntie Sakina.'

'Yes, this is Susan, thank you for ringing. Have you decided, Mrs Islam—can you give me my father's things?'

'Yes, I've thought about it, and I can give you your father's things—but I will keep some for my own remembrance. Where can I meet you? Perhaps for lunch? … There's a place called Oliva near the National Gallery …'

What place more appropriate than where she herself had gone with the girl's father.

'Thank you. That would be most convenient, Mrs Islam. Is tomorrow all right?'

The other day Susan, David's daughter, had called and said that she understood her father had left some stuff of his for safekeeping with Mrs Islam before leaving England with his family. Would Mrs Islam be comfortable relinquishing them? Yes, she was back in England, studying in Leeds. They would mean a lot to her and her mother. Sakina, totally taken aback, told her yes, she had a box from David, she would look at the contents and then let Susan know.

A few days before the Masons left, David had come to the door bearing, along with a bunch of flowers—the first time—a banker's box. He gave her the flowers, and when she went and placed the bunch on the dining table and turned around, he said, 'And this.' He put the box beside the flowers. 'I brought it for you,' he said, 'it has some memorabilia and personal items of value only to me. I hope you don't mind keeping it for me.'

'I will guard it safely. Any secrets?'

'No. Just some notes and memories. Some letters … photos … a pipe I don't use anymore … my first fountain pen …'

They laughed. It was understood that this was between the two of them.

They had tea at the dining table. Staring at that tall figure sitting up, the dome forehead, the long face and shy smile, she had felt sad. Over the months she had developed a treasured closeness to him. Whenever Nurul went away, David would come to take her out. She could recall six instances. Once, Mr Shah of the corner store, getting curious, came to stand at his door to have a long look as they waited at the bus stop. She didn't feel inhibited. There was nothing to feel guilty about; still, Nurul didn't know.

They would window-shop on Oxford Street, which she loved, and have lunch and they would talk. Once they stopped for a concert at a church near the National Gallery.

One day she asked him why he and Una were not to be seen anymore. Did he and Nurul quarrel? He had looked away before replying, 'A small misunderstanding.'

'Nurul is a good man,' she said.

'Of course he is. A downright decent man all the years I've known him.'

'You're a good person too, David. So why the misunderstanding? I'm sure you two will make up.'

'Yes,' he said. 'I would like that.' Then, with a smile, 'Your husband is a very complex person too, you know.' And apologized. 'I'm sorry. How can I say that to you.'

Now he was going away and had brought her this box.

She said to him, controlling her voice. 'Thank you for trusting me. I'll keep it for you, and you can have it back when you return.'

He smiled. 'All right. Whenever that is. I don't really need it. If I don't ask for it in, say, three years, keep what you want, you can throw the rest of the contents away. Sometimes you have to shed your past.'

She stared at him.

'Really? I'm not going to throw away anything of yours, David. This is a part of your life. I'll treasure it.'

'Thank you,' he said gruffly.

To say goodbye then, as they stood at the door, he leaned over and kissed her lightly on the cheek. Not the middle of the cheek but closer to the lips. And she thought she had kissed him too, at least in her mind. She put her finger on the spot now. There.

Since David had not told Nurul about the box, she did not either, keeping it in a bottom corner in her side of the closet, where it had lain innocuously in the dark under a shoebox. Her guilty secret, easily explainable. If Nurul saw it, he didn't ask about it. She had perused its contents after he left, and thereafter left it alone. Now she brought it out, put it on the floor next to the bed, sat down in front of it, and opened it. She took a deep breath, fought off the rush of grief. The box was about a third full. There were a couple of photographs of David as a boy—a skinny lad; in one he was standing in a garden with a spade, in the other he was stooped over a chessboard, the parting in his hair drawn like a line. In another photo, he was older and stood beside Una, when they were both in university, apparently; there was a photo with Nurul from about the same time, Nurul's trousers too flappy for him, she smiled; probably tailored by Abdul Mian in Pirmai, Pakistan. And there she was, in another one, standing between Nurul and David, and there with Nurul on the floor of their flat soon after she joined him. How dowdy she looked! There was a photo of David with an older woman, presumably his mother. Why hadn't he wanted these photos? Were they duplicates? And why would she want to throw them away? And then some letters. One of admission to Cambridge, another from America; a few from Una. There was the pipe, and the fountain pen, and a daily diary. And at the bottom of the box a thick folder containing some of his research notes, the papers now curled up at the corners, mathematical symbols and comments crawling all over them, handwritten in pencil, sometimes overwritten in red or blue ink. There was a draft copy of a letter to Nurul, and a reply. And then the friendship turned cold. If only …

Sakina decided to give Susan some of the family photos and the letters from Una, and keep for herself the remaining photos and letters as mementos of David. She would keep the pipe, pen, and diary, and hold on to his folder of research notes. They were incomprehensible to her, but still there was a personal touch in them, an intimacy.

She walked into Oliva, where she had made a reservation, with a large envelope containing the letters and photos and looked around. A waitress, or hostess, quickly intercepted her, asking, 'Can I help you?' and Sakina gave her a look she had by now practised. After all these years, you were still treated as an alien. A pretty girl looking tanned waved at her from a table near the middle of the room, and Sakina went to join her.

'Susan?'

'Yes! It's great to see you again, Mrs Islam—'

'Auntie Sakina, please.'

'Sorry. We spoke so often of you and your husband, auntie—we really missed you!'

'I didn't even recognize you! You're a young woman now! We missed you too,' Sakina said. 'It was a sad day for us when you left … but how is Africa? Do you like being there?'

'Kenya, yes. Sometimes it gets lonely in Nairobi, to tell the truth. But it's a beautiful country. But I'm now here, as I told you. At the University of Leeds.'

'That's nice!'

They ordered lunch. Poor girl, thought Sakina, taken to a foreign country without a brother or sister, and with a serious, diffident scientist for a father. Now she's uprooted again. The father dead. Suicide. She wanted to ask about David, imagine him as he would have been recently—was he well, wasn't he happy—but she couldn't. And David had never written. The girl was staring at her. A tall, athletic young woman, a striking round pendant made of tiny red, yellow, and black beads at her neck, the brown hair done up in many thin braids. She was not wearing a bra. The rebellious fashions of the young. Sakina remembered the day she was born, in Cambridge. And she remembered pushing her in a pram, ahead of the child's parents, wishing she had a child of her own. Nurul was Susan's godfather, but she hadn't asked to see him.

'How is your mother? How is she taking … it?'

'She is coping. The school keeps her busy. She is devoted to it.'

'You must have made friends there.'

'Yes, mainly English, a few Africans, some Americans and Canadians.'

Sakina handed over the envelope. 'There are some mementos from your family here—photos and letters. I'm sure they will mean a lot to you. I have kept some photos and a few letters—they were from my husband.'

'Oh, thank you!' The girl stood up tearfully and embraced Sakina, then sat down and fingered the stuff delicately, making a small pile on the white tablecloth and earning curious stares.

'Dad said … there was a file of his research notes in the box …?'

'Yes. I would like to keep it.'

'Oh why?' The cry came out more sharply than perhaps intended, and Susan fell silent, before continuing, 'They would mean so much to me, Mrs Islam, I would love to have some of his notes with me. They're a … a picture of how he thought …'

This was strange. Surely the old photos, the letters in his handwriting, these personal items should mean more? What could the girl tell from sheets of equations with weird symbols? Was Susan herself, like her father, studying mathematics, she asked. How marvellous, if that were so. Susan said no, she wasn't. She was studying Commonwealth literature.

'But anyway, he must have left bundles of research notes at your home there,' Sakina said. 'Since this work was done when he and Nurul worked together, I thought my husband would prefer to keep them as his own mementos. And you know … ,' she added, 'your dad gave all this to me to keep—not as safekeeping only. He wanted me to have them, but I thought the personal items would mean a lot to you.'

The girl nodded. 'They do, thank you. You're right, Mrs Islam … But why would he leave them with you?'

Sakina said nothing. Then she told the girl, 'Why don't you come home for tea one day? Don't you want to see Uncle Nurul?'

'Of course I do, I'll let you know when I'm free,' Susan replied. 'How is Dr Islam?'

As Sakina went home, she found the encounter with Susan even more unsettling. Why would David alert his daughter to the box? He had given it to Sakina, after all, had he forgotten that? Or had second thoughts? But Susan never said David had instructed her to ask for the box or its contents. Why were those notes there, for that matter, what did they contain—some secret research? Had he worked on the atom bomb? Couldn't be. She had heard him and Nurul discuss the subject once at the dinner table, and they were both vehemently opposed to that kind of research.

It was stranger still that Susan had shown no enthusiasm to meet Nurul. The uncle who had played chess with her, who was her godfather. She had called him Dr Islam this time; and Sakina had become Mrs Islam. Not uncle and auntie, as they were before.

When he arrived home that evening, Sakina decided to be at least partly honest and told Nurul she had met Susan that afternoon.

'Really? You met her? How is she? We must invite her home!'

'We will, when you return from Rome,' she told him with a smile.

On the eve of his departure she made biriyani and sweet vermicelli for dinner, and ordered samosas from a Punjabi restaurant. It was Sakina's formal goodbye to him until he came back, a gesture she had always made. Muni ate while sitting on his lap; the boys carried on a heated discussion about cricket. Afterwards, when the kids had received attention in their rooms, she asked him not to go to his study, to stay with her in the sitting room in front of the television. It was a good moment to reminisce about their life together, all the adventures, the ups and downs, their early years; the families back home. But surely this is home now, this house, the kids, your job. A good moment to cuddle up close together, in a show of love. No, he need not be different; he was her Nurul Islam, the kind and considerate genius.

When she was still new and feeling homesick in London, she'd returned to Pakistan to see her folks whenever she could. She would stay two months, and he would write to her regularly in a poetic Urdu; only once had he written in English, to tease her. In the letters he was affectionate, tender, giving her all the news that had happened in her absence. The greengrocer (the one who had owned the store before Mr Shah came from Kenya and took over) fell off his ladder while hanging Christmas lights outside; the old lady down the street had a heart attack when her terrier ran off with its leash; at Friday prayers there had been a fight. He told her about a neat little mathematical trick he had discovered. He wrote contritely that he had been sitting with colleagues celebrating the granting of a doctorate to a student and missed his midafternoon prayer as a result. The postman at Pirmai, Abdullah, enjoyed bringing her his letter, having announced on his way to one and all about the important khat he was carrying, and bringing along behind him a few of the town's layabouts, who perhaps expected a gift from the fortunate Begum from 'foreign.' Everybody in the neighbourhood knew that Nurul Islam had written to his bride. 'What does your lord write?' 'Does he miss you in the cold?' Her lord would end his letter with an oblique declaration of love; once he had written a ghazal. She would learn from him that he had composed it himself, and she wondered if it was recent or if he had written it long ago for someone else. It didn't matter.

He had ended his only letter in English with the words, 'My darling, in this foreign language I free myself from the shackles of conventional reserve and say simply, "I love you dearly."'

'Do you remember, that letter?' she asked.

'Of course I do.'

Hilary came out of the exit gate at the Rome airport and after a quick and nervous overview of the waiting crowd she spotted in the distance, standing next to a café, a small brunette holding up a sign, ROME CONFERENCE ON FUNDAMENTAL PARTICLES AND SYMMETRIES. She pushed through politely and headed towards the placard and introduced herself. The woman was called Rosanna, from the physics department at the University of Padua and secretary of the conference. They had corresponded. Waiting with her were several other participants who had recently arrived, two men who looked Indian or Pakistani—how do you tell?—a young man from Holland—she glanced at the name tag on his suitcase—and a loose-limbed, restless-looking man with blond-greying hair whom she recognized as Pete Sorensen. With him was a petite woman who looked like his wife. He ambled over with a friendly grin and introduced himself.

'I've seen you, when you gave a talk at Harvard,' she told him. 'I'm Hilary Chase, I'm a student of Abe Rosenfeld.'

'Ah, so it's you!' he exclaimed.

'Why, what d'you mean ...'

He was taken aback and immediately started explaining, 'I heard about you—any student of Abe Rosenfeld, well, well.'

Had Nurul spoken to him about her? Of course not. He must have heard rumours. He was eyeing her, sizing her up with a half grin. His wife, Jean, joined them and also gave Hilary a once-over, and then two other physicists arrived, a man and a woman from Kiev, and they were all marched off to a minibus waiting outside. Pete and Jean, perhaps to make amends, patronized her from across the aisle with kind advice for the young. No, Hilary said, to their astonishment, she had never left the

United States before, and Jean gave her advice on what to watch out for in Rome. Look out for solicitors, watch your handbag, don't attempt to buy antiques, they are imitations. Don't give friendly smiles or they might get misinterpreted.

The conference facilities consisted of a beautiful porticoed villa on a hill with an expansive garden in front and a hotel for the delegates at the bottom within walking distance. When she arrived in her room—she hadn't known how much to tip the bellboy, she had yet to understand the currency—she sat down on her bed, felt a sudden stab of loneliness and dejection. Have I done the right thing? Of course I've done the right thing. She had never been to such a congress before. The only large conference she'd been to was the annual Physical Society circus last spring in Washington, DC, with fellow students from her department. So American, so fun. She'd volunteered once at a meeting in Boston.

She called up reception and asked if Dr Islam had arrived. They misunderstood, taking her for a Muslim and asked if she needed something special, so she gave up and went up for a walk in the garden. Two clusters of physicists were out there, strolling about deep in discussion, oblivious to the beauty and colour around them. She herself had nothing to say, she mused. She had come for an overview of her discipline and to meet *him*. But there must be a few other people who'd come just to listen and get ideas. And for contacts. One of the Asian guys she had seen earlier joined her and introduced himself as Dr Abdullah Sood from Islamabad, the capital of Pakistan. She couldn't help noticing to herself that his suit was beige and the shirt dark brown like his skin; dark blue would have served him better. She shook the thought away. How silly. He said he hoped to go to London and work with Nurul Islam. He had done some calculations on Islam's and his student Patel's Greater Unification model and wanted to show them to the great man. What work was Dr Chase doing, please?

She was still a student, Hilary explained, but when she mentioned that Abe Rosenfeld was her supervisor, her legitimacy was restored as instantly as it had just dropped. Dr Sood's eyes lit up. As they rounded a path and came walking towards the villa, they saw a small crowd of people on the steps of the portico. It was Nurul, surrounded by four people. He looked up, saw her, and waved. Her companion fielded the greeting and waved back before she could respond. They went and joined the group.

Nurul Islam was giving a preview of the conference. Two journalists took down his words, and then he extricated himself to go inside to his room. The chosen few had rooms in the villa itself.

Had he glanced at her before turning around? Feeling a bit disappointed, she went back to her room where she thought she would take a nap, having reassured Dr Sood that yes, she would be down for dinner. He was a friendly guy, and also somewhat alone, and she had more than an inkling he would appreciate an introduction to Abe Rosenfeld.

There was a firm knock on the door. She woke up with a start, looked around to get her bearings, pushed back her hair and went to open it. There stood the figure of Nurul Islam, a beaming smile on his mustachioed face. He walked in, she closed the door, and for a hesitant moment they stood facing each other. And then they embraced.

'You didn't even acknowledge me out there,' he accused her when they untangled.

She gaped at him. 'And who had surrounded himself with fans, like bodyguards?'

'I waved at you.'

She laughed. 'Dr Sood pre-empted me.'

They sat down on the bed, and he took her hand in his; with the other he tenderly swept an imaginary strand of hair from her forehead, the way he had done in Boston. They kissed briefly.

She was all anxiety. How could he keep cheerful? 'We have to be careful,' she said. 'I have a feeling there are already rumours flying about. I think the Sorensens know.'

He gave a little smile, then said gently, 'We'll be careful.'

For how long, she wondered, and careful about what? She hadn't even thought about that.

'What are your plans the next few days?' he asked.

'I'll attend the sessions, of course. And I've signed up for the tour. I am so anxious to see Rome!'

Her hand was in his, and they had edged closer again. She leaned on him, and her head was on his shoulder, and then on his lap; she gazed up at him and her heart had stopped. She felt him move and was happy and yet frightened at the same time.

She got up. She had to change for dinner, and he said he had agreed to meet the conference organizers. There were a few people outside when he opened the door and walked out nonchalantly. She made sure she wasn't seen. She was happy, finally, and relieved. Somewhat. She had worried how this rendezvous would go, if their commitment in Boston had not been brief and impulsive and foolish. It was all of that, but more. They had just confirmed that. Surely it would work? What would work? And *how* would it work? She had been tormenting herself with these questions ever since they last met. She was not like the younger crowd, with free sex and thoughtless treatment of anyone who came in their way. But she had also wondered if her attachment to Nurul was not out of desperation because she had no one else and was lonely; or because he was famous and charismatic; or if this were not her bid for vicarious fame. But no, she had her own research and she was determined to make a name for herself in her field.

The welcome address at dinner that night was delivered by Dana Towner, a short and broad jowly woman with curly hair who had been a student of the famous experimentalist Madame Wu of Columbia University and was now at Berkeley. After her words of welcome and thanks she said, 'Let us remember our colleague David Mason, a talented physicist who passed away a few weeks ago and will be dearly missed.' There was a minute's silence, after which she continued, 'I did not know Mason well. He was a theorist, though who hasn't heard of Mason's Theorem? If you understand it, good for you. But Nurul Islam knew Mason personally and I am sure he will tell you more when he gets up to speak later.' She went on to extol the exciting times they were living in, listing recent developments in their subject, and concluded with an oblique prophesy: 'Remember, the spirit of Alfred Nobel hovers above this meeting.' There was applause.

The main course was traditional cacio e pepe, something Hilary had not had before, used to the lasagna and spaghetti and meatballs of university dining. For the vegetarians there was a gnocchi. Hilary thought it all looked exciting. Her previous qualms about the congress were subsided, she felt comfortable now. She was among colleagues, they spoke a common language. Abe had surely been wrong in putting it down. She perhaps had a glass too many of the red wine.

At her table there were, among others, Dr Abdullah Sood and his Indian counterpart, Dr Ramesh Garg. The latter, a cheerful, round-faced man wearing kurta-pajama, worked at the Bhabha Institute in Bombay. Both men had abstained from the wine but they did most of the talking.

'Bhabha, India's greatest physicist and the father of the Indian bomb,' Dr Sood commented mischievously when Dr Garg introduced himself around the table.

'There's no Indian bomb,' Dr Garg protested.

'There will be.'

'Does Pakistan have a nuclear bomb?' Hilary asked.

'It will, if India has one.'

'But what happened to Gandhi and nonviolence?' Hilary asked.

The two Asians looked at each other as if to say, What's this American woman about?

And did the Quran actually predict the theory of relativity? Hilary asked. She had come across that claim in her recent reading on Islam. The Vedas were two thousand years older, Dr Garg protested feelingly, and you can find modern physics—including relativity and quantum mechanics—coded in their verses. And the MIRV missile was definitely there in the Indian epic the Mahabharata, written long before the Quran and Homer's *Odyssey*.

'Are you serious?' asked Hilary.

Meanwhile *he* was having his dinner with senior physicists at what appeared to be the most cheerful table in the hall.

Sure enough, Abdullah Sood asked Hilary if she would introduce him to Abe Rosenfeld. She said she would. She wondered to herself how she would go about it.

Dessert was tiramisu or gelato, and coffee was offered also in American style, percolated or filtered, and decaffeinated if preferred; the Indian and Pakistani at their table asked for tea, as did Hilary.

Nurul Islam came to the front and was speaking. After his generalities, he said, 'I do have a few words about my friend David Mason. We all know he was a great theoretician; but he was also a gentle man, a kind man.' He related how David approached him in Cambridge while they were still fellows and invited him home, and when Nurul put his hand to his breast as a gesture of thanks the traditional way, how David's wife Una asked him if he had angina. That lightened the atmosphere in the hall, and Nurul went on to summarize recent developments in particle theory and fundamental symmetries.

At the end there were a few friendly questions, and then a young man asked, with all due respect, if the attribution of the Islam-Rosenfeld model was not perhaps too narrow, hadn't Mason already foreseen it in his PRL paper of 1963? There was a stir in the hall, then silence. Nurul Islam replied, 'Attribution is always tricky and sometimes unfair, I agree. But how far do we go? We all depend on the work of those who've gone before us. We never deny it. We stand on the shoulders of giants, as Newton said. There are those who say the theory of relativity can be seen in the Quran—and the Kabbalah. Perhaps, and I am a believer in the Quran myself, but I give Einstein the credit.'

He had fudged, and everyone knew it. Hilary wondered what else he could have said.

That night in her room she listened to music on the local radio, and she read the bestseller *Fear of Flying*, which had been highly recommended. Well, she was on a flight and she was afraid, taking a risk with her life. And someone else's. Surely Nurul risked nothing, he was a man. Just as she prepared to go to bed, he called. 'Shall we meet early in the morning? Say six thirty? We could take a walk in the garden.' She agreed, but with the comment, 'You mean I should walk up the hill?' He laughed. 'Use the steps!' he said.

She arrived in the garden early in the morning, and saw a few people already about, including the Indian, Ramesh Garg, who was bent over a plant, closely examining a flower. He looked up and wished her a good morning. Abdullah Sood was strolling around the periphery taking pictures with his camera. Nurul was standing with two other people, and this time throwing caution to the winds he excused himself and came over to her.

'How are you, Hilary? You look beautiful this morning—but you always have, since the first time I saw you.'

She appreciated that and showed it by her smile and her blush. To herself she was rather plain New England, plain as pumpkin pie or baked beans—substantive and no-nonsense, but still boring. But it mattered, his compliment. As it had mattered at the Chinese restaurant in Cambridge that evening. When it all began … did it begin then, or before?

They walked through the garden, down past the hotel, and out through the gate onto the winding country road outside the property.

She told him about her two visits to her father, and seeing her dropout sister, Jill, at Christmas after more than a year. 'I was always the steady one.' *I wonder what you see in me, the boring one.* 'I think Dad knows about you—about us.' He waited for her to go on, his hands behind his back as he walked. 'I think Abe must have told him—or Janis.'

'They've approached you, about us?'

'Janis did, she told me to be sensible.'

'She did to me too, when I was there. And what else?'

'That's it,' she lied. 'Just to be careful … not to get hurt.'

They walked thoughtfully together, she getting anxious. She thought she saw the gleam of a dim smile on his face but didn't prompt him. Finally, he said, 'As you know, I went to Pakistan and met my father.'

'The hush-hush trip?'

'The hush-hush trip, and most distressing. The folly of politicians—but I shouldn't tell you about it …'

'And how is your father?' she asked.

'Getting old. My mother too. He has a second wife, you might remember … who's a help. I worry about him. We're very close … always have been. And then there was the news of David.'

'I'm sorry …'

'That news, him killing himself, was the lowest point of my life in a very long time … He was a close friend … and it felt like … it was a betrayal.'

His face clouded momentarily, then he turned to her and suddenly grinned. He always tries to look cheerful, she thought, but he hides his deep feelings.

'Nurul—'

'Yes?'

'What about us now? We can't go on pretending when everyone seems to know? Does your ... I mean—'

'Sakina Begum.'

'Does she know?'

'Not yet. We should talk. I have a proposal.'

'A proposal? For what?'

He smiled. 'For us. If we're serious, if you're serious ... You'll see. Let's meet for dinner—we'll find a time. Tonight's busy, as you know. We'll find a quiet place where we can talk. We must.'

'I agree. We must.'

They turned and walked back, the objects of barely disguised scrutiny now; she didn't care, and she realized that Nurul didn't either. Breakfast was served in the patio at the back of the villa, where tea and coffee were served throughout the day. They sat down and were left alone for some minutes, before Jean Sorensen joined them, and a little later her husband.

'So, Nurul,' Pete said, 'do you still wake up at that ungodly hour? You know—' he turned to his wife and to Hilary, 'this guy begins work at four in the morning! That's when some of my experiments end!'

'Good thing I'm not an experimentalist, then,' Nurul replied. 'The human mind is at its most receptive at about four. It's a godly hour. I've woken up at four in the morning since as far back as I can remember! It is the stillest hour on the clock, when nothing stirs—'

'Except me, trying to sleep. And your father getting up! You told me about him.'

Another man joined them, thickset with white hair and a broad smile. He was chuckling. 'I couldn't help overhearing that. May I join you? I am Zaffar Khan, Pakistan.' He sat down.

'Which university?' Hilary asked.

'Government. I advise my government on atomic energy. Nurul and I go back a long way. I was his tutor in Lahore, where he was up to all kinds of mischief, including—' he looked at Nurul, 'shall I reveal?'

'Go ahead!' Nurul grinned.

'Where he wrote the most romantic poetry! The moth and the flame, that kind!'

'Well, I have to hear it!' Pete said.

'I don't have anything here with me, but I've kept some of his poetry. It may prove valuable yet …'

'Well, well, Nurul,' Jean said. 'You have a romantic heart after all.'

A meaningful silence, which Nurul broke by saying, 'Zaffar left for Birmingham, and when I arrived in England two years later he picked me up at Southampton and put a coat on me. I'll never forget that!'

'That's friendship,' someone said.

I would never have imagined—Hilary thought later—but wouldn't I? He does quote poetry, and doesn't he say the Quran is the greatest poem? He was hardly your stiff, one-track physicist. Even Abe Rosenfeld, she knew, had hidden sensibility. She had seen a Robert Lowell and a Melville on his shelves and there was a violin beside his armchair … his kids didn't play it, she knew. Feynman played the bongos, though she didn't think he was an artist. Einstein played the violin too …

A call had gone out for the first session, and they all headed towards the auditorium.

That day there were two lectures, the first one by Nurul Islam, and two workshops in smaller rooms. She realized she could have skipped the second workshop without missing much. That's how you survive a conference, she would learn. Lunch and dinner were served informally in the hotel dining room. The Sorensens joined her for lunch, and she had an early dinner by herself. In the evening the hosts had arranged a chamber music recital, but by that time she could barely keep her eyes open and retired to her room.

The next morning she tried not to show her disappointment at not finding Nurul in the garden. The rest of the day was similar to the previous one, but the evening was free. The first lecture was by Alf Greiner of Amsterdam, who had dropped by for a few hours on his way to somewhere else. Nurul avoided him, Hilary observed, and during the tea break she also saw Dr Sood and Dr Greiner engaged in serious conversation. Well, he does get around, she thought. And why not, young scientists have to hustle to get anywhere. The discussions this day had been more lively and continued into lunch and dinner. Friendships had begun to form. At lunch Dana Towner joined her with a sigh, plunking down her big form into a chair with her tray. 'Ah, an American at last,' she said, and a little later, she muttered, 'It's nice to see you here. Hilary, is it? Not many of our sex around, are there? We should work on that.'

She joined Zaffar at dinner. Nurul arrived in the company of two Africans and waved at her. 'Busy man,' Zaffar said, watching her with a smile. Fame and energy, Hilary observed, would create the slightest envy even in the closest of friends.

Early the next morning she met Nurul briefly in the garden—for five minutes, almost exactly, she noted—and they arranged to have dinner together at the restaurant outside the grounds the following night after the conference closed. That afternoon was the tour.

She had noticed that Dr Sood now avoided her. Was this a moral judgment or because now, as Nurul Islam's companion, she had become remote? Dr Garg on the other hand smiled knowingly every time he saw her, but without saying a word. He was somewhat vain, she had concluded, his matching kurta-pajama always bright and neatly pressed. It was as though she had not already spoken to the two men. Zaffar Khan was delightful, reserved but with a twinkling sense of humour. He kept his distance when he had to, approached her when he could. He had preserved a certain Englishness in his mannerisms; what a far cry from the awkward Dr Sood, for whom she felt a little sorry. He didn't have to keep his distance from her. Perhaps his encounter with the eminent Alf Greiner would produce results.

'You should tell me more about Dr Islam,' she told Zaffar. He had replied, 'Nurul? Yes, I'll do that!'

Nurul had said he would not join the tour, having been on one in the past, but he joined it nevertheless, the two of them seated together in the bus. They were met by a guide outside a hotel and taken on a walking tour of historical sites. Camera-toting tourists thronged the streets, many of them Japanese. After the Colosseum, Nurul and Hilary split off on their own and walked with the crowds along the road to the Forum, before finding refuge in a park. They sat down on a bench having coffee and Hilary consulted her guidebook. 'The Forum Romanum is not far, but I don't think I want to see any more, do you?' she said, and he replied,

'Not unless you want to.' 'I only want to spend time with you.' She moved closer and took his arm. He put his hand on hers. Happiness overcame her. Contentment. What else matters, his hand upon mine, committed. A new chapter in my life. A new beginning. We'll manage … But looking at that mien beside her closely she detected, she thought, a tension. Against her will, her happiness suddenly deflated. This was not going to be easy. Prepare for a heartbreak.

It was already dark when they returned in a taxi, she getting off at the hotel and he proceeding to the villa.

Later that night Nurul went to Zaffar Khan's room to catch up with his old friend. Zaffar had requested a meeting. He had been like an elder brother to Nurul in Lahore, and in England when he had felt utterly lost in a country he had thought he would know because there had been such a British presence back home. Zaffar had been a good physicist, but he knew he would never achieve the heights, so he had opted to advise. They sat in the two florid armchairs in the room under low lights, having tea. For a while they discussed the conference, then their families. Zaffar wanted to know all about Nurul's visit to Harvard. Nurul gave him the gist. Zaffar missed the excitement of research and the wistfulness was evident in his sparkling eyes. They spoke of low-key Rosenfeld and his hospitality. A good man. At this point Zaffar sat back and said, in somewhat fake innocence, 'That Hilary, she's a nice girl. Quiet for an American, I thought. Rosenfeld's student, is she?'

'Yes, and she's very good too.'

'I notice she has a thing for you … and you for her?' Zaffar now allowed the briefest smile.

'Leave it, yaar …'

'Ah. Something more, then? You're a famous man, my brother. Eyes upon you.'

'I know.'

'And watch out for that Sood fellow. A snake in the grass.'

'The one who goes around with the Polaroid?'

'And he has his eyes on you. Avoid looking at that Polaroid.' Zaffar reflected for a moment. 'These things happen, Nurul—infatuations—at our age especially, but don't let it rock your position … it passes … I know you'll be wise.' Before Nurul could reply, Zaffar interjected, 'But I have to tell you something important, Nurul—in absolute secrecy.'

Nurul looked up. 'You have a mistress? And you're preaching to me?'

'No. Of course not. I want to tell you that Project Babur is on. I thought you should know that.'

'You're sure? It's actually on? Funding and so on?'

Zaffar nodded. 'Yes. And I'm telling you this in strictest confidence.'

'Of course.'

Nurul swore in the choicest Punjabi invectives he could muster. 'And he told me—they told me—do you know, this messenger from Teymuri, Major So-and-so, came especially to my home one evening to reassure me? Project Babur is on hold, he said. Too costly. It's atoms for peace now. The bastards. I should have known. I had suspicions.'

Nurul didn't tell him about the presents. The bribe.

There was silence. Then Nurul looked hard at Zaffar. The question on his mind burning, but Zaffar took his time. He swallowed.

'I've considered,' Zaffar said. 'If the Indians test theirs, then …'

'Then?'

'Then I will join the project. Our bomb effort. I thought you should know.'

'Oh,' came Nurul's response. He felt his heart drop. He must have changed colour. 'You surprise me, yaar.'

'Well.'

Nurul got up and they embraced. 'Till next time,' he said. 'Khuda hafiz,' his friend replied. God protect you. Then Nurul opened the door and left, dark thoughts in his head. The door clicked shut behind him.

Am I so out of touch … the world passes me by … old at forty? All has changed. And me and my illusions. Science for peace, what bullshit. Even Zaffar has seen the light … or darkness?

The conference had concluded with a riotous lunch, and most of the participants had by now departed, exchanging addresses and promises. Such events are a success if only for that. Some collaborations would occur, some new friendships would last.

Hilary and Nurul sat on the closed terrace of the recommended restaurant down the road from the conference hotel. It was called Coppi, in honour of a famous Italian cyclist. The night was warm, breezy, the ambience to delight the heart. The waiter lit the candle on their table and reeled off a small list of specials, but first he brought two slim glasses and poured champagne: on the house, he announced, on this magical romantic night for a lovely romantic couple. They looked at each other, then picked up the glasses, toasted silently, and drank. It's Providence, he said to himself.

He chose lamb chops, she a bouillabaisse. Red wine came, a bottle. The server, who was also one of the owners, turned on music in the background, which they enjoyed very much, and when Hilary asked the man about it, he said, 'Why, it is Verdi!—*La Forza del Destino*—' Hilary responded with a wide smile. Obviously he had played it deliberately.

Initially they talked of anything but their situation. The conference, some of the people there, Alf Greiner's fly-in, some of the new ideas. Nothing earth-shaking, the big guns in America had stayed away. A mild controversy: were quarks, the constituents of neutrons and protons, real or imaginary? Could they be seen? They were fractional charges, one-third and two-third of the electron's charge, which was considered immutable. She had made some contacts and seen Rome, she couldn't believe it. Sent a postcard to her dad. Their rendezvous, though, was the real reason she had come, wasn't it? At some point his foot met hers under the table, and he squeezed her calf tightly. The server topped up their glasses; they could not refuse and look like philistines, having appreciated the music and accepted the recommended bottle.

'What time are you leaving tomorrow?'

'In the afternoon,' she replied.

He was staying for some meetings and would leave the day after. He would miss her, he told her.

Dessert came, she picked up her spoon, and then paused.

'What now?' she said, her eyes gleaming.

'What?'

'We have to decide something, don't we?'

'Here we are, under the stars, outside Rome, nothing else matters.'

'And then? … You go to London and I go back to Boston. That's it? Do you want to leave it like this, Nurul? In the middle of nowhere?'

'No.' He took a long breath, looked away. Then: 'I've thought of a solution. But don't judge too quickly. I want you to think about it before you hit me with that dessert spoon. Please put it down.'

'Tell me.'

As predicted, she blew up.

'What? Nurul! You want me to be your second wife, your junior wife, some chattel that you, you hide somewhere? Nurul! Is this you? I thought you were a civilized man!'

Eyes were upon them, the waiter hurried over to fill their water glasses.

'It's not what you think,' he said. 'It's not some Ali Baba story. It's a legitimate way to be together. A licence for me . . .'

'A licence.'

'Wrong word, sorry.'

She said nothing. He put out a hand, she did not take it. Tears flowed down her cheeks. 'I believed you.'

'I love Sakina. She's stood by me all these years. She's looked after me. Would you really want me to cheat on her, and her to hear about us from the world? Do you want me to abandon her? But I love you too, Hilary. Dearly. It's the only way for me.'

'So you get two wives, and I get a used husband.'

'That's what I am. Second-hand. You knew that.'

'And you think Sakina will agree.'

'I hope so.'

'You hope so.'

'What do you want me to do?'

'Nothing.'

She wiped her face. They got up and left.

Outside, she said, 'I know it's not easy for you. But what must you think of me? I'm an American woman, soon with a Ph.D. A student of Abe Rosenfeld. To be a second Muslim wife? A laughingstock? For your pleasure? Is this some kind of unification scheme for you, sometimes this wife, sometimes that? I am not a particle, we are not your … your forces to unite! We are people with feelings!'

He controlled himself.

'If you love me and want me, as I love you and want you. For that.' He added, 'Think about it. It's a means to be together. What the world thinks doesn't matter. It's what we want that matters.'

They parted with an embrace, an automatic instinctive one, a quick one. They didn't notice a light flash in the dark.

Back in his room, he thought, Well, that's that, Nurul mian. A showdown had to come. Taking stock. You can't spend what you don't have. You can't always get what you want, to quote from one of his sons' records. Beatles or Rolling Stones? He realized he should have been more careful right at the beginning, in Cambridge. He was older. This was not fair to her; he could go on with his life, his age and preoccupations would wrap up his pain. Her wound was deeper. But then she was younger, she would bounce back like a rubber ball. He would carry her memory, of what could not be, into the grave. But that last embrace—they had not broken completely. Yet. Her cutting remarks … had cut him. Good for her, if she could make them, she would recover soon.

Flipping through his conference papers, he saw the envelope he had inserted among them, which he had received in London just before he left. Missing the sender's address, it had not looked urgent. He tore it open, read the note inside. 'Professor Islam, you are a fraud.'

Well, whoever you are, you coward, Hilary Chase certainly agrees with you

He embraced Sakina at the door, which took her by surprise. She turned red, looked to see if they had been watched. Then she greeted him the traditional way, waving her hands over him, cracking her knuckles at the sides of her head and putting a sweet into his mouth. At the dining table, he accepted a cup of tea with biscuits. There was a weary look on his face. Muni entered the house in the company of her brothers and ran into his arms and lap. For her he had brought a Pinocchio storybook; for the boys, Italian football magazines picked up from the airport, for once nothing educational. Shouts of joy. A scarf for Sakina. Chocolates for everybody.

They gathered around the table, the five of them, excited.

'Was the conference successful?' Sakina asked. Always the same question.

'Yes, dear. And I've brought back some interesting ideas.' The usual answer.

She began preparations for a lavish welcoming dinner.

Something did not seem quite right, Sakina thought later that night in bed. The extra shows of affection hid a preoccupation. She could tell. The kids too. He had missed his prayer that evening.

'I would like to go to Rome someday,' she said. 'All that history.'

'We should go. And the food is excellent.' And the wine too, he could have added.

He was lying on his back, his eyes open. He picked up her hand and squeezed it.

'There was a letter from Rukhsana.'

'What does she say, your sister?'

'Am I keeping you happy? she asks. Now what got into her?'

'Of course you're keeping me happy. Am I keeping *you* happy?'

'In every way?' she persisted, not answering him. 'Do I keep you satisfied every way?'

'Now what does that mean? And why this interrogation? What's Rukhsana got up to, with this fitna, this interference?'

'I just want to know. You looked worried. What's on your mind?'

'It can wait,' he replied.

She rose up on an elbow, and to his great surprise, leaned over and kissed him on the lips. He held her soft body awhile. She fell back, they became silent, and soon she had fallen asleep.

In every way? He smiled. What to say.

From the beginning, they had never discussed sex. It was always 'it' or 'that.' 'You want to do it?' she would ask. 'Then all right. Go ahead. Gentle.' Where did it come from, this repression? Their culture? Was it the religion? Hardly. Among men the language could be so explicit … Punjabi seemed invented for that … to express emotion, lust. The first time he heard this sort of language, among older boys, he had been frightened. The terms, the gestures. He had asked his father, innocently making a gesture he had seen, and earned a sharp slap, his father assuming that he had begun to swear. Later Abba took him aside and gave him some explanations, using metaphors to assist him. 'Like those street dogs … ?' Nurul asked innocently, and almost received another slap. And when he started having cravings for sex, he was warned not to masturbate or he would go blind, lose his drive, never have children … that sort of thing, it came from the teachers.

A good thing, he thought, they'd not gone all the way in Rome. Done it. She was ready, he could tell. She wanted to. All he had to do was lean her back … He should have fucked her. And where would they be now? He would have become the proverbial louse. (Where did these delightful American expressions come from?) Not to say a sinner. Never mind the champagne and the wine. They were drunk when they quarrelled. They had not broken off entirely. Hilary, Hilary. Should he call her? No. Write, perhaps. But tell her what? *We are not particles, not your elementary forces.* That was a good one from her.

In the morning when Sakina came down she saw him saying his prayers; she brought him tea and watched him sit down at his desk, pick up paper and pencil. He was still in his pajamas.

How he likes his work. He lives for it, when most people in the world abhor getting up only to go to begin some dreary labour they do every day, in office or factory. That's God's gift to him, as he is the first to admit, and it's God's gift to the world and the people of Pakistan. That's what that Major Iftikhar said the other day, and it didn't go to his head, he seemed not to have even heard the compliment. And the next day his elation at receiving the Faiz copy was gone; when she brought it up, he called it a bribe.

Later that morning, Muni's hand tucked inside his, the two of them departed, strolling on the sidewalk this wet spring morning, a sight to warm her heart.

'Why does he favour Muni so?' Mirza asked.

She pinched his cheek affectionately. 'She is the youngest and the only daughter, that is why. That doesn't mean he doesn't love you, silly. Boys are loved differently.'

'With gruffness, you mean?'

'He wants the best for you, that's why. You have to see beyond the gruffness. It's just pretending.'

The head of physics, John Hemmings, intercepted Nurul outside his door. 'Could you come over a moment, Nurul. There's something I'd like you to see.'

Nurul followed Hemmings to his office, where the head had gone to stand behind his desk. He pointed to a sheet of paper in front of him. 'Take a look at this—it arrived while you were away.'

Nurul picked it up, read it. 'Yes, I've received a couple of them—'

'You have? Perhaps you should have informed me?'

'The second one arrived just before I left for Rome, John, and it came with me unopened. Best to ignore this for now, I think—someone with a grudge. Likely a former student.'

'They say the same thing? About the dates and so on?'

'Somewhat briefer, though. He charges me with plagiarizing Rosenfeld's work. He's wrong, of course—in case you want to know.'

'The dates …?'

'The dates don't mean a thing. Well—they do, but they are close and it's the work that counts. We approach the idea quite differently. Rosenfeld knows that, which is why he invited me. And I made it clear at the Oslo Symposium where I presented this work that it was from my old lecture notes—which extend what David and I began a while ago.'

'I see.'

'I spoke about it here too, at my colloquium, you might remember.'

'Of course I do. But how are you going to handle this, Nurul, if he goes public? This could be dynamite. The BBC will have a field day. They've celebrated you in the past.'

'I expect the university to support me, John. My record speaks for itself. Islam-Rosenfeld is only one thing. I'm on to Greater Unification now. And there's a lot more behind me, beginning with Cambridge and meson fields, as you know.'

Hemmings was a good man, but he was a geophysicist; he would know little about Nurul Islam's work except by hearsay.

'Of course, we all know that. Everyone knows that. Still, you want to avoid the publicity ...'

Nurul nodded, chose not to say more. That jury at Harvard; that former student of his, the Midlander who had piped up the accusation; and that challenge at the Rome conference. Then there was Alf Greiner, who disliked him and was conveniently present at both those occasions. In Rome they had briefly shaken hands.

'Well, it so happens that the BBC's looking for you. They've called a couple of times. It's about a panel they want to air on nuclear weapons. They want you on it. Please say yes and don't raise a fuss. Sarah's been speaking with them. Remember to say good things about us. And British science.'

Nurul took the message from the department secretary and rang the BBC producer who had left her number, and learned that she proposed to do a radio show on *Cross Fire* with him, on the idea of a nuclear weapons–free South Asia. She told him of a report in the press, based on a book by two American journalists, in which they revealed that both India and Pakistan were already on their way towards developing nuclear weapons. He wasn't aware of the book or that report, he told her. He had been travelling. His co-respondent in the show, she informed him, would be an Indian scientist.

Well, well. He agreed on possible dates and called Hemmings to tell him about it.

Nurul Islam was not surprised to receive a phone call from Major Iftikhar.

'Professor Islam, how are you? I wondered if you've had a chance to glance at that brochure I left you?'

'The one about the company called Universal Technologies, yes, I glanced at it, as you put it. Impressive, but I'm not sure exactly what they do—are you on the board, by the way?'

'Yes, I am. UniTech is an international engineering firm that runs projects in Pakistan and the Middle East. The major shareholders naturally are from these places, but the technical experts are employed from everywhere—including Europe and America. The London office offers consultants and procures materials for different engineering projects.'

'Well ... that's interesting.'

'We also hand out scholarships in science and engineering, Professor. We would like you to join us as a scientific advisor. Your prestige would be a great asset. We expect to develop a special scholarship program for Pakistani students to study abroad, and you would advise us on the application and evaluation process. Is that up your alley, Professor Islam? Please say yes. It would be greatly appreciated. There would be modest remuneration, of course.'

'I'm greatly preoccupied at present, Major. Let me think about it. I have a special interest in encouraging science in the, er, less-developed nations like ours, especially fundamental science, as you might know.'

'I do know that, Professor. And I applaud you. Mind you, there are others in our country who would take you up on that issue—do we need dams and bridges and more schools, or your quarks and electrons and abstract fields? Some other time, perhaps. But thank you for accepting my offer, at least in principle. By the way—how was the conference in Rome?'

Nurul paused.

'Don't tell me you are spying on me,' he said with a laugh.

'Word spreads, Professor. Posters for the conference have found their way even to Islamabad! We're not so backward. But we're proud of you.'

'Thank you. So these scholarship candidates would study abroad and return home?'

'Exactly, that would be a condition of the scholarship. To return and contribute to the nation. It demonstrates UniTech's commitment to science for peace.'

'Very good, Major. But give me time.'

'Excellent. One more thing. The BBC has announced this morning your appearance on an upcoming *Cross Fire* show.'

'Yes.'

'"Should South Asia become a nuclear-free zone?" That's a good topic, but in my opinion our politicians should be discussing it. They make the decisions, after all. What would be your position, if I may be so bold as to ask? On this issue, I mean.'

Nurul Islam took a deep breath. How disingenuous of the man, innocence itself. He had lied to him on behalf of his boss, the president, and brought a bribe. It was humiliating even to think about it.

'My position is, yes, South Asia should declare itself a nuclear-free zone. A nuclear war would be devastating. And in a populated region such as ours, even more so. All you need is one nutter to press the button. And we have enough of those.'

'You are right. Can I send you some points regarding Pakistan's position? Some nuances—that radio show can trip the unwary. The host is a wily one.'

'Please do.'

In Rome, Zaffar Khan had told him explicitly that Project Babur was on. By coming to see him that evening with the bribe, Major Iftikhar had been running interference for the president. (If that was the correct metaphor.) Nurul did not want to make accusations right now that would only be denied and earn him unwanted hostility. On the show, he would simply declare his pacifist position and defend it. If the Pak government was already going ahead with its nuclear program, so be it. He thought of Zaffar's revised position. If the Indians test theirs, then I will join the project, he'd said. How logical and commonsensical, except for the high stakes. A weapon with the potential to destroy entire cities, kill millions. Nurul Islam did not want a hand in it. But with the UniTech scholarship program—if the major had not lied about that too—there could be possibilities. He would be able to influence bright young minds, who would hold him in awe, to think of their country's development first. To think about peace instead of perpetual enmity with India. And perhaps UniTech itself might come on board on his international institute project. Now there was science for peace. But was that really possible? Was the world so civilized, so sane?

Shall I write to her now? Dear Hilary. I'm sorry it had to come to what it did ... What does a single young woman know of constraints, emotional and physical, that other people face ... what does a single

*American* woman know. I am tied with strings in all directions, and I can't just cut them. I don't want to. You said before that I was not direct in my communication, did not express my feelings. Well, this time I did. I said I love you. Love your reserve, your poise, your intelligence ... does that sound patronizing ... (Nurul Islam you are almost her *padrone*, wake up!) ... your everything, your freedom, your simplicity. Just you. Body too, I would not want to lie. How certainly you fell into my embrace ... like you belonged, it was our fate. Perhaps we should not have let it happen. But it happened. Shall we douse the flame? I gave you my option. You called it barbaric. Or did you actually say *uncivilized*? You made me out as some lecherous Harun al-Rashid, or a native in the jungle in some Tarzan film. I think that whether my suggestion is barbaric or not is how you apply it. You say it's the oppression of women. Whom am I oppressing? Why can't a woman have more than one husband, you may ask? Well, why not? And anyway, isn't that already happening in your world—what is free love, after all? Only you don't go to the judge or priest and officially marry more than one person. You divorce casually, acrimony and hatred replaces what was once celebrated with fanfare as love. Don't people have affairs in your world? Don't your presidents have mistresses? All I asked was that we make our love official and honest. According to my faith and according to what is possible for me in other ways. Sakina may not agree, but we didn't even get there.

Something like that. He sent it. A reply came immediately, their letters having crossed.

> Dear Nurul. I'll apologize first for some of my statements. My sarcasm and the scene I raised in the restaurant must have made you feel you were lucky to escape my clutches. You are not uncivilized. Far from it. Nurul, I realize you have constraints, based on your religious beliefs and your family obligations—your love for your family. But I have my constraints and beliefs too, based on my human rights. My American values. I do not want to be a second-class wife to someone. I don't know even if I want to get married. Nowadays a woman doesn't have to. That's unacceptable to you, and I understand that. But I do care for you dearly. I love you—and I'm putting myself out on a limb here, writing this. Perhaps we should not have gone this far. Rome was not a good idea.

You can write to me. Please do. I shall be attending the workshop in Trieste in the summer. (Madam Wu herself has invited me, and besides, I've got the travel bug now.) I'll pass through London on my way back.
Hilary

The moderator was Adam Foxx, a balding, paunchy veteran known worldwide—by those who listened to *Cross Fire* on BBC's foreign service—for his confrontational approach with his guests. Nurul's Indian co-respondent was Yogesh Bhatt, a political scientist at the School of Oriental and African Studies. A political scientist was not a scientist in Nurul Islam's book, and in any case why invite two people from different fields?

ADAM FOXX: Professor Bhatt, this is a quote from Mohandas Gandhi, father of your nation, an inspiration to many throughout the world: in Calcutta, on the eve of the country's independence, when a scientist asked him what people like him should do if the new India ordered them to develop nuclear weapons, he advised, 'Resist them unto death.' And yet India has embarked on a nuclear weapons program, which is certain to provoke its neighbour Pakistan to do the same. And other countries, that goes without saying. What have you—or what has your government to say to that?

YOGESH BHATT: India has not embarked on a nuclear weapons program, Adam. We have a nuclear research facility outside Bombay for energy production. India desires peace with all countries, especially our sister nation, Pakistan.

AF: But the facility—the Bhabha Atomic Research Centre—or BARC—does it have a bite? Surely it can easily be converted to a weapons program. Here is what Dr Bhabha, who died in an unfortunate plane crash a few years ago—a great loss for India—here's what he said on Indian national radio: 'Atomic weapons give a state possessing them in adequate numbers a deterrent power against attack from a much stronger state.'

YB: But that is not to say we are in production, Adam.

AF: Professor Islam. According to reports, at a secret conference in Pakistan, your president, Mr Beyram Teymuri, launched Pakistan's own nuclear weapons program. Were you, *the* eminent scientist from Pakistan, present at that meeting?

NURAL ISLAM: I was. I am not sure that a program was actually launched. It was discussed. I have been informed since then that Pakistan's atomic research is directed only towards peaceful purposes.

AF: But if India went on and developed nuclear capability—or arrives at a small step away from it, what would you say?

NI: Adam, I am resolved to work for a nuclear-free South Asia. We don't want to live with nuclear missiles pointing at each other.

AF: China is next door and has already fought a war with India, which it won decisively. And China possesses nuclear weapons. Surely India is justifiably nervous.

YB: Exactly, Adam. We are very nervous.

AF: And that makes Pakistan nervous. So you are affirming, Professor Bhatt, that India should go ahead and develop nuclear weapons too?

YB: As a deterrence. But before that we should talk about global assurances, in case India decides to stay on course and not go ahead.

AF: And what do you say to that, Professor Islam?

NI: The idea of nuclear development for the sake of deterrence makes me nervous. All it needs is some crazy person at the button, or an error—and I have heard reliable reports from scientific colleagues, told to me privately, about errors that have occurred in the American system that almost plunged us all into a nuclear holocaust. Thankfully that didn't happen. But it could happen. Don't forget the Cuban missile crisis. Or some organization like Ian Fleming's SPECTRE could mount an attack on a nuclear facility.

AF: International terrorists, yes. The capability could also spread, couldn't it? From India or Pakistan to elsewhere.

NI: It could. We know that it spread from Los Alamos to elsewhere. It is a frightening scenario.

AF: Professor Bhatt—what would your own stand be if your country decided to go ahead and explode a nuclear device?

YB: Let me say first that I believe the nuclear bomb was an abhorrent invention. India didn't develop it. We should all work to make the entire world nuclear-free. Ban the bomb—but everywhere. But if India were threatened, under the present geopolitical circumstances I would support my government's decision. We cannot afford to lose another war.

AF: And you, Professor Islam. Can Pakistan afford to lose another war? In conventional terms, it has the weaker military. How would you react if your country decided to go ahead with its nuclear program? You said that a program was actually discussed at that meeting.

NI: Yes. Project Babur was discussed. I do not support it. I will go on giving my voice to calls for a nuclear-free South Asia and world guarantees against China or any other nation that possesses nuclear weapons.

Nurul Islam had made a blunder, and he knew it the instant the words left his mouth: Project Babur. He had named it; he had made it a reality.

Major Iftikhar waited a day, perhaps awaiting instructions, before calling Nurul Islam at home. It was morning. There were hardly any preliminaries.

'Professor, need I say that you have let our side down.'

'Major, I was not at a rugby match. I had to declare my position. And I responded to that man's argument about deterrence. How treacherous and fragile it can be. You had told me that our nation was all for atoms for peace. That position should be made public.'

'You didn't have to name Project Babur.'

'That was a slip. But do you think the world's intelligence services don't know about it?'

'They can only guess. Your acknowledging it, the way you referred to it in the present tense—let's make no bones about it—was the clincher they needed.'

'So it's still going on.'

'My dear man, what do you think? Welcome to the real world.'

The major put the phone down.

The irony in all this was that he and Professor Bhatt had shared coffee and sandwiches at the BBC cafeteria after the show. In their friendly chat they had discussed their families and university politics. Professor Bhatt was from Gujarat.

In the second-floor apartment of the preacher Mowlana Sufar in Barakat Manzil, in a little alley off Lahore's crowded and bustling Anarkali Bazar, the old man waved his disciple Qadir Khan to sit down in front of him on the carpet. With Qadir was another young man. The mowlana sat, as usual, against the back wall of his reception room, one leg bent and half stretched out, the other crossed under him. There was a bolster on his right side for him to lean on. The carpet, Qadir noticed, was new, a deep red in place of the blue of his previous visits, the last one of which was a year ago. The room had been painted. There was the same framed picture of the Kaaba behind the mowlana, next to an elaborate large-scale calligraphy of a Quranic verse. There was a rosary in his hand. There was a sweet perfume in the air.

As he would write in his memoir, *Confessions of a Former Jihadi*, which he published thirty-four years following that visit, over the months since he heard Nurul Islam speak at MIT, Qadir Khan's hatred for him had only deepened. Recently he had heard the professor's comments on BBC's *Cross Fire*, as had Mowlana Sufar and others in their organization, Jang-e-Momeen, 'The War of the Faithful,' and concluded that Nurul Islam was not only a heretic, which they already knew, but also a traitor to Pakistan for his stand against nuclear weapons and the Islamic bomb.

After the greetings, Qadir introduced the young man he had brought with him. 'Mowlana, this is Abdullah Sood, a physicist. He was at the conference in Rome, Italy, that I spoke to you about on the phone.'

The mowlana glared at Sood. 'And?'

'The professor was also there,' Sood said, somewhat nervously.

'And? How do you know Abdullah here?' he turned to ask Qadir.

He seemed pleased, his gruffness only an act. By now Qadir Khan had learned the mowlana's mannerisms well. He himself was very pleased with his discovery.

'We were at Government College together, Mowlana. We became friends. And we both attended Friday prayers there … and listened to your sermons on the radio … and took part in discussions afterwards.'

'So. Welcome,' the mowlana said to Sood. 'You have brought information.'

'At this conference I saw the professor behaving in an immoral way with a woman, and I was very disturbed.'

'Same woman?' The mowlana threw a look at Qadir.

'Definitely the same, ji. Abdullah took photos and I recognize her.'

'*Astaghfirullah*. The sins of this man. He is a shameless dog. For this alone he should be stoned. What did he do?' he asked Abdullah Sood.

'He embraced her in the open. I happened to see them. He also drank alcohol—champagne—in a restaurant.'

'How do you know?'

'I saw them …'

Mowlana Sufar gave a deep and long cough and spat into a receptacle. He took a sip of water, paused to regain his breath, and cursed the sinner again. Then he said, 'You did a good thing by reporting to me. Our people are unaware of what's being done in their name.'

'I have photos, Mowlana.'

'Let me see them.'

Sood handed them over, three Polaroid shots, not very sharp.

In one, Nurul Islam was in a group of four where there was also a woman. The second one was of the woman with Nurul Islam in a garden, talking in earnest. In the third one, taken from behind in the dark, Nurul Islam and the girl were walking together. Heads close, hands just touching.

'Nothing more? Embrace, champagne—no photos?' Mowlana Sufar grunted. He kept the photos by his side. 'I will keep them.' There was a smile on his lips. 'Well done, son,' he said to Abdullah Sood. 'You can go, may Allah keep you. Allah hafiz.'

A tea tray came for him, with samosas, brought by a middle-aged woman. He did not ask the young men to join him, but signalled to the woman to serve them elsewhere in the flat. He struggled through another deep cough and remembered to praise Allah.

'What?' Janis almost shouted.

'Exactly my response.' Hilary smiled sheepishly, having quickly looked around. 'I couldn't believe it.'

They were once more at the Coffee Connection, with its bright-red metal railings and pine furniture, the steamy air redolent with aromas of the bean and the buzz of unending lunchtime chatter. In the background, coffee machines hissing and grinders shrieking. The occasional shout or call would hardly be noticed here, at this rendezvous, Hilary need not have worried. Across the table, Janis was all ears to learn about the latest development in the illegitimate relationship between her husband's student and his famous colleague.

'But that's medieval! I've always seen him as sophisticated and Westernized, a suave and well-travelled man of the world. Except for the Islam thing, I mean. The religion. It's inexplicable. Are you sure you heard him right?'

'I'm sure. No mistake.'

'And he expected you to go along? Maybe it was his way of saying bye-bye, I'm going back to the little wife and the kids.'

'I trust him to be more honest. When I'm with him, I know it's there—the love. You know.'

'The love. Remind me, I've forgotten,' Janis said, a little quickly, then added, 'But a second wife? That's not even legal!'

'He must have thought about it.' Hilary had wondered, only out of curiosity, what Nurul had in mind by his proposal. 'Anyway, it's unacceptable, of course. Ridiculous. Absurd. What must he think of me … just someone he could pick up and add to … add to his harem!'

On the verge of tears, she saw Janis's look and both broke into laughter. Nurul Islam was always a larger-than-life figure and easy to call to mind. Hilary went over to the counter on the raised floor and brought them refills of Colombian, which was all the rage. Then Janis went to the bathroom and soon returned. This had turned out to be an interesting afternoon for her.

'He could just divorce Sakina Begum. She's a darling—and one feels sorry for her, but they are universes apart! I'm sure it will come to that. If he really loves you, as he says. He would take care of her, of course. He's a decent man. She could even return to Pakistan.'

'He would never leave her. He loves her too—is that possible? The second marriage would be a licence for us to be together.'

'A licence to fuck.'

That choice of word shocked the younger woman. Janis trying to sound with it? It was so cheapening. Intrusive. But she rose to the challenge. 'There's more to intimacy than fucking.' Spoken softly.

'Yes. Sorry about that.'

'I've been thinking. How much worse is it than a man saying "I don't love you anymore" and dumping her for someone else, usually younger?'

Janis smiled. 'No worse, maybe. To get to another subject. I should tell you … it may come as a shock.'

'What?'

'Abe and I are separating. All amicable and so on.'

'Janis! … I thought you two were perfect complements.'

'Complements, yes. But it's gotten boring. Tedious. There's no fun anymore. I do care for Abe … and he for me … it's just that we've turned away from each other … like you do in bed. He has his own world to absorb him and take him into old age. What do I have? I'm thirty-eight now.'

'There wouldn't be someone else? Am I intruding?'

'I've intruded enough myself. There's someone I have in mind …'

'And Abe? Is there … there are always the groupies, I suppose …'

'Do you know something? Who is it? That postdoc he brought over from Israel?'

'Rachel Talmi? I don't know. She certainly clings to him.'

And when you're gone, she'll readily take your place. Look after him, traditional and so on.

'No wonder his new interest in Hebrew poetry. Andalusian. Hunh.'

Abe and Janis had been like a family to her; now she felt orphaned. The young stepmother, Rachel, would not want Hilary to be around. Later, at the end of their weekly Friday afternoon meeting, Abe surprisingly came with her to the door as she was leaving and said, in a quiet voice, 'Janis told you about us. It happens. At some point that old romance inexplicably runs its course … evaporates into thin air.' He made a gesture.

'I'm sorry,' she said.

'No need to be. How did you find Rome?'

She told him about the people she'd met. The discussions about the existence of quarks, were they real or imaginary. And she'd enjoyed the venue and the city tour.

'And personally? That's some proposal you came back with!—Janis told me about it.'

'She did? Yes!' As before with Janis, the laughter was also a cry.

'You refused, of course.'

'Of course. It's absurd!'

Abe stared at her for a moment, but said nothing further. She turned around and left.

She'd been hit twice, she thought, by men. Abe without Janis would grow distant, no longer the elder brother or father figure he had become. Janis would of course disappear from Cambridge. And Nurul, with his impossible proposal.

Ten days after Rome, she received Nurul's rambling letter. She guessed from the postmark that he would not have received hers yet when he wrote it. He called her once, in her apartment: she guessed it was him. He'd always called at seven a.m. His twelve. No one else called her at that hour. She did not pick up.

Normally so restrained in his emotions, this time her dad could not hide his great relief. She had spoken to him on the phone and now she'd come to visit. There was a spring in his step, a sparkle in his eyes, a warm energy in his voice as he pulled out a chair at the dining table and sat down where she was having her toast and coffee.

'I suppose it's in his culture. But how can a man love two women? Does he really believe that?'

'Come on, Dad. It's possible. *You* know that!'

He knew what she was teasing him about. His posting in England during the War.

'It's not the same thing at all,' he said, not offended. But he'd given the hint of an admission he'd never made before, with an even smaller hint of a smile: 'Not at the same time. You girls just imagined things and teased your mother no end about it.' He went to the sideboard and poured more coffee for himself from the percolator. When had he begun to stoop? It almost became him, the old doctor.

'So it's over. And you can get on with your life.'

'Not quite, Dad. I thought I would pass through London in the summer.' Her father waited. 'For a chat.'

'About what?

'Just talk. That's all.'

'He's given you a release, Hil. Take it and go on. He's from a different culture, a different religion. I know you don't believe in God—for the moment—but still. There's a long tradition to which you belong.' He threw a barely perceptible glance at the *Yardley* on the far wall. 'Just get on with your life.'

She told him about Abe and Janis. In the long pause that followed, during which he looked away, out the window towards the front garden, she could see him deflate. 'It happens more and more, I guess,' he said. 'Divorce rates going up. Abortions. People want to live to the full, they get bored and go after new experiences. Like travelling to a different country. I guess it's partly because we live longer now … and live better …'

He looked at her to say something.

'Just for the sake of argument, Dad … and don't jump to any conclusions.'

'Go ahead. I'm as open-minded as anybody. You know that.'

'People have affairs, men more than women. And men often go for younger women and divorce their wives—who have fewer prospects in our society. It happens. The wives then depend on alimony, they are not used to working. Although that's changing.'

'It happens, yes. I've seen it.'

'Which is worse, that or keeping two wives—'

'They both have to agree to the arrangement, Hil.'

That's the rub.

'How do you know that, Dad? You've been reading up on this?'

'Yes, as a matter of fact, I have. It's a practical arrangement in some societies, to rein in the men. It was useful during wars, when there were fewer men around. This happened in the early days of Islam. There was no love between men and women as we understand it. But for modern times … you're an educated, accomplished woman, Hil.'

However much she turned the arguments over in her mind, she knew that she could never live with the arrangement that Nurul had proposed. The sheer embarrassment of it would kill her. But they continued to exchange letters. Not gushing letters, but friendly, even affectionate ones; the love in them was implicit though strained, struggling out in a word or two, the mention of an incident they had shared. It was aching, this uncertainty, and she thought they should stop. She suggested that, he agreed; absurdly then she replied, to thank him, and the resolve was broken.

In early June, suddenly, he went to spend a day in Rochester, New York. Did she want to come over and meet him, he wrote. Talk things over. Hilary took a bus, and they spent a night together in his room, away from prying eyes.

A cable came from Zaffar Khan: *In London Friday, looking forward to seeing you. When can we meet?* Nurul replied immediately, *Come to my office at 12? Lunch.* Flights arrived from the subcontinent early in the morning. He had a graduate seminar till half past twelve, so that morning he left instructions for the department secretary to welcome his guest. When he breezed into his office following the seminar, Zaffar Khan was seated at an angle in the chair across from the desk, studying a paper. He looked up, stood up with a smile, and they embraced. There were two other men in the room, one of whom now turned from reading a conference poster on a wall, and the other rose up from the extra chair by the door. They looked younger, perhaps in their mid- to late thirties, and were clad in smart blazers and light trousers. They were Zamil Akhtar and Sajjad Khan, and came forward to shake hands. They were both with—Zaffar hesitated, having introduced them—the IAEA. The International Atomic Energy Agency. Zaffar himself, Nurul observed, with slight amusement, was in a dark business suit and had received a smart haircut that partially hid the grey.

'So, then, you must bring me up to date on recent developments,' Nurul said.

'That's exactly what we intend to do,' Zaffar replied.

Sajjad looked at his watch, took a moment, and excused himself. 'I'll be back soon,' he said and left the room.

'Friday prayer,' Zaffar explained.

'Shall we say ours here?' Zamil asked.

'Why not?' Nurul replied.

They spaced themselves out and said their midday prayer. The three visitors already had a lunch date at the Pakistan High Commission, and meetings thereafter, so it was agreed that they would visit Nurul Islam at his home at eleven the next morning. Zaffar would fly out that evening, the two others the following morning.

'Actually, I'm on my way to see my daughter in Boston,' Zaffar explained afterwards, brushing the dust off his knees. 'I thought why not stop over and see my old friend in London, bring him up to date, and I invited these two chaps to come over. They were desperate to meet you.'

Zamil looked embarrassed. 'Yes, sir,' he said sheepishly. 'This is an honour.'

Before Nurul could learn more from them, all three of his visitors were gone. Is this how far apart we've drifted, he mused, that he only drops in and out? The last time we saw each other was in Rome; since then, no contact. I haven't done much either, to stay in touch. Something happened there, the air between us altered, and we became shy of each other. And now? The suit, the pen, the shoes. The haircut. And he sounds different somehow. If India …, he had said … then he would join. And he has joined. Senior scientist, big shot. Government servant. Zaffar Khan, my friend. Used to be a regular chap.

Zaffar arrived with his companions the next day at five before eleven. Beaming smiles for Sakina Begum, with a box of special Lahori namkeen, presents for the three kids—an embroidered cloth bag, a signed cricket ball, a handcrafted pencil box. 'Bhabhi,' he said to Sakina, 'we can't eat lunch but we'll have your famous tea.'

Nurul watched in amusement as Sakina gave Zaffar Khan a glare. 'You'll have tea here and then lunch,' she said flatly and went away to prepare.

Zaffar threw up his hands. 'When will I learn?' Then he said, 'You're a lucky fellow, Nurul Islam.'

'I know,' Nurul replied.

The two young men said they wanted to do some shopping, they would be back at two, and they would eat out. So it was agreed.

After lunch—vegetable biriyani, chicken curry, daal, and roti—and when the two younger men had returned, the four of them sat down in the living room.

'You have a place I can lie down, after that lunch?' Zaffar joked as Sakina left them.

'You are always welcome,' she said.

'Well,' Nurul asked, 'what's going on in our holy homeland these days?'

'It's serious, Nurul,' Zaffar said. 'We've come with a special request from high up. A plea. And you must listen.'

'So it's not just to see your old friend?'

'That also.'

They began.

'Nurul,' Zaffar said. 'I'm telling you in confidence that we have information that Indira Gandhi during a secret visit to BARC in Bombay gave it a thumbs-up to go ahead and test a nuclear device. Deterrence is the only option for Pakistan. We must follow suit, and you must come on side.'

'How do you know about this thumbs-up?'

Zaffar picked up his tea, which Sakina had brought. He exchanged looks with his companions.

'I'll tell you, but in strictest confidence. Hear me and forget about it. There's an informer at BARC, not high-level, but enough to pick up the buzz after Mrs G's visit. And there's an agent in Delhi ... and an American spy also in Delhi who plays both sides, and we have partial access to his information. This is highly confidential. I repeat.'

Nurul gave a long sigh. His heart was racing. 'And these fellows?' He looked at Sajjad and Zamil. 'They are privy to this—'

'They are at the IAEA, which has been monitoring India's nuclear program. They know what's what, though they are here on personal visits. And it's true they were anxious to meet you. You know that Bhabha had declared publicly that India could test a device within two years if it desired.'

'I knew that.'

'So.'

'So?'

'Bhabha died, there was another war, there is a new regime—Mrs Gandhi. Hawkish.'

Homi J. Bhabha had always championed a nuclear-armed India. Nurul had met him once at Los Alamos and found him somewhat arrogant. BARC was named after him.

'In two years India will have tested a nuclear device,' Zaffar said.

'A peaceful one. A PNE?'

'As they say, the difference between a Peaceful Nuclear Explosive and an actual bomb is only the exterior paint. You know that. Deterrence is the only policy option, Nurul. They'll have the bomb, we must have ours.'

'What do you want me to say?'

'Join the effort, sir. Give us your leadership,' pleaded Sajjad Khan.

'If they had Bhabha, we have Nurul Islam,' said his companion with feeling.

'Not only your genius, but your name. It will make a difference. Our trademark.'

'If Bhabha becomes the father of the Indian bomb, Nurul Islam will become—'

'Yaaro, stop,' Nurul said with a hollow laugh, raising his hand. But the atmosphere had lightened and it seemed to his guests that he had acceded. Zaffar finished his masala chai with relish. In the brief ensuing silence, he sensed something different and turned to Nurul.

Nurul said, softly, 'Two years ago, Zaffar, you were against a nuclear Pakistan.'

'Well, now I'm for it.' Spoken a little harshly.

'You seem to have done well by that decision.'

That came out too quickly, thoughtlessly, and Zaffar's mouth opened in disbelief. For a moment no word emerged. The eyes that had sparkled with pleasure only moments before seemed to pop out. He exploded.

'My friend, if you are accusing me of—' His voice rising, he stood up, almost frothing, waving his finger. 'You've not done badly yourself either, sir, sitting on your arse, getting fat, forgetting … forgetting your close collaborator … flirting with young women—does *she*'—he pointed to the door—'know of your goings-on …'

Nurul had hit a raw spot. He'd been flippant; no, cruel. If his friend's information was correct, and it seemed to be, then he had a strong case. And he had stopped over in London to convince Nurul Islam to give the project his blessing. How could he have made that crass insinuation? He raised his hands in apology.

'I'm sorry. I overstepped. Forgive me. How could I say such a thing. You may be right about deterrence … but I don't feel it in my conscience to be part of a nuclear weapons project. You have enough smart people with you and I know you will succeed. But I would still like to speak for a nuclear-free world.'

'All right. You will be ostracized and left behind. You could at least have agreed for the sake of your beleaguered community.'

They embraced warmly, emotionally, forgave each other repeatedly, and parted.

'What was that about?' Sakina asked. 'I've never heard Zaffar Sahab shout like that. What did you say to him?'

'The world has left us behind, Sakie.'

He was bothered too by Zaffar's taunt, *forgetting your close collaborator* … David Mason. Zaffar should know better. Their mutual taunts were different … or were they? To agree to build a bomb, even if it made sense, was no small capitulation. And then to live fatly by it. A daughter in Boston. The fees. But so what? We could all do with some help. He's a good man.

Am I simply a coward? Seeking cover behind an illusion? There will never be a nuclear-free world. Deterrence could prevent a war, any kind of war, and therefore save lives. And yet how long can such a face-off last—you shoot and I shoot and we both die? The image of his tutor Mr Rajan came to his mind. Murdered during a frenzy of communal hatred. And Sharmila. Play, Nurul Islam! He wouldn't.

Now I'm an enemy to my nation.

Sakina Begum had been tense all evening, not said a word of greeting when he returned from the college, and later made a few perfunctory remarks, said nothing during dinner except when she snapped so sharply at Muni that she herself came to tears.

'What is it, jaan?' he asked. 'What's troubling you?'

Later, when the kids were in bed and they had retired to the living room with their teas, he asked, 'Something happened? Someone die? A letter from home?'

The news came on but neither showed interest. She was still quiet, sitting upright. Once she stifled a sob.

'Come on, you have to tell me what's up, Sakie. I'm your husband!'

'Husband?'

She got up and returned after a moment, threw three photographs on his lap and sat down. 'This, my husband.'

Two of the photos slipped to the floor and he picked them up. Four by three inches, colour. Of him and Hilary. He felt sick suddenly; it was as if the ground below had tilted, nothing was quite the same, nothing would ever be the same. He remembered the man with the Polaroid in Rome, but these in his hands were sharp, professional prints. Such an invasion, such an attack, what to tell her, he wasn't even sure where the affair was going, how to explain that this was a mere possibility, a proposal, I would have come to you for permission as required, I still care for you, I've realized how much I love you, but there are certain needs and it's not *that* but an understanding, an ability to communicate in a different way, seeing the world with different eyes … Oh God.

'Will you let me explain?'

'What is there to explain? You were planning to give me a talaak, just like that!'

'No, my dear.'

'Then what is this?' The anger restrained, like a taut string ready to snap. When had he seen her like this? Not once. Sparks in her eyes, mouth firm. 'What have I done? Have I been short of anything? Have I not been a good mother and wife?'

'You have been everything to me, meri jaan. Let me explain—'

'Explain.'

As though she were foreign to him. All that love and affection had, only briefly, he hoped, melted away.

'First, tell me. How did these come to you?'

'Motorcycle courier.'

'Any address on the envelope? Any note?'

'No. Just the photos. I don't need more.'

'I met this girl … this young woman, student of Abe Rosenfeld … when I went to visit him in Cambridge—the other one. And just that. There was something.'

'What something? Something you don't get from me. What all you men want. *Chut*.'

He was stunned. She continued.

'Yes, I know that language too, I am from Pirmai. That's what you Punjabi men want, a white woman's *chut*! I was not refusing. You didn't want to do it.'

'I did not do *it* with her. And please don't use such language. It doesn't become you.'

She waited.

'I could talk to her—about other things. There was just the attraction …'

'So you thought, Give the wife a talaak-talaak-talaak like a good Muslim, let Sakina Begum go.'

'No.'

'Then?'

'I thought I could marry her.'

She paused, taking this in, breathing hard.

'And have two wives. One to do the chores and one—'

He stopped her before she could get into that trove of Punjabi expletives that seemed to have emerged from some hidden vein.

'Your brother has two wives. You did not say anything then. You welcomed the new wife.'

'My brother is my brother, and I am I.'

'Yes. You are you. And I would never give you talaak.'

'And she agreed, this wonderful white woman you can talk to?'

'No.'

In bed, both on their backs looking up, wide-eyed, sleepless, entertaining this monster that had appeared between them in their thus-far flawless married life. Flawless? He knew that she was crying, while defending the fortress that was her married home.

'What can she give you that I can't? I was always ready. Ready with food, ready with love. Ready for *it*. You didn't want. Ready for children. Always waiting for you. Proud of you.'

'Yes.'

'Did you do it with her?'

'No. I told you.'

'But in the photo …'

'Just an embrace.'

'Some embrace. I am too Punjabi for you.'

'Yes. But I love you for it.' He heard her barely audible *hm*. 'It's just that there is something else—'

'I am not educated.'

'It's not that.' But in a sense, yes. 'It was something different …' How to explain.

'What's her name?'

'Hilary.'

'Hilary. Like hilarious.'

They both started giggling.

'She said no. Now what?'

'I don't know …'

After a moment's silence between them, she cuddled up to him and he held her close. She fell asleep. This Punjabi wife of his had been his anchor; such a solid anchor that he was not always conscious of it. A habit, a pleasant lovely habit he woke up to and returned home to. Now he was adrift in the vast ocean of life.

He thought of Hilary and her shocked expression when he proposed to her in Rome. Her tearful face. Betrayal, she called it. Uncivilized. Did he regret having encouraged her? No, they had drifted and then just flown into each other like magnets. Hard to explain, impossible to rationalize, it just happened. Like lightning. Back in Pakistan they might have sent him to a sheikh to be exorcized … his success after all had been attributed to God's grace. Had it spoilt him in the end? Things had just come to him … and so did he think he could just take without a thought about its goodness? But he was a good man, he believed that.

Where could those photos have come from? They were sharp and focused, taken by someone who had been watching, someone other than that Polaroid man. Someone sent to watch? This was a personal attack on him. He thought of the anonymous letters. But from an argument in physics regarding precedence to something so personal? Why not. Even that argument about precedence was about his personal integrity. He had been called a cheat.

The next morning she woke up with him, but she waited awhile before following him down. She made tea for them while he said his prayers in his office, and brought it for him when he sat down at his desk. She took the extra chair in his office. They sipped their tea, dipped their biscuits. He observed a stiffness in her manner, a resolve. He smiled at her.

'So you are going to give up on this girl?'

'I don't want to. I explained to you what I would like.'

'What you would like may be different from what you will get.'

Again the Rolling Stones. They sat in silence for a while.

'You realize that those who sent you the photos will make them public?'

'My shame, my whole *izzat* hung out like laundry.'

'I'm involved too, Sakina. I too have izzat.'

On his way out later, holding Muni's hand, he embraced her at the door. She was awkward.

The boys hustled out a few minutes later and the house fell silent. Sakina Begum sat at the dining table for a while, brooded, then with a resolve made she went upstairs and took her shower. Having dressed, she went to the wardrobe and removed David Mason's box and took it to the bed. She mulled over the remaining contents—what she had not given to Susan—a few letters, a number of photos, and the notes. Among the letters was the incomplete draft of his letter to Nurul, and Nurul's reply, dated a few days later. Nurul had once confessed to her that he felt guilty not acknowledging David enough and up front regarding the unification theory. And she had said to him that David would have told him if he thought so. She wondered about that now. His letter began, 'Dear Nurul, of course I understand. It's the different ways we are—' then stopped. Nurul's was short, begging David to think again about his decision. He would be missed at the department. He didn't say he would be missed as a close friend, but that was the implication. They should have made up, she thought.

Why did Susan want the notes?

This was her secret, her memories of their outings, and this box—a part of him. Her own small guilt regarding herself and David, but they had stayed within the bounds of respectability. But not Islamic respectability. She touched the spot on her cheek.

There were two urgent phone calls from Pakistan the next morning—they had to call back from London each time, it being cheaper that way at both ends and with less likelihood of the line breaking. The first was from her parents and sister Rukhsana, who immediately began by scolding Sakina Begum.

'I've done nothing!' Sakina cried. 'He just went to America and found this gori ...'

'Are you sure you've done nothing, given him everything he wants, satisfied all his needs?'

'Yes, I have,' she sobbed.

Her father came on.

'Nurul Sah'b, you are wise. An understanding, renowned personality. You should forgive her, if she's displeased you in any way, she's not a bad girl—'

'Abbas Sah'b, my dear father, she's done nothing wrong! She's an exemplary wife. She's perfect, she's done nothing wrong. It's just that—'

'Then what's the matter, son?'

'I've only asked her if I could marry again.'

'Then explain the photos in all the papers? Embracing that American woman. The rumours we hear ...'

'What photos?'

'Two photos. In all the papers. English, Urdu, Punjabi, Sindhi. They can't be explained away. You know zina is a sin.'

Nurul was struck speechless, Sakina watching. 'How—' Nurul began and stopped. 'I have to see these photos myself.'

'We will send them to you.'

'All right, but don't worry, Abbas Sah'b, Sakina is a good wife. She will always be with me.' He squeezed Sakina's arm beside him.

He put down the receiver and they made their way to the living room and sat down in silence. The children were still in their rooms.

He was stunned by the intensity of the attack on him, its pointedness. Anyone in Pakistan who could read in any language now knew of Professor Nurul Islam's transgression. The great scientist, pride of the nation, cheating on his wife, with a white woman to boot. An ordinary man after all. He wondered what the newspapers had actually written. He wondered what they were saying in his community, in Pirmai.

The phone rang again, as it had to.

His father, Ghulam Ali, said they were all embarrassed by the publicity. But the hullaballoo would soon die out. What was Nurul's intention?

'I've asked this woman to marry me, Abba.'

His father paused a moment.

'Second wife?'

'Yes, Abba.'

'Does she agree, this woman?'

'No.'

'And Sakina Begum, does she agree?'

'No, Abba.'

'Well then. What is your intention now? Talaak?'

'No, Abba. I don't want a divorce. Unless she wants it. But why is it anybody's business? This is my private affair.'

'Son, for a mere perfumer and book-hawker like me, it is OK, nobody cares. Private is private. But you are famous. You are public. You are a hero. And therefore there is no private. You have enemies, you told me so. And here, too, there is agitation against you. They will not let you be.'

And his mother said, 'You go ahead, Nurul. Don't worry. Sakina will understand. It is a woman's lot. You've given her a good life over there. We are praying for you both. Look after yourself, and give a *nice* little pinch to little Muni—'

His father snatched away the phone. 'Khuda hafiz, Nur,' which was echoed by his mother in the background. God preserve you.

A London paper carried a small item. Nurul Islam was not that famous in England, politicians' sex lives were more titillating. But at his department there were smirks and knowing smiles. Embarrassing, but nobody thought it a shame. There was some envy. He shouldn't have been caught. Past the first lecture, when the students gazed at him in disbelief, and he said, 'I'm still the same person! No horns yet,' and they laughed, it all returned to normal.

Pete Sorensen called.

'Pete, you heard.'

'Wait till you hear this piece of news, my friend! In your world you hear only about the other woman. In my world the excitement is about the other current, the neutral current. We've found it, Nurul! The neutral has been discovered!'

The neutral current was the key prediction of the Islam-Rosenfeld model besides the God particle. It was a version of the weak force not known before, in which the initial particles were the same as the final particles—unlike the long-known version in which a neutron emitted a proton, an electron, and a neutrino.

'It has? Well, well. That should give the buggers something to talk about. Nurul Islam is still batting!'

'You're not out. Now what's this about … Hilary? You two were going on a bit too openly in Rome, I must say, Nurul. Everyone knew.'

'Yes, but photographs? Who would be crass enough to do that, not to me only but our families—mine and Sakina's.'

'They found out over there, in Pakistan?'

'Yes, the photos were sent to newspapers in Pakistan. The entire nation has seen them, so to speak. And I'm wondering who's responsible.'

'There was that young Pakistani guy taking pictures in Rome …'

'Only with a Polaroid. These are professional-quality. They were sent also to Sakie.'

'Wow. You have big-time enemies, Nurul. But enjoy the glory of the neutral current and forget the rest. The world will forget about it soon.'

'What was Abe's reaction?'

'More excited than you. "God exists!" he said. And he's usually the calmer one.'

He called Abe, who said, 'You've got your bottle of champagne out?'

Nurul chuckled. 'In a manner of speaking. Now what?'

'We celebrate—and we open a bottle when we meet.'

'Yes, we celebrate.'

But how? When he would pick up his pencil and stare at the pad in front of him, he could not find that drive. As though there were an impediment in the brain; or the arm or finger muscles had atrophied. Could this be possible? In all his life, since he got over Sharmila's betrothal, he had never lost that inner energy, the fever that pushed him, even when idle, to write an empty formula on a pad; a simple number sequence and wonder if it had a meaning; a geometric pattern and wonder if it was continuous; an algebra and wonder if it was known ... or to attempt to derive from a known algebra some expression, some Lagrangian equation that contained in its concision some secret of the physical world. Now he felt impotent, shuffling papers, reading student reports or journal articles, pretending he had ideas. He would think of David. I should have told him that I had developed and extended the formalism we had worked on, that it became my part of Islam-Rosenfeld. I would like to acknowledge that joint work, our collaboration ...

He was aware of Sakina's eyes upon him from some angle behind him as he fumbled with his mind at his desk, and wondered if she were gloating, celebrating his decline. Could that be, could love turn to hate or indifference after more than twenty years together bound by destiny, it seemed, to spend their lives together until he or she, more likely he, would die? All those years of a bonded life couldn't be washed away. Something would remain, some residue. They had children ... He had hurt her terribly, and he would never be able to undo that.

She had embarrassed him at first, with her ill-fitting dresses on a dumpy figure, the clumsy hair and wrong lipstick, the horrible accent like a frog from the mouth, as he had imagined it in his frustration. He would scold her and she would cry and he would apologize, aware that outside of physics he himself hardly fit into English society, but his accomplishments had earned him a respect and confidence and he could cope and learn and maintain a thick skin. Once, at a formal dinner hosted by the dean of sciences, to cut a chop she inadvertently held the wrong knife—the butter knife—and stabbed at the piece on her plate and it slid off. Utter silence, which a faculty member fielded expertly, but one of the other guests, a woman, broke off into a peal then stopped.

'Give me talaak,' she had sobbed back home when he scolded her. 'I'm not fit for you, just an embarrassment. You're ashamed of me!'

'Yes, you make me ashamed, sometimes, but I'm not going to give you talaak—just learn! Be careful when you are not sure how to go about something, observe how others are doing it. Practise if you must.'

They were painful moments. He had actually thought of sending her back home, fearing she would thwart his career. But they had survived. Una Mason had helped. Sakina slimmed down. And then the kids came, and they were a family of Londoners.

One day, the same woman who had muffled a laugh at the dean's dinner, Mrs Alarakhia, called for a favour. 'I would like to invite you and your wife to dinner. A small, informal one. We need advice for our son. You see, he's good in maths ...' Nurul declined, asked her to come for tea instead. Sakina's territory, and she had done admirably. Nurul couldn't recall what he told the boy, in the fifth form, perhaps that he should follow his dream, but the women became fast friends, laughed about that incident. We're in the same boat, aren't we. We all started like that, we all had to learn, at home or in schools or by experience. You think the English knew how to behave in India? Just watch them eat curry with roti.

She was on her way to attend a summer school in Erice, Sicily, and had allowed herself two days to spend in London. She'd walked into Imperial College like any student, and surprised Nurul outside his office, even though he was aware she was coming. He let her in.

'Nurul, you must be delighted. The neutral current has been found, and your theory has been renormalized by a Dutch genius. Everyone is talking about it!'

He grinned. 'I guess.'

'But you look terrible. What's happened to you?'

'It's really nice to see you, Hil. You think you'll get that fellowship in Cambridge? You'll be close by.'

'Too close? Abe wants me to consider Austin.'

'Still trying to protect you? How's he doing—after the separation?'

'He looks happy. Janis too. She now lives in Newton.'

'How amazing. Some of us just mess up our private lives.'

'Do you think you've messed up your life? Or I have messed up your life?'

'It just became more complicated, with you in it.'

Messy and painful, how to admit that to her? Why do we walk with open eyes into trouble? But we do. Something in us drives us on. Dares us to jump. And we jump. I had a perfect marriage, a balanced life, then you came along. And that balance was gone.

'But I want you in it,' he said.

She smiled. 'Would you like to meet this afternoon?'

What was it that just drove him to her, reservations and guilt aside?

'I'll be free at four. Where?'

'I'm staying at the Hargraves in Russell Square. Meet me outside.'

They had tea at the British Library. He reached out and they held hands briefly, sparely, only their fingers, tentative. Now why did they do it, when it was not working out?

They discussed the photos, which had caused only a ripple of amusement where she was (Janis had called, Abe had wagged a finger at her). He told her of Sakina's reaction when she received them in London, and the scandal back in Pakistan when they were published there. She pressed his hand.

'How did we end up like this, neither here nor there?' he asked.

'You tell me.'

'I'll tell you. What I proposed was the only solution possible for me, for us to be together. You didn't like it, understandably, and so here we are.'

'You didn't spell it out.'

'You didn't give me a chance.' Called me uncivilized.

'Can you meet for dinner?'

He shook his head. 'Same time, here tomorrow? You have no reason to, I know. I shouldn't ask.'

'I'll wait for you,' she said. 'We can then decide what to do.'

She knew exactly what she wanted to do. That night she had dinner by herself on Russell Square, and in the evening she perused the program of the summer school. It was named after Ettore Majorana, an Italian physicist who had disappeared without a trace in 1938, while on his way from Palermo to Naples. He had not been seen, until recently someone claimed to have sighted him in Venezuela. She had studied his equations.

She mused over the names of this and past years' lecturers. The summer school had quite deliberately ignored Nurul Islam over the years; he had never been invited. His commanding personality apparently rubbed European decorum the wrong way. She had wondered if his manner was a front, the pre-emptive tactic of the alien, always the alien. He had told her emphatically that science, especially physics, had no boundaries; that was true, of course, but only in its purest sense. Scientists were humans, after all, mostly men. They could be vindictive, jealous, bigoted. As a woman she herself often felt like an alien in her field, but without the confidence of genius to shield her.

The next morning Hilary took the Tube to Harrow-on-the-Hill station, from which she went by taxi to go see Sakina Begum. She went unannounced, reaching the house at half past ten.

Sakina Begum opened the door and stared for a moment at the white woman, who said, 'Sakina Begum? Mrs Islam?'

'I know who you are. Hilary.'

'Yes.'

'Come in.'

Sakina Begum took Hilary to the sitting room, and Hilary looked around, thinking, This is his space, this is where he lives and comes home. This is his wife. Yes, she would have tea, she replied to the query, and Sakina Begum brought tea for them, in separate cups, mixed with milk and sugar. He had described the tea and the ritual to her. Sakina put down a plate of cookies.

'This is our special chai,' Sakina Begum said. 'With spices. He likes it. With biscuits.'

'It's very good,' Hilary said. She did like it.

'Mrs Islam—can I call you Sakina Begum?'

Sakina Begum nodded. Her husband of course called her Sakie or jaan.

'Sakina Begum, you know why I am here ... I wanted to meet you ... to know you. I love your husband and—'

'I love him too. I was first.'

Hilary thought she would laugh. And cry. It was difficult for her. In front of her was a beautiful, solid, traditional woman whom her husband had brought to England. Hilary nodded under that appraising look.

'And he loves me. He loves you too, of course. Very much. Which is why I've come.'

'He wants to marry you.'

'Yes.'

'We have been married twenty-three years. I have been his wife and cared for him.'

'No one can deny that. You have been absolutely ... wonderful,' Hilary said, just managing to avoid a guilt-ridden emphasis. *Perfect* was perhaps the right word, she thought.

A long silence followed, in which she felt she was being judged, evaluated. The sound of a sip; the tinkle of a cup. Was it right to come?

But I had to see her, I want to know her. She smiled inanely at Sakina Begum, who spoke finally.

'And you will agree to marry him and become a second wife? You are an educated woman, an American lady. Do your parents agree?'

'My mother is dead. My father discourages me—but he will not coerce me. I understand your position, Sakina Begum—as much as I can, please believe me. But sometimes—'

Sakina Begum spoke quietly in a flat voice.

'You talk of love. What do you know of love? You are young. In your society love can come and go. On and off like with a switch. It is not love. Love is what you grow from a little seed, and take care of, and let it grow, and there are flowers and fruit. Love is when you grow old together. In sickness and health, as you people say in church, but you people don't wait, you just leave—'

'Please, Mrs Islam. Not everybody is like that. My father nursed my mother until she died.'

'Your father. Did he marry again?'

Hilary said nothing. She looked around. The living room was small, modest. There were family photos on the walls, and a piece of Arabic calligraphy, also framed. A pleasant odour. And everything in its place. She turned to Sakina Begum and said, 'You keep a very fine house.'

Sakina Begum asked her about her family, then asked when she was leaving for Boston. Hilary explained she would depart London tomorrow at two, and go to Sicily for two weeks before returning to Boston. She stood up to leave. Coming out of the living room she saw, on the right, at the foot of the passageway, a study. 'His?' Hilary asked. Sakina Begum nodded. 'Go, look,' she said, in a sudden inexplicable act of kindness. Hilary stepped towards it. A medium-sized room, the curtains at the window facing the desk were pulled aside and looked out on the street, letting in the midmorning light. A bookshelf. His certificates from Government College, Lahore, and Cambridge hung on one wall facing the desk, which had two photocopied articles on it, and two books, one of them the Quran.

This has been his everything, she thought. Everything he's been, his universe. And I intrude.

'Thank you, Sakina Begum. And I am truly sorry for having intruded.' She tried to explain but stopped herself at the ambiguity of what she'd just said, and asked hesitantly, 'If he asks your permission to marry me, what will you say?'

'He has already asked.'

She was too afraid to inquire what the answer was. As she walked down the suburban street, she felt those dark eyes upon her back, and saw two neighbours who had come to the door. One was an Indian or Pakistani woman in traditional dress. An Asian man stood watching from the newsagent's. Hilary felt strange, accused. But I did it, she said to herself. I had to do it. Dad would be proud of me. But I won't tell Nurul. She can, if she wants to.

Sakina Begum brooded long over the visit, over her situation. The kids came home and had their snacks, and as soon as they were finished, the boys wanted to go to the park to play cricket, and she said yes. The neighbourhood was safe and friendly. Nurul Islam had on two occasions gone to speak to students at the high school, and he had judged a science contest. A pretty girl, she thought of Hilary, not actress-like, just good-looking. Young, and men are men. She was a physicist too, Sakina smiled. So Nurul didn't lose his mind over some gum-chewing, dolled-up fluff. Father was a doctor. Went to church. And she herself? Father selling shoes on Muhammad Ali Jinnah Road. A brother with already two wives.

Nurul came home an hour later than usual, as he had the day before. He hardly touched the pakodas she had fried earlier. Looked a bit guiltily at her.

When the kids had rushed upstairs, while they were still at the table, she asked, 'Are we still going to see the James Bond film at the Carlton?'

'Of course,' he said. 'I don't want to miss it.'

Then she said, quite out of the blue, 'Do you love me?'

'What kind of question is that? I'll not answer it.'

She paused. He smiled at her.

'If you love me, what would you give up for me?'

'Anything. I'd give up anything for you, Sakie. Except my faith and my physics.'

He could have said, and except Hilary, but she already knew that painful fact. He didn't ask what she would give up for him. But she answered it. 'If you want to go ahead and marry that Hilary, then you have my permission. That is my love gift to you.'

The next morning he met Hilary at a small café in Bloomsbury. It was his second breakfast. When they had ordered, he stretched out his hand and took hers.

'So you are leaving today … it was nice seeing you again.'

'Yes … And now? What?'

He took his moment.

'She has agreed,' he said slowly. 'I can marry you—if you want it.'

'Are you sure?' she asked. 'Sakina Begum agreed to that?'

I was first, she had said to Hilary. What do you know of love? Twenty-three years of marriage.

'Of course, I'm sure. I'm sorry—I forgot you had not accepted my proposal. But she brought it up herself and gave me permission, so I'm telling you.'

Her love gift to me, she said. But if I tell you that, I'll probably never see you again.

She replied softly, 'Then I accept, Nurul. I accept. You knew I would, or I wouldn't have come to London to see you.'

'You'll be my wife?'

'Yes. I won't deny I'm nervous. What would I have to do as the other wife? Cook? Press your feet at night?'

'Just love me. And accept my love and trust me.'

'Really?'

'We'll work it out. As long as you love me.'

He went to her and she stood up and went into his arms. A few eyebrows got raised. And their owners didn't even know that the woman had just accepted to become the second wife.

Sakina Begum was hurting deeply, yet she knew this was what it had to be. A calamity had fallen on her, like a landslide in those remote cold areas of Pakistan. She had often wondered, how do you pick yourself up from such disasters, when you've lost your home, and go on? She knew he loved her, but she was no longer exclusive. Had she ever been exclusive? There had always been his physics to take him away from her. She had joked with him sometimes, 'Physics is your second wife.' Now fate had played a joke on her. Now there was the shadow of a third person on their relationship. Did this American girl see the first wife's shadow on her relationship with Nurul? What was it like, this relationship, this intimacy? She shuddered to think about it. She cried when the thought came.

But then she had her own little secret, her own shadow from the past.

It was afternoon when she picked up the phone a few days later and called Susan Mason in York.

'Susan? It's Mrs Islam. How are you? … I've thought about the matter we discussed, and I can give you your father's notes, if you are still interested.'

Come what may, she thought. Come what may. I will keep the memory of David Mason alive. All else is in God's hands now. 'Bismillah.'

It was a simple Muslim ceremony in London, at the house of Nurul Islam's colleague John Hemmings, conducted by the imam of a liberal London mosque. The marriage would not be legally recognized in the UK, which fact was irrelevant to the couple. Hilary's father had come over and, much to Nurul Islam's surprise, Abe Rosenfeld, making a stopover on his way to give a lecture in Sweden. A few of Hilary's fellow graduate students had also made it, using this opportunity to tour Britain. A handful of faculty from Imperial's physics department were present, and the imam had brought members of his own family and a few friends. Rather shamelessly, Major Iftikhar had sought an invitation, ostensibly to bring his government's good wishes. All were seated on the floor in the formal drawing room, where the larger furniture had been moved to a side. The imam, Sheikh Sadiq, insisted that the male and female members separate into two groups, then beckoned the couple to come forward and sit beside him, facing the congregation; when they had done so, he began the ceremony.

Nurul Islam had left his house that morning wearing a light-grey, freshly pressed suit; the shirt and red tie were new. Sakina Begum followed him to the door and there, as he turned around to face her, she managed a thin smile and, reaching out, cracked her knuckles on the sides of her head to bless him in the traditional manner. 'So long, jaan,' he said and walked over to the waiting taxi. The three children stood some distance behind their mother, watching. Closing the door behind him she went and sat down in the living room and softly cried. He would be returning home, but for how long? And not the same man. She had volunteered to help Hilary with a saree, but Hilary had declined, she would wear a white dress, not showy but good enough for the occasion, and a light headscarf as instructed by the imam.

The imam began by reciting the Fateha, the first sura from the Quran; then solemnly he announced that they were all gathered to witness the marriage of Professor Nurul Islam and 'our sister' Mumtaz Begum. Uttering a few quotes, he proceeded to give a small speech about the sanctity of marriage and the duties of the husband and wife towards each other. He ended with 'Now you take your vows. Are you ready?' They were ready, and in a raised voice he asked the bride, three times, 'Do you, Mumtaz Begum, of your own free will, accept Nurul Islam as your husband before these witnesses and before God?' She answered, 'I do.' He repeated the process for the groom. When that was done, he drew out a ledger book and asked them to sign their names under a long list of those who had preceded them in taking the marriage vows. John Hemmings was the witness. The imam announced that the couple were now married, and concluded with a verse from the Quran. Nurul and Hilary got up and thanked the guests and the Hemmingses for their hospitality.

The guests now stood up awkwardly and with obvious relief from the floor, wonderstruck at having just witnessed an unusual event, and began introducing themselves. Photos were taken, and food was served, a modest English repast of sandwiches and a pie. Mrs Hemmings had refused to smell up her house with Pakistani cuisine, but she allowed a recording of joyously sensual Punjabi wedding songs to be played.

Dr Chase was the first one to come bless the couple. He embraced his daughter and shook hands with the groom, whom he was meeting for the first time.

Abe Rosenfeld came over, followed by the students, to wish the couple a happy life together.

'You've taken a brave step, you two,' he said. 'Good luck and behave yourselves. Don't worry what the world says.'

'We won't,' Hilary replied, then broke down briefly when he embraced her.

'So, have you become a Muslim—Mumtaz, is it?' he asked her.

She laughed. 'Of course not! The name was only a formality.'

She knew instinctively that she had goofed there, but there was little choice with such a direct and sudden question. It would be added to the charges being toted up in Lahore against her husband.

'Janis sends her best wishes,' Abe said.

Dr Chase, on a walk the next morning, convinced an Anglican priest at the small St. Mary's in Bloomsbury to bless the couple inside his domain. So that afternoon Nurul Islam and Hilary Chase also took the Anglican vows. The following day, the doctor took a train to a town in Dorset, and when he returned he had on him a placid, dreamy look. Over dinner with Hilary and Nurul that night, when his daughter inquired about his journey, he gave the briefest nod, with as close to a blush as he was capable. Without saying a word, she stood up and gave him a hug. Something in her father's past had been laid to rest.

Out of respect for Sakina Begum, there was no honeymoon, except for the three days he and Hilary spent together at a hotel, during which they visited museums and roamed about London, exchanging stories about their lives. It was the longest he had gone in many years without touching his pencil to his pad. He accompanied her to the airport when she left to defend her thesis. Back in her department, she was apprehensive at first about receiving strange looks and facing hostility from faculty. But this was the early seventies. She was as likely to be accosted by an orange-clad, tambourine-banging Hare Krishna devotee on Harvard Square as a Jesus devotee standing outside her apartment building with the Book and the Message. Everything was kosher in the social realm of the day.

At her graduation, her father and Jill were present, and after the ceremony, when she brought him her diploma, wearing gown and mortarboard, saying, 'Another doctor in the family, Dad,' he replied, 'I'm proud of you, girl. So would your mother be.'

Jill added, 'Yeah, at least one success story. Not bad.'

They went for lunch at a Buddhist restaurant that Jill had picked.

Hilary Chase took the fellowship she had been offered by Cambridge University, with the life-modelling group. She had been recommended by Freeman Dyson, who had missed the Nobel Prize in physics by a whisker, being the fourth of the eligible candidates when the Nobel limit was three.

He was at Princeton and had read and liked her thesis. Nurul Islam helped her settle into a small house in Cambridge, where he would come to spend weekends with her. Later he added a weekday to these visits.

His relationships at home inevitably altered. He could not have predicted how, but he tried hard to keep things close to the norm that the house had known. It was impossible, of course. That world had broken like an eggshell. A new presence had come around in their lives, affecting everything. To the boys he had revealed a depth in himself they could not have imagined, he had become a stranger, someone they both felt they had not known at all. Was this the same father who had made them study, brought presents for them every time he travelled, discussed cricket with them? On his good days recited Urdu poetry in the house, teased their mother? Nothing was the same anymore, and they resented that. Mirza threw a tantrum once, throwing things around in a frenzy, until Sakina Begum screamed at him and broke down. Rahim, who always took things quietly, told his father of the taunts they had received in school about their lecherous Muslim father, and the snide remarks they had read in the newspapers. When he said, 'You know the story you told us about Abraham putting a knife to Ismail's throat ...' Nurul drew a sharp breath. To be judged by your offspring. He replied, 'You have a whole life in front of you, son. You too, Mirza. But adults have lives too, they are all too human, and they do the best they can.'

He grieved for their pain, a sadness he couldn't share with Hilary. She had made a big sacrifice herself, for the sake of their love. What girlhood dreams of marriage had she not abandoned?

Muni, his darling Muni, absorbed this new reality without chiding him. To her he was the same father, and occasionally, at what always seemed the right moment, she would come and put her arms around him. She was visibly growing up, and sometimes when he arrived home he would ask for her as 'meri maa,' my mother. Rahim, tall and lanky with the body of a cricketer, was preparing to go to the University of London, to stay close to his mother. Mirza wanted to follow in his father's footsteps and go to Cambridge to study mathematics.

Sakina Begum's relationship with Nurul acquired distance. She became more involved with women of her extended family who were in London, and in community events related to the Shirazi Islamic mosque that had sprung up. But she remained a proud Mrs Islam, the original and authentic—as she would sometimes quip. Between her and Nurul was a partnership, built on familiarity and experience, and occasional nostalgia. He always claimed to love her, but there was no longer that gentle glowing fire between them that had kept alive the humour, the security, and the warmth in their home.

It was Wednesday morning, and he was at his London home preparing to depart for his office. While perusing the *Guardian* with his second cup of tea, he saw something that startled him. 'Arré—look at this.' He sat upright as he read.

Professor accused

Amidst the speculations and rumours preceding the current year's announcement of the Nobel Prizes, a statement was released to the press by Professor Alf Greiner of the University of Amsterdam with the title 'The Truth about Islam.' He argued that Professor Nurul Islam of Imperial College, London, should not be considered for the Prize for physics for two reasons. According to Dr Greiner, Professor Islam claims credit for the theory known as the Lesser Unification of forces; but he revealed his work on the theory six weeks after receiving the formulation by the American physicist Abe Rosenfeld in a widely distributed preprint. 'He therefore cannot claim discovery,' Dr Greiner wrote. 'Professor Islam had also, in his work, suppressed vital contributions by his junior colleague David Mason,' he continued. David Mason, who was at Cambridge University and Imperial College with Nurul Islam, without explanation left for a teaching job in Nairobi, Kenya, where he later took his own life. Professor Greiner claimed to have in his possession research notes and letters in Dr Mason's writing which substantiate his claim. The letters express his disenchantment with his colleague's practices. 'The Nobel committee for physics should pay heed to this revelation,' Professor Greiner said. Professor Islam, who recently got married unofficially to his second wife, Dr Hilary Chase, an American …

'My, my, my …' Nurul Islam spoke after a long silence. 'Wah. So now they say not only that I copied Abe's result but also suppressed David Mason's contribution. So which is it? Can't be both. Junior colleague indeed!—he was a month older. At least they're out in the open field, where I can meet them. I knew that old man had something to do with that accusation all the time.'

Sakina Begum, who was sitting with him at the table, gave a hiccup. 'What happened? What old man? What accusation?'

'They got hold of David's research notes … and apparently some of our exchanges after he left. Come read this article.'

'Really?' she exclaimed shrilly and came to read over his shoulder.

'Yes. Good, now I have a chance to clarify. He's done me a favour, this man. Don't worry.' He grinned at her startled face and pinched her cheek. 'Don't worry. I've been expecting something of the sort.'

Sitting back, he continued to stare at the paper. 'But how did Greiner get the stuff? And what letters? There were a few, to Baltimore, I think, in which I begged him to come back … It could only be Una … or Susan. How did the girl sound when you spoke with her?' He turned to look at Sakina Begum.

'A little formal … she didn't seem keen to come by to visit us.'

'She didn't have the courtesy even to phone me. How could it end like this? We were so close once.'

'You are her godfather.'

'Yes. How she could go on to gang up with that viper in Amsterdam beats me. There could be another explanation.'

She said nothing.

There were calls at home from two science reporters, which he didn't take. At the department he had a long chat with a very worried John Hemmings—who had also been reached by reporters—and reiterated his position. Finally he allowed the head to reply to any inquiry with the statement that Nurul Islam would come up with an appropriate response in due time. In his graduate classes he sensed a hostile air. How fickle the human heart—they will not even wait for me to say something. One of his students dropped him as an advisor, according to a note from Hemmings. 'Professor Islam is vague in his instructions and then criticizes us.'

After two weeks, Nurul Islam wrote up his response. John Hemmings sent it off on official Imperial College letterhead to the media. First, Nurul Islam stated his birthdate and asked the press to check who was junior, he or David Mason. 'This bit of mathematics does not call for higher algebra'—a sentence deleted by Hemmings. Nurul Islam admitted that when he released the results of his work on Lesser Unification in Oslo, he should have clarified David Mason's contribution in BOLD LETTERS. He had failed to do that and for that he was contrite. The theory was not considered the great breakthrough it became later. He pointed out that since his work with Mason, which had been introductory and speculative—Mason himself did not want it published yet, and others had reached the same stage—he had gone ahead and extended it, using recent breakthroughs by Goldstone in Cambridge and Higgs in Edinburgh; it was this fuller work that he had presented in Oslo. It was true that his Oslo presentation came a few weeks after Abe Rosenfeld's preprint, but his work had already been done and presented at a colloquium at Imperial College. If David Mason had approached him, they would have worked out the credits. David Mason was a dear friend of his and his family's. As for the Nobel, he had already sent a message to the committee through a colleague that he did not wish to be considered for it, and if nevertheless he was ever awarded the Prize, he would decline it. Dr Alf Greiner should not lose sleep over this matter. Nurul Islam had not gone into physics for prizes, though the kudos were welcome encouragement. The privilege of being able to work with some of the great minds of physics was prize enough for a boy from Pirmai, Pakistan. But he, Nurul Islam, did not appreciate the anonymous letters with which he had been pelted, nay stalked, over the last two and a half years, about which Professor John Hemmings of Imperial College, London, and Professor Pete Sorensen of Lund University were well aware, having seen samples.

The *Guardian* published this response in abridged form in its letters section. *Physics World* published the full version post-haste in its next monthly issue. Half a dozen eminent scientists, including Feynman and Rosenfeld, released a joint statement declaring that anonymous accusations had no place in the world of science, whose methods involved proof and evidence. Alf Greiner vehemently denied responsibility for them, saying moreover that he had not intended any double entendre in his reference to Professor Islam in his statement.

Nurul Islam received no more anonymous letters. But then, something pleasant happened. Sakina Begum's attitude towards him suddenly changed, as though a magician had appeared before her and waved a wand. When he arrived at his London home one Monday morning, she greeted him with a smile and gave him his chai with a cake she had specially made. She fed him biryani that evening. This attitude prevailed and he even worried a little that perhaps she was getting soft in the head. Later he realized that this change was in response to the accusations that had been made against him. She had come to stand by his side. She bore his name, she was still his wife with three children.

She could not tell him that the research notes that Alf Greiner had spoken about to the media were most likely those that she had handed over to Susan Mason. She had done that in a huff, and never imagined the intent of their use, to attack her husband in public. This was not what the quiet and decent David Mason would have wanted. He would have been horrified. She had let down his memory, involved him in dirty dealings. Susan Mason had thanked her perfunctorily, as though the material were hers by right. She was wrong. Sakina Begum was left with the feeling that she had handed a dagger to an assassin.

Nurul Islam and Hilary Chase went on to have two children, Jonathan and Aisha. On some weekends, when the two kids were old enough, he would take them with him to London, though it never seemed appropriate for Hilary to be there with him in that other home. Sakina Begum was gracious when the Cambridge kids visited. Muni in particular enjoyed taking Aisha under her wing; the two would go skipping down the street to buy sweets, Muni with her hair now cut short, and Aisha with two small ponytails bobbing behind her. Mirza and Rahim were much older and, if anything, Jonathan was a tolerated pest. At the few public functions where Nurul Islam accepted invitations, the two wives greeted each other warmly and yet with reserve, then kept largely to their separate corners like opposing football coaches.

He doted on the younger kids, especially Aisha, little more than a year younger than her brother. They were the magnets that pulled him towards Cambridge full of anticipation of their welcome, of seeing their happy faces at the window waiting for him, then the two running out to the door to greet him. He now only reluctantly travelled abroad. The tug of home was stronger.

His heart was not into research as before. He was war-weary. 'I've had my run, Hilary,' he said. 'I've no more left in me, and there are all these brilliant young guns cropping up, hungry for glory. Let them go for it.' He read the journals in his own field and tried to keep up, but his grasp on emerging developments grew steadily tenuous. His graduate students completed their degree requirements one by one and left. He did not accept more. He continued to teach but was mellower. Less exciting, some said, but less challenging. Student egos stayed intact.

Hilary, who had fallen in love with the driven, ebullient, competitive Nurul Islam whose mind never stopped ticking, devising questions and answers, always confident yet with doubts, appreciated his stepping back from it all to be with his new family. Yes, he had had his run, and it had been an enviable one. He was not young, had to watch himself. She knew, however—though she never brought it up—that the media controversy had affected him deeply. She had often wondered if he would have been judged so quickly if he had been 'one of them'—a throwaway phrase she had heard him utter only once, and in a flight of humour, but understood instantly. He was different in every way: an Asian Muslim in a white country, a devout Muslim scientist among mostly atheist or agnostic colleagues of Jewish and Christian backgrounds, a persecuted minority in his own country. That nation had made a meal out of his troubles, more so than his host country.

The only big ambition he had remaining now was to fulfil his dream of an international institute of fundamental physics to host scientists from developing countries, for which cause he continued to write letters and travel when required. He shunned public recognition. When the Italian government conferred an honour on him, he politely declined. He made two exceptions. He accepted, after some cajoling from Abe Rosenfeld—a man hard to refuse—a science medal from the president of the United States. It was a private ceremony, but both wives attended. He also accepted a knighthood from the queen of the country that had given him a home; he would not be called Sir Nurul because he remained a citizen of Pakistan.

News of these two honours provoked unexpectedly strong and opposite reactions in Pakistan—'back home,' as he had often thought of it. The English-language papers there exulted in the news, and his small Shirazi community held public celebrations with processions in Shirazi colonies. There were calls to name a street after him in Lahore, where he had attended college. Far as he was from the scene, Nurul Islam knew that the celebrations were foolish and ill-advised; a community like the Shirazis needed to keep a low profile. A lull followed, thankfully, and it seemed that he had slipped out of the public eye. But then a flurry of articles descended upon the Urdu pages, questioning his faith, his morality, his professional integrity, his patriotism. 'Nurul Islam likes wine, white women, and glory,' said one. 'English physicist Paul Dirac is the incarnation of Allah, says Nurul Islam,' said another early headline. 'Allah not aql-e-kul says our hero,' said yet another one, going on to explain that according to Nurul Islam—who belonged to a sect following the notorious heretics of the past, Ibn Arabi and Avicenna—modern physics knew more about the universe than God Himself. And this: 'Nurul Islam writes an equation to describe Allah'—someone had gone to the trouble of digging up the problematic short story he had written for the college magazine. The list of his perfidies went on. His second marriage to a non-Muslim woman was declared haram, and therefore the children were illegitimate. He was called a traitor because—and this was surely classified information—he had refused to work on the development of a Pakistani, so-called Islamic bomb. The final insult, carried in an article in the main English daily, questioned his contribution to the Islam-Rosenfeld theory, with quotes from Alf Greiner, Duncan Harvey, and Susan Mason.

He rang Zaffar Khan to ask how his refusal to contribute to the bomb project could have leaked out. They had long made up since that acrimonious, painful meeting in London, where Zaffar had come to invite him to join the effort. Now each respected the other's position, and they never forgot to call each other every few months. Hello yaar, salam my friend, how are you doing? Gossip, nostalgia. Soon after the wedding Zaffar had come to call on Nurul and Hilary in Cambridge, on his way to the States, and the reunion had ended in laughter and tears.

Zaffar had no answer for Nurul, except to say, 'Fame has its price, yaar. Let the bearded ones have their day. Your reputation will outlive them.'

That was hardly comforting.

'And Nurul, dear friend, closer to me than my heart and liver—control yourself. Stop talking about Dirac, Einstein, and the others. Stop calling them gods. Here the word *god* carries a different meaning. Allah has no partner, if you remember your Quran.'

'That was a long time ago, yaar. And I was saying what I had felt as a fresh student at that time in Cambridge. Surely—'

'Well, they remember. And they know how to dig up. And they have no idea of context. The next time you are interviewed, bring up Allah liberally and with praises. Please.'

'I will.'

Nurul Islam could hardly confess that nowadays he tended to be a little less religious, a little more eclectic. He sometimes forgot to pray. He sometimes went to the church at Trinity or King's with Hilary, not strictly to pray but to listen to the choir. And—

'And,' echoed Zaffar at the other end. 'That comment you made about an Islamic bomb. "Does it carry a Quran on its back?" And "Do the neutrons emerge from the explosion crying, God is Great?"'

Nurul Islam laughed. 'It was when you visited me with those two dapper young men. Surely—'

'They talked. It's not the kind of thing you say, or even think or even dream! It's seen as blasphemy.' Do you know what trouble you're in? But Zaffar didn't say that to be heard.

One evening, having just returned from a walk with Hilary, Nurul Islam heard on the BBC nightly report that a small but influential conclave of Pakistani clerics had declared him a heretic and apostate. At the same time a riot had occurred in Pirmai and Lahore, resulting in three deaths. Three invitations to Nurul Islam by Middle Eastern governments to discuss funding and venues for his dream institute were soon after retracted. When he entered the London mosque where he had often gone to say prayers for close to twenty years, he was politely turned away, with 'Professor, we don't think it's appropriate at the present time.' In the Cambridge mosque, where only the previous month he had led the prayers, people stayed away from him.

Nurul Islam, the Light of Islam, as his name proclaimed, was now, according to religious authorities in his so-called Islamic country, not even a Muslim.

Late one night the phone rang at the London house. Nurul's sister Zainab informed Sakina Begum that her father, Sakina's father-in-law, Ghulam Ali, was seriously ill, and he wished to see Nurul. He would also dearly like to set his eyes upon his grandchildren, if that were possible. And the two daughters-in-law. The family did not wish to impose, but if any of them came, his joy would be uncontainable. Sakina Begum immediately called Cambridge.

It would be a visit that had been postponed long enough. Nurul called Pakistan to reassure his mother that he was on his way. He explained that Hilary couldn't come, due to work; but she hoped to meet the family soon at a better time. Sakina Begum was disabled with arthritis. The older children were busy with school or university, but Hilary had agreed that little Aisha could go, as a treat for his father and for the entire family. If anyone could, Nurul told his mother, his little Aisha would cure the old man. Wait till you meet her! But it would be a short visit, he warned. She said she understood, the situation there was stable but tense. According to the doctor, the chances of his father's recovery were zero. He might not see his father again.

They got the child a British passport. Nurul Islam travelled on his Pakistani document.

He had noticed changes during every previous return to Pirmai. Now it was fully grown, a ripe, bustling, noisy city with multi-storey buildings and wider roads. The former modest Ames Street, long since renamed Muhammad Ali Jinnah Road, had transformed into the busy stretch of highway bringing him home from Lahore airport. Over every scene he passed he superposed a sepia print from his past life. The simple shops with modest owners' names replaced by two-storey buildings with balconies. A restaurant in place of a chai stand. An apartment complex in the distance, presumably where the old ruins lay to which he would cycle with his school books. Tangles of electric power lines; they used oil lamps then. All the women in chador. Aisha sat pressed against him in the back of the taxi, perhaps a little fearful lest this alien life swallow her, yet drawn to the window on which her arms and forehead rested. Eyes wide with wonder, a smile on her lips. A child in the front seat of a stationary car waved at her. She waved back, uncertainly. There was a special satisfaction in having brought her with him, the place of his birth. Her roots.

The adults he had known were old and sick or dead, the kids now had their own families, and some had gone away to the larger cities or abroad. His Shirazi community, he knew, was in a state of shock from recent attacks. They had celebrated too loudly, too confidently. Too foolishly.

He was greeted with joy and sadness, Aisha with pure joy. The family looked beleaguered, awaiting Ghulam Ali's departure from this world. Nurul's mother had become a shadow of herself, diminutive and darker than he recalled, sitting by her husband most of the time with words of comfort. The second wife, Hanna Begum, ran the household like a general, supervising comings and goings, seating guests, shouting orders for tea and instructions for cooking. A sheikh would come by every morning and afternoon to cheer them up; once, a little boy from the family, seated quietly with his mother, sporadically burst into verses from the Quran. Nurul had never imagined he would smell death, but now he did, as he sat first on the bed and then beside it, holding his father's limp hand. The medicines, the stale breath, the dust motes in the air where the sunlight streamed hopelessly in. Aisha was shown to the old man, who put his hand lovingly on her face, and then she was taken to play outside with her relatives. The adults doted on her, looked at her in wonder, a little girl from another planet. Her attire had already been changed, specially made for her in anticipation of her arrival. Nurul was given the largest bed to sleep on, supplied with a new mosquito net, and Aisha slept next to him.

Ghulam Ali lingered, the family said he would get better, but not with much conviction, and the doctor merely shook his head at Nurul, with a muttered proviso, 'But miracles happen,' or 'God knows best.' A few family members, with Nurul's mother, had visited Sheikh Fariduddin Ganjshakar's shrine in Lahore and brought back blessed water and sweets for the patient, though diabetes was one of his ailments.

Even here, mused the son beside his dying father, Ghazali knocks heads with Averroes: can God interfere with His Creation, with the laws of physics that He Himself put in place? One said yes, the other said no. And what do you say, Nurul Islam?

His presence in Pakistan could not possibly have remained secret. Within two days, students from Government College in Lahore and other institutions had quietly arrived to see their idol. The minister of science and technology paid a visit. And finally his friend Zaffar Khan arrived in a chauffeured white car. He now walked with the aid of a stick. After he had paid his respects to the family and to Ghulam Ali, he and Nurul walked over to a local tea shop. Aisha trotted along.

'Well?' Zaffar began, when they'd sat down and he'd given a disapproving shake at their rickety table, to Nurul's amusement.

'Well. You tell me. I've been declared a heretic and a traitor in my own country. All of a sudden. What else? How do you explain that?'

'I don't know what to say, Nurul. I'm truly sorry. But all this will subside—it will go away—times change. You know that.'

'Nobody's come out to defend me. They were eating out of my hand previously. Even the president of the country.'

'You've made enemies, Nurul. And there's envy at your success out there in the West. People are afraid to speak out.'

'And that leak ... that I refused to participate—'

'I don't know who's responsible for that, Nurul.'

'Someone high up, surely? The project is not even public knowledge—it's still on?'

Zaffar gave a slight tilt of the head to indicate yes. Then: 'After India exploded its Smiling Buddha device ...'

'We had no choice, I know. What a name to give a nuclear bomb.'

'Ironical. The next one they might call Mahatma Gandhi.'

'Weeping Gandhi. And ours?'

'Don't even think about it.'

'Do you regret … agreeing to work on the …'

'The bomb? No. And you … any doubts about dissenting?'

'I've had doubts. When politicians speak about "first strike," when another war looms. But I just couldn't put my hand on such an instrument of destruction. We should have worked harder for a nuclear-free zone.'

'A dream. It was never possible, with all the unresolved issues we have with our neighbour. And world peace is surely an illusion. The world is a war zone—deterrence is all we have to guarantee survival. If some madman presses the button and we all get blown to bits, so be it. Perhaps we deserve it.'

He asked about Hilary. He had always been fond of her, ever since he met her in Rome. And he asked about Bhabhi, as he called Sakina Begum, of whom he was also very fond. He had lost his own father recently. For some moments, with paternal smiles on their faces they watched Aisha playing at the doorway, other kids coming to join her, if only to hear her speak. 'What joy they bring,' Zaffar murmured, 'and what a dirty world we leave behind for them.' Finally he took both Nurul's hands into his and said, 'You've done us proud, my friend. You'll ride this one out.'

'You're right. But you must know what's behind this campaign—it's well organized. You must have heard something. Tell me.'

'There's an outspoken mullah at large, his name is Mowlana Sufar. He heads an organization called Jang-e-Momeen. And apparently he's been following every crazy thing you've said, for a long time. You've lived away too long. These people are a force to be reckoned with. Everyone's afraid of them. They can unleash a riot outside your door within minutes!'

'So I'm a foreigner now?'

Zaffar smiled.

'Let's be honest. You can't begin to understand how it is to exist here. Three wars. A hostile border to the south. An army and intelligence presence, the God presence, the crazies. One treads carefully. Do you remember someone called Qadir Khan? He boasts that he heckled you at MIT a while back—challenged you, is how he puts it.'

'I recall a student shouting from the back of the hall. He was escorted out. What about him?'

'He's a disciple of Mowlana Sufar. His chief lieutenant. And there's a physicist called Sood—Abdullah Sood—you might remember him from the Rome conference?'

'Polaroid.'

They shared a laugh.

'The same one. A fanatic. If only you had said yes, Nurul, given your name to the project—you had the generals' protection. We pleaded with you, when we came to see you in London. You always were an arrogant bastard. Life is not mathematics, you can't always be consistent.'

'Was I really … arrogant?'

'And our genius. Our pride.'

As they walked back to the house, embraced and parted, Zaffar told him, 'I've asked for discreet police protection for you. I don't know if you've noticed. I insisted.' He gave Nurul a box of sweets to take with him, and the girl a smaller box, wrapped in green and red and tied with gold ribbons.

There were lengthy goodbyes; more boxes of sweets were proffered for him to take, of which he took only one, promising to his tearful mother finally that he would return before it was too late, and he would bring the young wife with him. And both her children. The entire neighbourhood turned out to see him off, therefore any prospect of secrecy was non-existent. A police car with dark windows and a blue light on top waited to escort Nurul and Aisha to the airport.

Before they left, they walked down to the old mosque for the afternoon prayer. Nurul walked with the men, Aisha was with the women behind them. The blue paint on the mosque exterior was faded, but a new loudspeaker had been installed for the call to prayer. The call, which carried throughout the neighbourhood, sounded formal and distant, lacking the warm, crackly intimacy of the ancient contraption. Everything changes.

They had arrived inside the compound. It was paved. The doorway to the prayer hall was to the left. The imam was waiting to welcome him and stepped forward. Nurul Islam would remember greeting the young imam with an adab, then turning towards someone else to his right, and then the deafening sound of explosion, and chaos. The only thought in his mind, which he would hear in his nightmares long afterwards, was 'Aisha!'

Later, in hospital, he learned that in the melee she had been carried away by the crowd and thrust against a concrete water fountain and killed.

Refusing to see anyone except his mother, he returned home to London and Cambridge accompanying the coffin of his daughter.

On the evening of the bombing at the Shirazi mosque in Pirmai, Sheikh Qadir Khan writes in his memoir, *Confessions of a Former Jihadi*, celebratory laddus were distributed to a crowd of followers gathered on the street outside Mowlana Sufar's residence in old Lahore. 'Mowlana had struck a blow against the arrogance of science,' writes Sheikh Qadir.

A few days earlier, when the mowlana was informed about the professor's presence in the country, his eyes had gleamed like a predator's.

'He's here?' he had exclaimed. 'In Pakistan itself?'

'Yes, Mowlana. College students are going in droves to see him. Even a cabinet minister has gone to pay respects.'

The old man grunted. 'The country's deviated to the ways of Satan. We should show the world the wrath of Allah against blasphemers, heretics, munafiqs, infidels … Start a dangal,' he said, with a nod at the three uncouth types, his hired agitators, who stood together waiting to a side.

He was able to give that instruction because, says Sheikh Qadir, 'Mowlana Sufar had been made aware that the government's protective hand no longer shielded Professor Nurul Islam.'

'We can arrange a disturbance,' one of the three agitators said. 'There is a girl from his community who is accused of insulting the Quran—'

'Laanat upon them all …'

Sheikh Qadir had been a follower and a lieutenant of Mowlana Sufar since his student days, and had constantly fuelled the latter's hatred by keeping him informed about the heresies, blasphemies, and indiscretions that he ascribed to Nurul Islam. Yet in his book he absolves himself entirely of any responsibility for the Pirmai bombing. 'I did not agree with Professor Islam's views on science. He was an arrogant, proud man. I abhorred how he equated the laws of physics with what he called manifestations of God. God has no manifestations, no equals. He is the One. The professor flouted God's laws and the Sharia. His idolatry and blasphemies in themselves deserved the wrath of Allah. But I did not and do not believe in violence. Which is why, after my release from Guantanamo prison, where I spent fourteen months on false charges, I split from Mowlana Sufar's organization.'

Nurul Islam buried his daughter at the Cambridge Islamic cemetery—the fact that he had been declared an apostate in his own country having been quietly overlooked by the cemetery authority. Outwardly, his life had returned to normal. He taught his classes, though the new chairman had understandingly reduced his load. He was aware that he carried an aura around him—he was not only the famous one in the duo of the Islam-Rosenfeld unification theory but also had suffered a tragic personal loss. He could hardly avoid that momentary awkward look in a colleague or student. Perhaps at times he imagined it, but he had to live with it, as he lived with the memory. In his appearances he attempted to invoke his former ebullient, arrogant self—for example, with an impertinent question at the weekly colloquium—but always seemed to be seen through. Soon after he returned from Pakistan, in a bid to resume his life, he had accepted an invitation to the annual physics meeting in Washington, DC. When he got up and started his keynote address, the audience had stood up spontaneously and applauded. It was hard to go on after that, but he did, beginning with a quotation from an Urdu poem that went 'We will see.'

His detractors persisted with their attacks, but more quietly. Duncan Harvey, the man who had challenged him at Harvard, had added a new charge to his list, that Nurul Islam was working secretly with Pakistan's nuclear weapons program. Not only was this patently false, but Dr Harvey left implicit the moral basis of his accusation, that Islam (the religion), and its proxy, Pakistan, could not be trusted with this weapon—which five or six other nations of the world already possessed. From the other direction, Susan Mason, now a professor of postcolonial studies, carried on her vendetta, with an article here and there. His goddaughter, Nurul

Islam realized, had never gotten over her father's suicide. Perhaps she was the one who had discovered him having hanged himself. She needed someone to blame, and Nurul Islam was convenient. Alf Greiner did not follow up on the public accusation he had previously made, but in his revised monograph on particle physics, Nurul Islam remained a footnote, an 'also,' while Abe Rosenfeld was there in all his glory in a half page with a new photograph.

At home in Cambridge life proceeded. There was young Jonathan to take care of, to distract, bringing moments of joy and parental anxieties. The two parents carried their grief between them like a tender baby—or something lethal like an explosive that had to be allowed time, unprovoked, to lose its potency. Which it would never do completely, they both knew. Sakina Begum had come to visit, along with Muni, to express her condolences; after that she had left them alone to nurse their grief. Nurul had visited her on a day of Eid one day, when he spent time with his entire London family. The undue attention, the sympathetic pauses were unbearable, it was impossible to assume his former role as the father. At the end of that visit, as he was leaving, Sakina said to him at the door, 'No need to come. I understand. She needs you more over there. She may not show it, but she's a mother. I have my life here. Come when you are more comfortable.'

One day, a full two years after the incident, a Pakistani dignitary named Riad Ansari came to visit them in Cambridge to bring his government's condolences. He brought sweets and a small package wrapped in delicate light-green paper. 'Open it later,' he said. He wanted to invite the couple to a Maulid celebration in London. It would take place at his house, a qawwali-fest in praise of the Prophet on his birthday. Nurul couldn't help retorting, 'Over there they've called me an apostate and a kaffir, and here you invite me to your house to celebrate the Prophet's birthday!'

Riad Ansari blushed. 'Believe me, Nurul Sahab, we would like nothing better than to cancel that fatwa. But you know … the different factions in our country … they are hard to control. Accept this invitation as a first step.'

They declined politely. This was not the right time, they said.

When Riad Ansari had taken leave, Hilary got up and picked up the parcel from the coffee table. Tenderly she unwrapped it, peeling back the tape, leaving the green paper as intact as possible. She opened the box, and choked. Nurul took it from her, brought out its contents. Aisha's sneakers, pink and white, the ones she had worn during that blast. They stared at each other.

Five years after that tragedy that broke him inside, he received a call from Sakina Begum.

'Professor, I want to see you.'

He laughed. Imagined her deadpan face on the other line. How he knew that look of half sarcasm, hiding a smile.

'Yes?' he replied. 'What's up? One of the boys ready to marry?'

'I'm still your wife,' she said. 'The original one.'

'Of course you are, my dear.' Now what was up?

'Then I'm telling you, come and see me. Come to London, to this house. By yourself.'

'Of course, jaan. I will, on Saturday. Can't you tell me what it's about? Anything serious?'

'Nothing serious. Just come.'

And so he had gone, a little worried, somewhat intrigued. Perhaps one of the boys was seriously thinking about getting married, and she wanted to consult. They were still young, he thought, and Muni certainly.

When he arrived, she let him in as usual with her usual gesture of blessing at the door. The table was laid inside and she bade him sit. She brought from the kitchen two cups of special chai that he liked, which she was confident Hilary would never know how to make. She had ready for him jalebis to start with, samosas and channa, and a cake, Lahori-style. She had hardly spoken two words when she finally sat down in front of him.

'You have something on your mind, jaan?'

'Two things.'

He got nervous. That alternative universe, with its own laws, where he feared to tread and often blundered. With Hilary it was not the same; Sakina had a different claim on him. She was the mistress of this different reality. He smiled.

'OK.'

'I have cancer.'

'Are you sure?'

'Two tests. Pancreatic.'

They shared a long moment's silence. He felt something clutching him inside, felt a shiver up his spine. It happens, why to us, why to her? Finally he let out a gasp and stretched out his hand and grasped hers. These hands, this touch. His life's partner. He stood up, went to her and squeezed her soft shoulders, put his head against hers for a long moment.

'Are they sure?'

'Yes.'

'Treatment?' he asked.

'It's too painful. Anyway, I'll die in a year, guaranteed.'

'I'll move in here, to be with you. You can rely on me.'

'No. You stay there. Muni is with me. And the boys come.'

'Are you sure? Let me come.'

'Yes. No.'

'Doctor Khan—'

'He comes and visits. Advises me. Talks too much as usual.'

She allowed a smile. The doctor had attended to the family for many years now. And yes, he talked a lot, and before you knew it he was telling you his own news. And before he left he always accepted chai.

Another long moment. Then, back in his chair, he said, 'I know I hurt you. I couldn't help it. For that, Allah will never forgive me.'

'He will. You always had your way with Allah.'

'Except in the matter of Aisha,' he muttered.

'That was the work of Satan. But she is with God. An angel.'

They discussed news from home. The births and deaths, the marriages. She looked tired and he got up to go. Paused at the door. 'And the second thing you had on your mind?'

She came and stood beside him. She looked up into his eyes. 'It was I who gave David's papers to that girl—Susan. I lost my mind. I'm sorry, I hurt you—' Tears ran down her full cheeks, painting them with kohl. He opened his arms and embraced her.

'But you did nothing wrong, jaan. You did nothing wrong.'

He noticed traces of grey in the parting of her hair. And he put a name to the perfume she was wearing, the one she knew he liked. Seduction. He smiled.

As he turned to depart, he ran into Muni.

'Hello, Daddy. Not staying for me?'

'Your mum's had enough of me.'

She put a hand on his cheek. 'Can I come and see you sometime—this week?'

'Please, yes.'

# Coda

Hilary Chase, now Dame Hilary, drives up to her house in her little Smart car and parks on the gravel driveway. She gets out, tries to disguise a stab of pain before she starts walking, and smiles at me where I'm waiting for her at the steps. With a quick look towards the garden, which evidently needs a caring hand, a wet spring having arrived, she comes over towards me. I apologize for having arrived early.

'Hi, I'm Sofia Ali, you agreed very graciously to speak with me …'

'Yes, come on in,' she says, opening the door. She takes our jackets and places them on the back of a chair. 'Have a seat.' She indicates where. 'I'll be a moment.' She goes off inside, returns a few minutes later. I look around. What do I see, what do I expect to see, the intruder?

The house is where she's always lived in Cambridge, since her marriage to Nurul Islam. The living room is modest, the furniture functional, the loveseat cover—beautifully floral—faded. I sense memory preserved. Decor consists of an orchid on a stool, a few reproductions on the walls, including Monet's *Sunrise*, a half wall of framed photographs beside the defunct fireplace, and an abstract bronze on a corner pedestal table. At the foot of the bronze are a pair of child's sneakers.

Sitting down, she asks, 'Why this interest in Nurul Islam, may I ask? He's been long forgotten, the science has moved on, the world has changed …'

I explain to her my interest, which began as an idle curiosity. This past autumn I happened to be in Zanzibar visiting my family; it was a torrid afternoon and I was sitting by the pool of a tourist hotel when I picked up a well-thumbed magazine and got intrigued by a small news item. The grave of a Nobel Prize–winning scientist, Nurul Islam, had been desecrated in his hometown in Pakistan.

The woman sitting in the other chair—the upright one—has a beautiful face, as only the aged can have, drawn smooth, sculpted long and thin; the white hair is short and combed straight back. There's an amused, somewhat patronizing—or is it indulgent?—look on that face as she leans and listens to me.

'And this was not the first time that happened,' she says, crowning my account. 'Every now and then someone comes on a motorbike and defaces the headstone with black paint, and later someone else—paid by me—goes and cleans it up.' She gets up. 'Let me get us some tea.'

'Let me help you.' I go with her as she stands up and heads off shakily towards the kitchen, and we return with a tray of tea and biscuits.

'He liked that.' She gives a small chuckle. 'Tea and a biscuit or two to start the day with. Fed his brain, he said.'

'You yourself did work on—' I begin, not sure how to go on beyond the niceties.

She smiles. Mischievously, perhaps detecting my amateurish ploy to get her talking.

'I worked on how—at what point—an inanimate soup of atoms and molecules develops into life—reproduces, uses energy, and so on. Using the same idea that Nurul Islam and others were applying in particle physics … symmetry-breaking, it was called …'

She drifts off, and then: 'What do you want to know?'

My eyes fly to the gallery of pictures to the right of the fireplace. There he is, the mustachioed Nurul Islam with the thick black wavy hair, the sparkling eyes, and the confident smile; another of him and her, he wearing a sherwani and a turban, she in formal gown, elegantly decked out. There is another of them together, taken much later, outdoors at a café, both turned to stare at the camera. A boy of about twelve in a school blazer standing between his parents. And in the centre of the gallery, the little girl, perhaps five; full-length, in overalls, challenging the camera like her father. Her mother, tight-jawed, follows my gaze upon the child, says nothing, gives a slight nod.

What must it be like to lose a child, especially at that young age? Hilary Chase had prevailed, diligently continued her research and sat on committees, including the one that designed a curriculum and physics textbooks with girls in mind. For this she was honoured in the British fashion. He taught for a few more years, canvassed for his favourite project, gave up and then retired.

She prompts, 'Yes?'

'Tell me about when you first met him. Just for a start?'

There was a lot of excitement that week he went to Cambridge—the other one—she says. Nurul Islam, one half of the duo of the Lesser Unification Theory, was in the department; two other people would be around later that day—Richard Feynman and Murray Gell-Mann. It was like the gods had descended from Olympus. Her eyes twinkle as she describes the scene. 'Students would walk by Abe's office to take a peek at this glamorous mustachioed genius. And I got the chance to escort him around!'

I wait as she looks away, smiling. 'I was young and naive then. A lowly graduate student. Abe Rosenfeld was my supervisor. So I volunteered to escort his guest, Nurul Islam of Imperial College, from his hotel to our department on his first morning there. And later to take him shopping! Just to brag about it. He didn't know that, of course!'

She flashes a smile. 'I fell in love the moment I met him,' she adds quietly, and stops. 'And you?' she asks after a modest silence. 'Tell me about yourself.'

I tell her. My parents are from East Africa. She, of Persian and African heritage, he, Arab and African. They came to Britain soon after the revolution on the island and divorced some years later. My mother teaches accounting at a technical college, and my father runs a small travel business. I am studying medicine, but have taken a year off to find out more about Nurul Islam.

Now I take the plunge.

'Tell me about your lives after you lost your daughter.'

She takes a deep breath. Looks at the picture. Before I can apologize, she begins, 'Yes. After we lost Aisha. What is there to say? You ask yourself, why you? Why her, a beautiful life? It happened, it happens to people. I didn't blame him, though I had qualms about him taking her there. I know now that if I had gone with them, she would have been safe. He was swallowed up in the crowd of adulating men and she was among adoring female relatives. So many things one should or should not have done. But it's destructive to think like that. It was over, a joyful period in our lives. A dream, for which I'm grateful … We had Jonathan.'

The face reveals much. Not a day goes by, I imagine, when she doesn't think of her daughter; sweep a gaze over that wall of photographs, feel her heart momentarily give way.

'He was taking her to see her ailing grandfather. What could be more natural? He was so proud of her … Prouder than he'd been of anything else, he said.'

He did not excuse himself so easily. He had known about the libels and slander rampaging against him and his community. He was aware of how easily violence could erupt in that country. How could he have been so blind, then? Arrogance. Nothing could happen to him.

'It seemed to him at the end that he had been gifted since childhood, but then—as though by design, as though to teach him a lesson—everything, his entire world, collapsed upon him. But I was with him—we were there for each other all the time … and the few friends … Zaffar would call, and visited once … his health was not good. Abe would drop a line or two to me.'

She is holding back her tears now. I wait until she recovers, then get up to leave. She allows me to visit her again, for which I am grateful.

She took three months off from her university duties, and Nurul Islam took a month from his. They each needed time to look away from each other, to ask themselves where they were in their lives, what had they just done, what was the future. She went to Boston to be with her father; he was coping well and helped her recover. Her sister, Jill, was living not far away in Connecticut, she was a teacher and married, and Hilary spent a week with her. She visited her old department and was welcomed warmly by her mentor, Abe Rosenfeld. There was still a lot of excitement in the world of physics, with an expanded theory of unification that included the third, the strong force; black holes were also the rage. Life went on, though Cambridge like everything else had changed. Nurul also appreciated the space; having Jonathan was a balm to him, it helped him control his rage and sorrow. When she returned, they were both ready—and anxious—to get on. They had missed each other. A year later in the spring, leaving Jonathan at the London home, they went on a tour of southern Spain and Portugal—Andalusia—which he had always wished to do. The region had once upon a time been under the rule of Muslim sultans and fostered a golden age of unfettered speculation and creativity, of philosophy, aesthetics, and poetry, that he'd often spoken about. Averroes, the rationalist, and Ibn Arabi, the mystic, were both from Andalusia. So was Maimonides.

'There's an open-air café outside the city wall of Cordoba in Spain, and facing it is a statue of Averroes. Not far, on the other side of the wall, is a statue of Maimonides, the Jewish philosopher. In the late afternoons, after a day of strolling about, we would inevitably end up there exhausted—and sit at the café till sunset. The river Guadalquivir flows close by. That's an Arabic name. Nurul enjoyed that. The following years he would return there by himself for a couple of weeks and tour around the region, discovering evidence of Moorish presence. I sometimes joined him, worried about his health. I often imagine him sitting at our table outside that wall in Cordoba, in communion with the philosophers ...'

'We recovered. We had each other, and we still had Jonathan. We couldn't let Nurul's enemies destroy our relationship—our love.'

His enemies? She throws me a sharp glance but doesn't elaborate. The fundamentalists in Pakistan, I presume, his defamers in England and Holland, and the army major in between, linking them. Major Iftikhar had felt slighted by Nurul Islam. Surely it was he and the entity he represented that had commissioned the surveillance on him and sent the telltale photos from Rome to Sakina Begum, who in a huff gave David Mason's research papers to his daughter, Susan. And regretted and apologized thereafter. And it was that powerful entity that sent the photos to the media in Pakistan and removed the protective hand it had held over him.

'Perhaps it all started with me,' she says. 'The evil American second wife.'

'Did he ever question his faith? ... after the tragedy?' I ask. She ponders awhile.

'I think he became free of it ... unburdened. He had paid his dues, you see. He had paid his sacrifice. He didn't have to prove anything. There was almost a defiance in him.'

'Yes?'

'Early one morning when he thought he was alone, I heard him muttering—expostulating. In Urdu, of course. I asked him what that was all about, and he looked up embarrassed. Just talking to the Maker, he said. A piece of my mind. And what did you tell him? I asked. He said he told God, Don't remind me to praise you. You sent a goat to save Ismail from the knife. Where was my goat when you sent me your fanatics!'

'That's a very bold comparison,' I venture.

'It was something he would say. Ismail—or Ishmael—was saved by a goat, his Aisha was simply sacrificed ... on the grounds of a mosque ... I feared he was losing his mind sometimes, but then he would be back to normal again. And he would have that glass of champagne or a glass or two of red wine when we went out. And he liked his sausage roll—don't tell me what's in it, he would say, I will claim ignorance.'

'And the Scotch?'

She pauses.

'Yes, occasionally.' She looks away, remembering, a dim smile on her face.

'And physics and God?'

'Two separate worlds. God does not interfere with the laws of physics. God should mind his own business, he quipped once, and that too went into the charge sheet prepared by those fanatics.'

'But blaming God for the tragedy was ...'

'A contradiction, I agree. And he knew that too.'

'But he continued to believe in God.'

'Yes. But he'd lost his former rapport with Him, you see. That intimacy he had—'

She stops, looks away, and I try to follow. 'There's something else ... please?'

She says, 'When we married, he would wake up with the Islamic credo on his lips. Years later I suddenly realized one morning that he was not doing that anymore. I never brought that up. Too sensitive a subject.'

'Did he also stop praying?'

'He did pray—in the morning. It was a habit, I thought, like stretching your arms or brushing your teeth ... some quick gestures. I think for him God had entered the realm of uncertainty. He didn't matter too much.'

They lived a normal life, albeit carrying a small bubble of ache inside; listening to music, going to concerts—he was calmed by chamber music—and films and reading poetry. He enjoyed the way the different instruments came together in a quartet, each unique in itself and yet part of a unity. 'Like the laws of physics?' he would say. Physics had not left him, he saw wonders all around him, even in the shape of a cloud formation or a trail of rainwater on the ground. On Sundays they might walk into a college chapel to hear the choir service. He called it Sufi music.

The Cambridge mosque invited him to lead the Friday prayer, but he declined.

He corresponded with some former students, and followed his field from a distance; he would discuss wistfully with her the recent successes of the Standard Model, which had accomplished the unification he had worked so hard on—taking forward, of course, the work he and others had done. The older children came to visit, especially Muni. Pete Sorensen visited a couple of times, without giving notice, as was his wont, as did his former student and collaborator C. D. Patel, who gave him a short lecture on his recent work.

'And the Nobel?'

'Pete Sorensen tried to convince him, as did I, as did Sakina, but he insisted he would refuse it. So we waited to see what would happen.'

'Then he changed his mind ... he relented.'

'He relented. It was Abe who called and pleaded, "Nurul, if you're not there they'll never give it to me. I can live with that. But I'm calling at my old father's request. *Tell that Muslim or Islam or whatever he is not to be a jackass!*" So Nurul said yes, for my people. And my father. And Abe's father. And the rest of those who love us.'

Sakina had already passed away and he regretted she would not be at the ceremony. He would have taken both wives, he said. But he took Hilary. He in a sherwani and traditional Shirazi turban; Hilary, quiet elegance personified, as in the photo in the wall gallery. Her father had passed away by then and her regret was that he could not be in Stockholm.

It was Jonathan who found his father, upon his return from school. Nurul Islam had had a heart attack while sitting at his desk. The boy called his mother, who arrived immediately. 'I would swear,' Hilary says, 'when I saw him, still sitting at his desk, there was on his face half a smile and half a grimace. I wonder if he could have called for help—the phone was right there by his hand—and chose not to.'

She concludes, 'It's his God I feel sorry for, when they meet.'

# Author's Note

This novel was inspired by the life of the mathematical physicist Abdus Salam. He was born in pre-independence India, in what is now Pakistan, attended Cambridge University, graduating as a 'Wrangler,' with a double first in mathematics and physics—and went on to become a professor at Imperial College, London, where he did his major work for which he won the Nobel Prize. What intrigued me about Salam was that while most physicists of that calibre, working towards a 'Theory of Everything,' would have been—reasonably, in my view—agnostics, Salam was a devout Muslim. And so this work of fiction. I did not know Abdus Salam personally (he was of a different generation), nor did I know much about his immediate family or his religious community—which, ironically, is now regarded as heretic. Whether Salam was part of Pakistan's nuclear bomb project depends on whom you talk to. My character Nurul Islam, however, is against it. All the characters and incidents in this book, including cameos by Feynman, Dirac, and Gell-Mann are my fictions. Only the physics is real. One caveat: the electroweak unification theory is actually attributed to the independent work carried out by three physicists, including Abdus Salam. In this novel, with apologies, it was convenient to have two.

I am grateful to the Forman Christian College in Lahore and Pervez Hoodbhoy for their hospitality and kindness. And to Munir Pervaiz for introducing me to Syed Tayyab Razza, who went out of his way to pick me up at Wagah and show me around Lahore. I am also grateful to Munazza Yaqoob and Sofia Hussein for their hospitality in Islamabad. Rajkumar Hans, my friend with whom I roamed around Gujarat at one time, hosted me in Amritsar and took me to the Wagah border—and waited until I got through. My boyhood friend and co-conspirator in physics, Adil

Hassam, checked the Dirac Equation for me in case I had been blinded by time. None of the above knew about this novel or is responsible for its contents.

I am deeply indebted to the Rivendell Foundation for providing me a retreat in Bowen Island, British Columbia, where I put my finishing touches to this novel in idyllic isolation.

Thanks to Bruce Westwood, for his boundless enthusiasm as my agent for so many years, and to Carolyn Forde, who's taken over with equal enthusiasm.

Finally my gratitude to my editor Kiara Kent for her friendly, cheerful, and potent observations. This novel is undoubtedly better for that. Also thanks to Melanie Little, as before, for her astute, sensitive copy-editing. And not least on any count, gratitude to Nuru for her patience and for encouraging me to wander about in search of detail and quiet, wherever they took me.

A RANDOM, INCOMPLETE LIST OF WORKS SOMETIMES CONSULTED

Weinberg and God: https://www.pbs.org/faithandreason/transcript/wein-body.html
Avicenna on God: https://en.wikipedia.org/wiki/Proof_of_the_Truthful
Steven Hawking on God: https://www.washingtonpost.com/news/acts-of-faith/wp/2018/03/14/im-not-afraid-what-stephen-hawking-said-about-god-his-atheism-and-his-own-death/
Einstein on God: https://www.npr.org/sections/13.7/2010/06/10/127754688/can-newton -and-einstein-teach-us-something-about-god
Ibn al-Haytham, scientific method: https://en.wikipedia.org/wiki/Ibn_al-Haytham#cite_note-{{harvnb|sabra|1989}}.-63

So, naturalists observe, a flea
Hath smaller fleas that on him prey;
And these have smaller still to bite 'em;
And so proceed *ad infinitum*.
JONATHAN SWIFT

Attacks on Ahmadis:
https://www.dawn.com/news/1123873/ahmadis-on-the-run-fearing-death-in-peoples-colony
https://www.dawn.com/news/1591426/teenage-boy-guns-down-ahmadi-doctor-injures-3-others-at-their-home-in-nankana
https://www.dawn.com/news/1583413/professor-belonging-to-ahmadi-community-shot-dead-in-peshawar-allegedly-after-religious-argument

Abdus Salam:
https://www.dawn.com/news/1589090
https://www.dawn.com/news/1519654

*Cosmic Anger*, Gordon Fraser
Weinberg PRL paper, my library

Paul Dirac: *The Strangest Man*, Graham Farmelo

Tirmidhi on family: https://www.abuaminaelias.com/dailyhadithonline/2012/05/28/best-of-you-best-family/ (Tirmidhi 628 and 3252. Google.)
Physics:
https://www.economist.com/leaders/2021/08/28/fundamental-physics-is-humanitys-most-extraordinary-achievement
https://www.forbes.com/sites/startswithabang/2019/02/12/why-supersymmetry-may-be-the-greatest-failed-prediction-in-particle-physics-history/?sh=5ad0626d69e6
https://www.britannica.com/science/supersymmetry
*The Infinity Puzzle*, Frank Close
*The Second Creation*, Robert P. Crease and Charles C. Mann

Pakistani bomb:
https://nuclearweaponarchive.org/Pakistan/
*Eating Grass*, Feroz Hassan Khan
*The Islamic Bomb*, Steve Weissman and Herbert Krosney

Indian bomb:
https://nuclearweaponarchive.org/India/

*Islam and Sciences*, Pervez Hoodbhoy

Philosophy (Ghazali, Avicenna, etc):
*Philosophy in the Islamic World*, Peter Adamson
*Stanford Encyclopedia of Philosophy*
*The Cambridge Companion to Arabic Philosophy*, edited by Peter Adamson and Richard C. Taylor

Bombing of an art exhibition:
https://www.dawn.com/news/1565617/society-the-fakir-and-the-mullah

Assassination:
https://www.dawn.com/news/1584316/jamia-farooqia-head-maulana-adil-driver-shot-dead-in-karachi
see 'bombing in Lahore' etc. on Google

Blasphemy re Quran:
https://www.dawn.com/news/1661873/the-mutawwa-are-coming
https://www.dawn.com/news/1664535/essay-the-politics-of-blasphemy-and-lynching
https://www.dawn.com/news/1674960

Also by M.G. Vassanji

Fiction

*What You Are*
*A Delhi Obsession*
*Nostalgia*
*The Magic of Saida*
*The Assassin's Song*
*When She was Queen*
*The In-Between World of Vikram Lall*
*Amriika*
*The Book of Secrets*
*Uhuru Street*
*No New Land*
*The Gunny Sack*

Non-fiction

*Nowhere, Exactly*
*And Home Was Kariakoo*
*A Place Within: Rediscovering India*
*Mordecai Richler*